The Shaman

A Novel

David Nees

ISBN 9781721169184
Manufactured in the United States

For Carla

*As always, you are my greatest supporter
and encourager when courage falters*

My thanks go to Ed, Carla, Chris S. and Rob for their early (alpha) feedback. It helped to refine the story. Thanks also to Chris M. for his very helpful beta read. And many thanks to Eric, my writer friend. You didn't let me rest until the book was the best it could be.

It was a challenge to bring this book to completion with my cancer battle intruding in the middle of writing it. You don't fight cancer without paying a price. Many of you know that. The disease comes in many forms, all pernicious, all evil, and all destructive. The treatments can be effective but are brutal. Recovery from them can be longer than the fight to kill the cancer itself. I can't thank enough everyone who encouraged me to not give up, to win, and get back to writing. You all know who you are and how much I am indebted to you for your support.

The Shaman

*"We come here with no peaceful intent,
but ready for battle,"* William Wallace

*"The spirit-world around this world of sense
Floats like an atmosphere, and everywhere
Wafts through these earthly mists and vapours dense.
A vital breath of more ethereal air."*
Henry Wadsworth Longfellow

Chapter 1

The dreams came, night after night. He had learned a long time ago to pay attention to them. Now he was having the same one every night. That was significant to the old man. He lived in the Mexican desert with only a raven and coyote for companions. He was ancient, uncounted years old. He had followed the path of the shaman learned from his father and his father's father. They were all gone and he was alone. He was tired. He had fought many battles in his life; now the dreams called him to action once more. He would have to go to battle again.

His name was Tlayolotl which means "Heart of the Earth". He had watched his grandfather fight the battles, trying to stem the tide of darkness and evil that wanted to spread itself over all of creation. His grandfather had died in his last struggle against these forces. As a grown man he learned more under his father's tutelage and had watched him spend the last of his life's energies engaged in the same battle.

Then he was alone for so many years he could hardly remember the company of humans. The raven and coyote were his only friends. He was getting more and more frail with each passing year. How many years did he have left and who would follow? Even though he had not the strength of his earlier years he knew he would respond to the call. While his body might let him down, he still had the shaman's power. He would use it as he had learned over so many years. Would this be his last battle? He didn't know but as a shaman, son and grandson of shamans, he could do nothing else. The forces of darkness were gathering and he had the ability to see, to understand, and to fight them. He would do his part.

Someone was coming, someone evil, and they were bringing darkness with them. Yet there was another coming, from the north. That one would fight the darkness. That was what his dreams seemed to tell him. And that someone would drop out of the sky. He was called to find the one from the north and help him. He was to show the northerner his true role in the fight, to help him drive back the darkness. The wisdom of his years had to be imparted to this visitor. That was his purpose.

The cargo bay of the C130 is a loud, uncomfortable place. Even with earphones on the sound assaults his senses. It's a hollow metal tube and the roar of the plane's four Allison turboprop engines, each developing over 4,000 horsepower, flood the space with their fury as they pull the plane through the air. The cacophony is only partially relieved by the load of supplies that help to dampen the sound if not the vibration.

The cargo is tied to pallets and locked down on the loading rails that run front to back in the cargo bay. The plane is old and beat up, the result of years of hard work hauling men and equipment around the world. The engines and operating systems are maintained, but the rest of the plane has not received much attention. Dan

Stone sits in a seat made from aluminum tubes with a canvas material strung between. The seats are arranged against the wall. Behind him is the uninsulated skin of the plane, cold to the touch. The heaters only slow down the encroaching chill from the outside air which at this altitude hovers around minus 25 degrees Fahrenheit. The metal ribs of the air frame run vertically up the walls of the tube and across to the other side. The sound is relentless, hammering his senses and, along with the uncomfortable seat, killing any hope of relaxing.

The plane had taken off from Denver a half hour ago, headed for Mazatlán, Mexico where the cargo of relief supplies for the flooding taking place south of the city near Acaponeta are to be unloaded. A company named Disaster Relief Fund has leased the plane. They deliver relief supplies all over the world where needed. It just so happens that these relief missions are usually near areas of conflict.

While en route to Mazatlán the plane will cross over the desert north of Chihuahua. It will fly at 21,000 feet and not be noticed from the ground. Most importantly, the flight plan will look normal to the controllers.

Two men, a loadmaster and a jumpmaster, sit across the hold from Dan. They could all converse over their mics but neither man seems interested in small talk, which suits Dan just fine. He has his own thoughts to wrestle with.

The Disaster Relief Fund is a front for the CIA. It allows them to get into or near areas of conflict while providing useful supplies. The pilots and the two men in the back are staffers of the agency. Even so they know nothing about Dan's mission. All the pilots know is that they are to alert the men in the cargo bay when approaching a certain point on the flight. They have been told to expect the rear cargo ramp to be opened and then closed. The pilots have no idea what will be going on back there. Neither of them knows that the plane carries an extra passenger. The flight will continue to its destination, unload its cargo and return home to Denver.

The two men in the back with Dan are also separated from him by more than the mission. They are employees of the CIA while Dan is a newly acquired asset, a maverick to be used in the field on almost suicidal missions. He is and will remain an outsider no matter how long he survives.

Dan will jump out of the plane at its cruising altitude. He will perform a HALO, a High Altitude Low Opening maneuver. No one on the ground looking up or anyone looking at a radar screen will notice the jump. Dan has practiced this type of parachute jump only three times. While he is well-practiced in parachuting, this is a new endeavor, one with much risk attached. There will be no instructors waiting for him on the ground. He will be all alone: no support team, no extra resources, only what he can take with him. And if something goes wrong he is on his own. If caught, he will be completely disavowed by any agency in the U.S. There is nothing to identify him as an American agent. He is a man without connections.

He has an insulated jump suit, sturdy boots, gloves, and a helmet. None of the gear bears any markings of U.S. Military. In addition to his parachute, Dan carries a separate facemask and oxygen bottle. He also has a fifty-pound rucksack strapped between his legs. The pack has a lanyard which when pulled releases from his legs allowing him an unimpeded landing.

The bay is illuminated in red light. It paints the jumpmaster's face a sickly green. Dan goes over his gear for the fifth time. It will be another two hours before he has to jump, plenty of time to worry. His mind goes over the jump repeatedly. This one will not be as straightforward as his practice ones, he reminds himself. It is a dangerous maneuver in uncertain terrain and he has no margin for error—no backup if things go wrong. Dan is worried.

He is also worried about the mission. He hadn't expected his first assignment to be in Mexico. He had listened to Jane's explanations along with her boss, Henry. He understood the points they had made, but he felt this was a throwaway mission; something cobbled together quickly without much planning. That fact made him feel expendable. *Is this how they think of me?* He tries to sleep, his mind filled with troubled thoughts.

He is jarred out of an unpleasant dream of being lost in the desert by words from the cockpit coming through his headphones: "Thirty minutes out." The jumpmaster, who doubles as the Physiologic Technician, or PT, gets up and steps over to Dan.

"It's time to switch you over to pure oxygen."

Dan will breathe one hundred percent oxygen for the next thirty minutes to purge his system of nitrogen to protect against the bends from the decompression and rapid recompression he was going to experience. After checking the airflow and seal around the mask, he gives Dan the thumbs up. Dan responds in kind. The man goes back to sit down next to the loadmaster, leaving Dan alone on his side of the plane. The sitting arrangement exemplifies his isolation. He will be leaving the plane, stepping out into a dark void to disappear, perhaps forever, from the crew while they will complete the flight and return to Denver and their families, all known activities with known results. The outcome of Dan's activities is far from known or assured.

Oh, well. This is what I signed up for. It still feels lonely to him.

"Two minutes out." The voice jars Dan back to the present. A light near the rear bay door starts flashing amber. He goes over his harness again. He checks the heavy rucksack to make sure it was secure and the quick release isn't fouled. The pack carries his survival supplies, food, water, and camouflage gear along with his weapons. He will be on his own so he has to pack in everything he needs to complete his mission.

The jumpmaster comes over to him and sticks his face in front of Dan.

"Tell me your name," he shouts through the noise.

"Steve Mason," Dan replies using the alias he had been given for this mission.

"Where are you?"

"In a noisy C130."

"Where did you take off from?"

"Denver." Dan's responses are crisp and clean. The man is looking for signs of hypoxia that, if detected, will cause him to abort the jump. He gives Dan a thumbs-up and sits back down. Then he and the loadmaster put on their oxygen masks.

"One minute," comes the announcement.

This is it. On my own. My first mission. Dan quenches a sense of panic or dread, he isn't sure which. *Don't think about it. Just execute.* He stands up as the rear ramp begins to lower. The wind buffets him as it curls around the rear of the fuselage and strikes inside. They have slowed to around 220 knots. Dan knows it will be a shock to step into the abyss. He can see the end of the ramp and then...only darkness. An altimeter is strapped to his wrist. His chute is set to open automatically at two thousand feet if he passes out on the way down. He will be dropping at nearly 130 miles an hour and will open his chute at 2,500 feet. Once on the ground he will hide his gear and begin the trek to his objective.

"Thirty seconds."

The colorless voice drones over his headphones. Dan pulls them off of his head, hangs them on a hook behind him, and waddles towards the back of the plane. He carefully shuffles to the edge of the ramp. The jumpmaster is tethered by a safety strap but still grips a handhold. He flashes five fingers in Dan's face. His hand curls into a fist; then he flashes four fingers, then three, two, one. He shoots his hand out to the rear and Dan flings himself into the dark.

Chapter 2

Instantly the roar of the engines dropped as the plane receded away from him. It was replaced by the roar of the wind rushing past him. Dan twisted his body into a forward, partly face down position. His heart was racing and he had to force his breathing to slow so he wouldn't hyperventilate. The night was pitch black. There were no lights on the ground. There was just desert somewhere below him; the desert and his objective. At his rate of fall it would take him less than three minutes to reach the ground. He kept his eye on the altimeter as the dials spun around. The hand measuring feet spun in a blur so he focused on the arm marking each thousand-foot interval.

It was cold. The exposed parts of his face felt frozen. He flexed his hands, trying to keep them loose. He had to be able to pull his chute open and drop the rucksack. It was critical to find an open spot to land without breaking a limb. A good landing was the last challenge of his jump. The night was dark and he would have very little time or light to see by before he hit the ground. He had to aim for a boulder-free spot. Small rocks, while painful, would not inflict serious injury, but twisting his ankle or breaking a bone by hitting a boulder would end his mission in failure.

The twenty-five hundred foot mark came up. Dan pulled his lanyard and his chute opened with a slap, jerking his feet down under him. The ferocious wind dropped to a breeze. He grabbed the control lines and peered down, trying to penetrate the darkness. To his right he sensed more than saw a large rock formation; the shoulder of a hill. He looked left. The ground seemed flatter. As he closed in on a thousand feet, he could make out scattered large rock outcroppings reflecting up at him from the starlight. He steered to the left more and saw the ground open up. *That's the spot!*

As the ground rose up at him, he pulled the rucksack lanyard. It dropped away below and behind him. At the last minute he pulled both control lines to flare the chute and slow his descent. His feet touched the desert. His left foot twisted outward over a boulder he hadn't seen. He dropped onto the sand and rolled. The chute collapsed away from him. There was little wind so no danger of it trying to drag him.

"Damn." Dan cursed under his breath. He lay on his back and pulled his left leg up with his knee near his chin. His ankle started to throb. After holding it up for a moment to assess the damage, he got up, unclipped his rucksack and limped forward gathering in the parachute. With the chute bundled in his hands he shuffled back to his pack. He sat down, slipped off his parachute pack, and stuffed the chute back inside as best he could. Then he pulled his ankle up again.

Got to keep it from swelling. He removed his facemask and took a deep breath of the desert air. It was clean and dry. The silence was so complete as to be almost a presence, having weight to it. From the top of his rucksack, Dan took out his Night Vision Goggles and clipped them to his helmet. He surveyed his surroundings. Nothing showed but rocks and sand. Nothing moved in the greenish light of the NVG goggles. Next he checked his position against his GPS mark.

Crap. He was way off target. *Two strikes and I've barely started the game.* He was two miles off target. *How the hell did that happen?* That meant more walking. Something that now was going to be problematic.

The first order of business was to tend to his ankle. He had no ice and limited bandages. The best course seemed to be to keep it elevated for the present and then put a wrap on it to support the joint. It would swell but he'd just have to live with that. It was important to not allow more damage to the joint. He had two days of hiking to complete over unknown and uneven ground.

Still he should leave his landing site in case anyone saw or heard him. *I don't think that's happened.* But he remembered Jane's admonitions to not take anything for granted. He dug into his rucksack and found some tape. Carefully he wrapped his ankle the way his high school football coach had done to keep him on the field. After twenty nervous minutes he hooked his parachute pack to the rucksack, gingerly stood up, and shouldered it. At fifty pounds, it was going to be a heavy load to carry, especially with his injured ankle.

He lumbered off looking like an alien with his pack making a large hump on his back and the goggles strapped to his head with their single intake lens sticking out from his face. After putting two miles between him and his drop point, Dan stopped to take off his jump gear. Night was beginning to fade. He could see the darkness begin to recede in the eastern part of the sky. Soon it would be dawn, which would bring new challenges as the heat rose. It was June and the desert would get to over one hundred degrees in the daytime; possibly too hot to hike while fully loaded. He'd go as far as he could and then hole up until the evening.

Dan changed from his insulated jump suit into brown pants and shirt with a soft-brimmed, tan hat. He jammed his parachute and its pack in a rock cleft and donned his tactical vest, made to look like a civilian garment. Next he strapped on his side arm, a Beretta M9, and shouldered an M4A1carbine with its telescoping butt stock. His sniper rifle, a Barrett MRAD, remained disassembled in his pack. He ate an energy bar and drank deeply from a water bottle. Then, with a look over his shoulder towards where he had landed, he set out south towards his objective.

Jane Tanner, his CIA handler, had mentored him through his agent training and given him this assignment. Dan considered it a diversion from his core mission. The task had an impromptu feel to it. Jane, however, considered it business to be done. The point of the black ops they were setting up and why they had recruited Dan was to strike any target, anywhere. Two days from now, if all went well, Dan would be at the rim of a mesa overlooking a hacienda nestled in a river valley. The house and the ranch surrounding it had the uninhabited mesa to the north and hills to the east. South and west the land stretched away flat for miles. The approach road went through the eastern hills. It was actually a multi-mile driveway. There were no other dwellings along its route which ended at this isolated ranch.

From the mesa, Dan was to assassinate the current most powerful drug lord in Mexico, Jorge Mendoza, leader of the Sinaloa cartel. He had called a meeting of the other cartel leaders to convince them to stop their fighting one another, set up some rules, and increase the flow of drugs and money. All the major cartels would be represented: Beltran-Leyva, Gulf, Juarez, Tijuana, and Los Zetas. Mendoza's goal was to create a super council to partition territory and resources, eliminate infighting, and to open up new channels of income. Working together he felt they could consolidate their hold on the government and increase their control over the *Policía Federal* as well as the local police forces.

Jane's sources were from NSA communication intercepts. Additionally she had limited corroboration from the CIA informers on the ground, HUMINT resources. She was worried about the damage the cartels could cause if they stopped fighting one another. She knew how effective the US mafia had become after they apportioned territory to the ruling families. Mexico was nearly a failed narco state at this time and Mendoza's plan could push it over the edge. The intel was imperfect, but the threat the plan could present to the U.S. was enough for Jane and her boss, Henry Mason, to decide to do something about it. If Mendoza was taken down, the cooperation amongst the cartels would collapse and infighting was sure to break out.

Chapter 3

On the West Wharf was the Karachi International Container Terminal. It was the main terminal in the port city of Pakistan. One evening in May, five tractors pulling forty foot containers drove onto the piers. The containers passed through customs. The declaration paperwork indicated the boxes held a variety of textiles and bales of cotton fiber bound for Mexico.

These containers were special however. They did hold cotton fiber in bales, stacked firmly up against the doors five feet deep and along the sides to provide sound insulation. But just behind the rear bales, six thousand kilos of heroin were stacked and strapped in place. The remaining space in each box housed twelve men. The tops of the containers were modified to provide a concealed gap that allowed air to enter. There were panels along the lower sides that allowed air to escape. These would remain closed until the containers were in place and the ship sailed. Since the boxes were lighter than most freight, they were scheduled to be packed high on the deck, not down in the hold. This insured a good flow of air to the men inside. They would endure a thirty-day voyage to the Mexican port of Veracruz in the Gulf of Mexico.

The men were prepared for the deprivations of the trip. They had trained for six months. They would do a partial fast for the trip to minimize the human waste that had to be dealt with inside the containers. It would be a brutal experience but these were brutal men. Their mission was to sneak into the U.S. via the southern border and disperse throughout the country. They were the test case; more would be sent along if they were successful. They would implant themselves into Muslim communities and connect with the members of the local mosques. The men were taught to seek out and identify disaffected youths who they could begin to radicalize. These men were the advance guard of a multi-year invasion planned by al Qaeda.

Others who would arrive had orders to plan and execute terror attacks on designated targets. The two-pronged approach, infiltration and radicalization along with direct terror operations were certain to sow disruption in American society. Along the way the men would rely on Muslim apologists and activist groups to lecture the public about rights and freedoms as the terrorists went to work tearing down the society.

The heroin was to cement the connection between the terrorists and the Sinaloa cartel. It would be a financially lucrative connection, both for the organizers back in Pakistan and the cartel. The drugs also greased the skids for the infiltration plans of Al Qaeda.

The men in the container could not tell exactly what was going on. They felt the trucks stop and then minutes later they were abruptly lifted up, swung to one side and put back down. The men looked at each other wondering what was going on. They could not be aboard; they hadn't been lifted high enough. For the next four hours they sat without moving. Then the men heard the metallic sound of something clamping to the metal box. This time they were lifted up, higher and higher and then swung outward. More slowly they felt the container lowered and clamped into place. They were on the ship.

At the docks Tariq Basara watched the containers under the glare of the floodlights; they would be among the last to be hoisted aboard. When they were finally loaded high on the deck stack and locked down, he breathed a sigh of relief. The first part of the plan had been accomplished. His driver looked over his shoulder at Tariq who nodded. They drove off.

They rode through the dark labyrinth of streets in the Gulshan E-Sekandarabad section of Karachi. It was not far from the docks but seemed removed in time from the modern, urban setting of the container terminal. It was run by one Sikandar Jadoon, a gangster that controlled this section of reclaimed land. The driver had picked Tariq up in the northwest section of Karachi called Manghaphir. It was a Taliban controlled area, nearly a "no-go" zone for the overworked Karachi police. The driver took them across the sprawling city and now navigated the labyrinthine streets with assurance while Tariq was soon lost.

The man he was to meet made him nervous. He was a wealthy, shadowy figure; an Arab with an international reach who did much of his legitimate business in Pakistan. He also was a benefactor and conduit of funds to people like Tariq; people who had a vision of how to change the strategy of the war with the west. The man liked new ideas that kept the enemy off balance. He understood, as Tariq did, that they waged a multi-generational war. They would do their part to weaken the west and then pass the fight on to another generation.

The benefactor, Rashid al-Din Said, liked Tariq's idea of men who would plant seeds for future, home-grown terrorists with the U.S. It was this idea of smuggling men into the U.S. who would do more than commit acts of terror that had caught his attention. Tariq was one of the few people who knew of Rashid's connection to terrorist groups. That fact made him nervous. If any agency were to close in on Rashid, Tariq knew the man would take any step to quickly eliminate any possible ties and he was one of those ties. But this risk was just one of the many Tariq took in his war against the west. He had grown up poor in the disputed territories in the northwest border area with Afghanistan. He was too young to have fought the Soviets but many of his uncles did so and told exciting stories of driving the infidels out. Now there was another infidel to drive out; not only from Afghanistan, but from all the mideast. And since joining Al Qaeda, Tariq set his sights on the U.S. and the west in general. He would play his part and, god willing, rise to higher levels of leadership.

Tonight he was to report the successful insertion of sixty men aboard a container ship that would unload thirty days later in Mexico. The start of their journey to America had begun. Tariq would also pick up a half million dollars to transfer to a certain bank in the Caymans. It was his down payment for the smuggling operation.

The car turned the corner into an even narrower street. The driver slowed. Tariq noticed two men at the corner who observed his vehicle. Halfway down the street the car stopped. A man stepped out from a doorway and walked up to the car. Tariq could see the bulge of a handgun in his jacket pocket. He peered into the car and stepped back to open the door. Another man appeared in the doorway. He held an automatic rifle held in his hands.

When Tariq stepped out of the car, the first man motioned for him to hold up his hands. He patted him down carefully, to his ankles, front and back. After a word to the driver, the car pulled away and the man motioned Tariq forward to the door.

After entering the dark doorway, he climbed two flights of stairs in between the two guards. No one spoke. On the second floor the lead guard stopped at a door and knocked quietly.

"*Udkhul.*" The Arabic word for "enter" came from within.

The man opened the door. Tariq stepped into the room. It was softly lit. There were fragrant smells of lamb and spices. At the far end of the room was a low table with his host sitting on a large cushion beside it. He motioned for Tariq to come forward and join him. The man did not get up, a sign of his greater stature. He gestured for Tariq to sit across from him.

"Come, sit. You have had a busy evening and I trust it was successful."

"Yes *Sayyid.*" Tariq used the Arabic expression of respect.

"Well, let us celebrate." He clapped his hand and a veiled woman brought a tray with sweet tea to the men. The two body guards stood at the corners of the room, not taking their eyes off of Tariq.

Tariq savored the tea. Soon plates of food were brought to the table. He ate out of politeness. He was not hungry. He only wanted to get back to his own group and depart this city which offered so many possibilities for trouble.

"So the men will endure? It will be a long time. They will see neither the sky nor the sun."

"They will endure, *Sayyid*. They are well trained and ready. They are not soft like the west."

Rashid smiled. "No they are not...and you are not. But will they find it difficult to be in the heart of the decadent west?"

"No. We know we can use the freedoms of the west against them. This is our way. We don't adopt them but use them and look forward to a time where we will purge all the faithful of such ways."

"And my ways, do they offend you?"

Tariq caught himself before he could register any shock at the question. "No, Sayyid. You fight in the manner you are accustomed to. That benefits all of us."

"But you hope to see all of us return to purer ways."

"*Inshallah.*" Tariq said no more. The direction of the conversation seemed dangerous to him.

"It is all right, my young warrior. We all have a part to play. There will be need for businessmen to operate, but we do want to purify the faithful and break their infatuation with the west, just as we want to cripple the west so they can't control us anymore. That is a common goal we can work towards."

"Indeed. We have the same goals." Tariq focused on the food.

When they had eaten and the table cleared, Rashid motioned to one of the guards who went into another room and returned with a briefcase. He set the case down next to Rashid.

Rashid flicked open the latches and turned the case around. Tariq looked at the neat stacks of one-hundred dollar bills; five thousand of them. "Here is the down payment for your work. You have to deal with a dirty man. Try not to contaminate yourself."

Tariq nodded. He didn't like doing business with the drug lord. "But it has to be done."

Rashid closed the lid and slid the case to Tariq. He leaned towards the terrorist. His voice came low and sharp; almost a hiss. "When this is done, someday you must kill him. Do it for me, and I will reward you well."

Tariq looked up at the rich man, his *patrón*. He had harbored his doubts about Rashid's orthodoxy, but accepted the fact that the man wanted to help his cause. Now he saw a glimpse of perhaps a deeper motivation; perhaps a deeper commitment to the Islamic cause. "It will be an honor, when the time comes." He sensed dismissal and stood. After thanking Rashid, one of the guards opened the door and Tariq went out as he came in, between the two large men, only now with a briefcase of money in his hands.

Chapter 4

Dan stood six feet tall with brown hair and hazel eyes that seemed to change color depending on what he wore. He looked fit but not that muscular. His body though was more powerful than one might have suspected. In high school a coach taught him to concentrate on core muscle development along with the major muscle groups. The result was that Dan had a deceptively strong body that could absorb a lot of abuse without injury.

He had joined the army after school and quickly came to the attention of his instructors for his shooting ability. He was encouraged to try out for sniper school and made it into the ranks of snipers. Dan relished not only the shooting but also the physical challenges encountered during the course.

He had been hiking for an hour when the sun broke over the horizon. Almost immediately he could feel the temperature climb. *Going to have to stop soon.* There was no way he could hike through the day burdened with a fifty-pound pack when the desert heated up to its full extent. It would be a waste of water resources and he would risk exhaustion. Two hours later, he slipped off his pack and nestled himself under a rock ledge that gave him some shade. He propped up his left ankle as best he could and tried to relax. The ankle throbbed. He could feel the swelling and didn't dare take off his boot. *Only if it begins to go numb.* He began to relax; his mind drifted back to the days after his recruitment.

Jane Tanner worked for the CIA. More specifically she worked for Henry Mason who had maneuvered himself into a small sub-section of the SAD, Special Activities Division. He headed a five-person team that included Jane. They were technically under the Psychological Operations section but Henry reported to Roger Abrams, an old friend and CIA veteran who was the director of SAD.

Jane had discovered Dan during his vendetta against the mob family in Brooklyn that had killed his wife and unborn child. He had been so successful in taking down their operations that his actions had come to Jane's attention. She was charged with recruiting someone to pilot this new black ops program. To that end, she had enlisted several agents she knew in the Crime and Narcotics Center and HUMINT Coordination Center to keep their eyes out for potential assets for recruitment. Jane didn't mention the mission objective and no one asked. A field agent stationed in New York City due to its attraction as a terrorist target noticed someone taking down members of a mob family in Brooklyn and brought it to Jane's attention.

After some work, Jane was able to make contact with Dan. When they finally met, Jane explained the operation and its objectives to him. The point was to take out the enemy terrorists *before* they struck, not after. As intel identified terrorists Dan, an ex-military sniper, would be sent around the world to eliminate the targets.

Jane had arranged for Dan to disappear after his vendetta, making a deal with the FBI and spiriting him away to Camp Perry near Williamsburg, Virginia to train for his assignment. When she presented him with his first assignment after completing his training, Dan thought it didn't fit the mission objectives and expressed his concerns.

They met on a clear early spring day in Washington, DC. The air was crisp with still a winter's bite to it but the sun was shining stronger as spring approached. Brave daffodils, always coming out early, were showing off their yellow, announcing the arrival of a new season. The ground greedily soaked up the sun's warmth even though people were still bundled in their coats.

Dan had spent the night in the Key Bridge Marriott just across the Potomac River from Georgetown. In the morning he walked south through Gateway Park and down Lynne Street to a Starbucks. Along the way he stopped to look into store windows, using the reflection to check to see if he was being followed. He scanned the pedestrians as they passed by on their way to work. After purchasing a juice in the coffee shop, he checked the sidewalks and then crossed the street to enter an office building. The building spanned the narrow block and opened on to the adjacent street as well as the one where he entered. He traversed the lobby and exited one block to the west on North Moore Street. Within a minute Jane drove up and Dan got in the passenger seat. He glanced over his shoulder as they pulled back out into traffic.

She circled around and headed back across Key Bridge into Georgetown. She drove north weaving through the neighborhood streets and finally headed west on Reservoir Road. They crossed back into Virginia over Chain Bridge Road and took the George Washington Parkway west to I495, the beltway around DC. Going north they crossed back over the Potomac River, took the Clara Barton Parkway back east to Glen Echo Park. The park, usually deserted this time of morning, had one car in the lot. Waiting in it was Henry Mason, Jane's boss.

Henry was sixty-one. He stood about five feet, nine inches with thick, white hair and glasses. He had a portly build and looked more like a professor than a spy. His eyes usually held a glint to them that hinted at a lively sense of humor. Today he looked serious and concerned. They all got out of their cars and started walking through the empty parking lot.

"So, you recruited me to go after terrorists. You spent a lot of time and money training me for the past eighteen months. I'm now fluent in Spanish, passable in Italian and German with a smattering of Russian. Why send me after a drug lord?" Dan asked.

Henry smiled. "There's more to this than meets the eye." He looked at Jane before continuing. "We are concerned about a growing interface between drugs and terrorists."

"You said, 'growing'. Aren't there terrorists we know about right now that I could go after?"

"Yes," Jane said, "but this situation is getting more urgent and we need to act on it."

"What the hell is more urgent than killing known terrorists, especially leaders?"

"Jane told me you were a bit difficult," Henry said. "I understand you gave the instructors a hard time at the Farm."

"I don't think I'm difficult. I just need for things to make sense to me. And this doesn't."

The three stood huddled against the wind which had come up, driving away the warmth of the sun's rays. Jane stood noticeably taller than Henry in her low heels. Dan at six feet was the tallest of the three.

"Look, this wind is chilly on my old bones. Let's go into Bethesda. I know a restaurant that has some private corners where we can talk out of the wind." Henry turned and led them back to his car and they drove off.

They settled into a booth in the back corner of the Town Diner and took off their coats. The restaurant was warm and inviting. The aroma of fresh coffee and bacon fill the air. It was comfortably dark and worn; a place that invited you to relax. The waitress brought menus but everyone just ordered coffee. After the coffee was delivered she left them alone.

"A little history might help," Jane said. "Henry, would you mind going through it?"

He nodded. "Since the sixties and the cold war the Soviet Union has had a program to undermine the west through drugs. It wasn't all that new of an idea; Mao had used it against his enemies in the thirties in China. What was different was that Khrushchev wanted to insulate the soviets from any connection to the program. They used their satellites, mainly Czechoslovakia in this effort. Cuba was brought into the program as well. They were enthusiastic about it because the drug smuggling generated hard currency for them. None of the participants were allowed to keep all the money, though. It was directed through offshore banks and dummy accounts so that most of the money could wind up back in the Soviet Union untraced. The program used known drug smugglers and dealers; again as a protection against tying the operations back to the Soviets."

"So when did we find out about this...and how? Seems like this would be pretty volatile information. I never heard about it."

"We found out about it in the early seventies. There was a defection of a very high-ranking Czech who had been heavily involved in the planning of this operation. We debriefed him but no one wanted to know about the problem."

"Why the hell not?"

Henry sighed. "We were entering an era of détente; the opening up of China, working to get along with the Soviets, lower the tensions of the cold war, all of that. Alexandr Janacek's information didn't fit in to where the State Department and administration wanted to go."

"So they ignored him?"

Henry shrugged. "Pretty much. If the information got out, the public would have been furious and would have demanded action."

Dan thought for a moment. "Okay, that's interesting history, but what does that have to do with now? I mean the Soviet Union is gone." He leaned back. All this information still didn't address why he should be going to Mexico.

Jane touched his arm. "Do you think this ended with the downfall of the soviets? Where did Putin come from but the KGB? They were heavily involved in this drug scheme along with various interior ministries. While the plan was highly secret, it involved a lot of agencies, just not many people in each agency."

"And now we know that Venezuela is connected to the terrorists," Henry said. "They have a known Syrian-born terrorist in their administration and we know he's involved in the cocaine and marijuana smuggling business."

"I get that drugs could be a good way to try to undermine the country, although it doesn't seem to have worked all that well with us. I get that it provides money for other operations, but I still don't see why this assignment."

Conversation stopped as the waitress refilled their cups. Henry had her bring the check. When she was gone again he continued.

"Recently we were appraised of an NSA intercepted a transmission that indicated al Qaeda was working on some kind of deal with Jorge Mendoza. We don't think it's about drugs."

"Who's Jorge and what's it about?"

"Jorge is the head of the Sinaloa cartel. It's the most powerful of the Mexican cartels. And this deal seems to be about smuggling terrorists into the U.S. They do it already with low-level operators, *Coyotes* who are loosely connected to the cartels. This is going to be something bigger."

"So taking out Mendoza will derail this deal?"

Henry nodded. "That's what we hope. The added benefit is that the cooperation plan between the cartels may also disintegrate. Mexico is too close to being a failed state and we have too large a border with them. Columbia was bad enough, as is Venezuela now; we don't want that on our borders."

The shadows had lengthened while Dan had been lost in thought. Suddenly his attention turned to a scorpion advancing towards him. He flicked a pebble at it. The scorpion didn't run. It backed up and arched its stinger in the air. He could see that the arachnid understood its power and was not going to be easily intimidated. *Wonder if they're territorial?* The thought made him uneasy. Sighing, he got up. There would be no more lying about and relaxing while wondering if the scorpion was going to come after him. He hoisted the pack and, testing his ankle, started limping south.

Dan struggled through the night. His ankle got worse and finally around 3 am he had to stop. He found a level spot against a rock wall. After scanning carefully for scorpions he settled down with his pack under his head and his left foot propped up on a rock.

The dawn woke him. As he looked around he noticed a large black bird perched on a boulder about fifty feet away. It would not have drawn his attention except that it seemed odd to see a bird perched so close; all the other birds he'd seen either flitted away before he got close or were soaring high in the sky like the hawk he saw yesterday. The other odd thing was that the bird seemed to be staring at him. The sun glinted off of its eyes and he thought one of them looked to be black and the other red. *Is that normal?*

He studied the bird for a few moments and then ate an energy bar and drank some of his water. He relaxed and let his eyes close again. His foot was throbbing less and he hoped spending the day off of it would allow him to walk all the next night. He could not be late for his rendezvous with Mendoza.

Chapter 5

Jorge Mendoza pushed the off button on his phone. He was standing behind his opulent desk in the private office of his mansion in Mexico City. He was a thick man about five feet ten inches tall; built like a fireplug. He had a broad face without elegance. It spoke of Indian blood in his lineage. It also hinted at a brutal nature. He was not a subtle man nor did he look like one.

Hector Ortega, his close friend and lieutenant stood across the room watching his boss carefully. He was taller and thinner than his Jorge. He had an angular face and sharp eyes that shifted around, looking and evaluating. His hair was black and slicked back. A hint of cruelty showed in his mouth even when he smiled.

The two had had a long relationship. Jorge came up through the ranks of the Sinaloa cartel by being smart, efficient and ruthless. He started out as a *sicario*, a hit man, but he had a knack for making things work and was soon elevated to higher positions in the cartel. He could be relied upon to carry out any task whether it was opening another smuggling route into the U.S., taking out a competitor, or enforcing discipline within the gang.

Jorge could be charming and pleasant, to men as well as women. When he turned on the charm, people felt comfortable and warmed up to him. Although he came from peasant stock, he found it easy to relax in the company of the elites. They, knowing his power, enjoyed how urbane he appeared to be. The women seemed to be attracted to his power as much as his charm. He enjoyed their company and was reputed to have a huge sexual appetite. But all this masked a dangerous, vicious nature and, when crossed, he was ruthless. Actual enemies as well as perceived enemies disappeared as a result of his orders if not directly by his hands. People who got involved with Jorge had to be very careful and, once involved, they had little chance of backing out. He trapped people with his favors and then demanded adherence to his dictates.

Hector had recognized Jorge's ascendance and attached himself to the man. He watched Jorge's back every step of the way. Hector didn't have the vision Jorge had, but he knew his friend was destined to be a big man in the cartel and Hector knew how to protect him. He had an ability to sniff out deception and disloyalty and quickly dealt with it. Jorge had learned to trust Hector over the years and considered him his special advantage in this dangerous business. Hector soon was taking care of all the dirty work for Jorge.

When the previous boss, Miguel Rivera, was captured, all the cartels were worried that he might give up information in exchange for protection against extradition to the U.S. Winding up in a U.S prison was the worst fate a drug kingpin could imagine. In Mexico one could bribe the jailers for many special favors. Life inside the prison was made easier by special food, liquor, and prostitutes. The funds also bought off not only the guards but other inmates who helped enforce the drug lord's orders. But in the U.S., the regulations were stricter. Life was not so easy and there was no hope of escape or release. To many it seemed worse than death.

A delegation from the other cartels came to Jorge to ask him to intervene. Jorge struck a deal with the other drug lords that if he took care of the problem, they would acknowledge his leadership over the cartel. They were happy to oblige him. Next he convinced all of Rivera's lieutenants, of whom he was the most powerful, that their futures were at risk and he could protect them if they pledged their loyalty to him.

With everyone set up, Jorge had Hector smuggle a knife into prison to a street level cartel member who, two days later, stuck it into the base of Rivera's skull, through his brain stem. Then Hector got the word out about who had done the killing and let the prison inmates take care of the rest, leaving behind no evidence of his or Jorge's involvement.

He was in his private office in his Mexico City mansion when Hector had come in.

"You called me. What's going on?" Hector asked.

"The Pakistani, Tariq. He's coming to oversee the transfer of the men."

"He'll get in the way. We don't need him around."

"I agree, but he's bringing in the heroin along with the men. I guess he wants to be present to protect his goods and not do the transaction at a distance," replied Jorge.

"Is this still a good idea?" Hector asked.

Jorge looked sharply at him. "The drugs?"

"No, smuggling the men."

"We will deliver the goods."

"But you have the cartel meeting in the middle of—"

"Which is what I want. I will show the other bosses how we can broaden our incomes. They need to see we are leading the way and have serious allies around the world.

They need to see I have the vision and the international connections. There are many around the world who will work with us if it's against the U.S."

"But making peace between all of the cartels, won't that be more effective?"

Jorge paused. Hector meant well but he had no vision. "This helps to cement the peace. The others need to see my strength and influence. I will lead them to cooperate, but I will be in charge. Do not question me. I have made my decision." He pointed his finger at him. "Just make sure this goes well—both the meeting and collecting the terrorists."

Hector nodded. He knew when to keep quiet. His boss was not a man to oppose. "I will meet the ship in Veracruz and transport the cargo to Chihuahua. I'll put them in one of our warehouses to let them recover. I think they will be in bad shape after living in a steel coffin for thirty days."

Jorge shrugged. "Good enough. They are zealots. They'll survive." He looked over at the side wall with its shrine to Santa Muerte. "We survive as well."

Tariq's plane landed in Veracruz. He carried with him a bearer bond in the amount of $250,000 taken from the half million he had received from Rashid. He checked into a small, three-story hotel two blocks from the waterfront. It was inexpensive but that wasn't the reason Tariq picked it. He chose it because it was anonymous and he could blend in as a limited budget tourist.

He had shaved his beard and wore western clothes; a long sleeve shirt and pants, suitable for the hot climate. He had stylish sunglasses and wore a brimmed hat. He carried an Egyptian passport and passed himself off as a single man with a good job on an inexpensive vacation. His only issue came with the taxi driver who wanted to drive him by all the tourist traps where he would get stiffed for overpriced drinks. When that didn't work, the man offered to find a woman for him. Tariq declined and the driver glanced suspiciously at him throughout the rest of the drive to the hotel.

The ship wouldn't arrive for two more days. His communications with Jorge about the arrangements weren't comforting. Jorge wouldn't meet with him and told him he would be dealing with Hector. He assured Tariq that the containers would be picked up and trucked to Chihuahua, to a safe warehouse where the men could recover their strength and get ready for the final leg of their journey. Tariq insisted that he ride along with one of the trucks and after a tense argument, Jorge agreed. Now Tariq had nothing to do but wait.

It was near dawn on the third night when Dan reached the rim of the mesa. The rim consisted of a jagged line of broken boulders offering good concealment with crevices through which he could place his rifle. He chose a spot that would offer some protection from the sun and set up his hide. He strung a camouflage net across the space covering his resting and shooting area. He had pushed hard and was a day early but waiting was part of the job. Patience had been drilled into him in sniper school. You waited for your opponent to expose their position, for the enemy to show up, or for a clear shot; always you waited. After screening his hide with the netting and arranging his gear he propped up his sore ankle and tried to relax. A few hours of sleep would be nice before it got so bloody hot.

He would have to wait out the day while keeping his eyes on the target area. If the plans had changed and people arrived early, Dan had to be ready. He would get very little sleep in the coming day.

When the sun cleared the hills to the east the temperature began to rise again. Dan stirred, thankful he had fallen asleep for a couple of hours; there would be little chance of that for the rest of the day. *Better look at my ankle.* He was dusty, dirty, and nervous about taking off his boot. If the ankle started to balloon up, he'd have to jam it back on and use it like a cast. It wasn't throbbing deeply so Dan figured he could safely examine the injured joint.

Gingerly he unlaced the boot and slipped off his sock. The ankle was swollen and discolored. The tape had supported it well through the two nights of hiking. Dan decided to leave his foot out for a while, making sure to keep it elevated. A half hour later, his patience ran out. He was thirsty, hungry and he had to pee. He put some more tape over the original wrap, rolled his sock back on and carefully maneuvered his foot back into the boot. He kept the laces loose for now but would tighten them when he had to move...after the shot. When he had gotten the boot on, he crawled out from under the netting and limped away from the rim to relieve himself.

Then he saw a black bird, either a crow or a raven. The size of it made Dan think it was probably a raven. It was like the one he saw the day before. It was farther away but looking at him, like the other one had done. *Are ravens that interested in humans? Enough to study us?* He knew they were smart, but the idea of them being interested in human beings seemed to be a stretch.

After taking care of his business, he limped back to his hide to survey the target area with his binoculars. The road came from the east, through some rocky hills and ended at the ranch. To the north of it was the uninhabited mesa where Dan lay in wait. West and south the ground stretched away to the horizon. It was a hot, dry land. He could see dust devils already starting to swirl around on the flat ground. They appeared out of nowhere, spun up and then fell apart. Some were more robust and danced across the parched earth. Very little grew here. There was a shallow river at the base of the mesa flowing east through the hills. Dan guessed it dried up regularly but it offered enough moisture to support a line of willow bushes along its banks.

The entrance to the building faced north towards the mesa. The drive turned up towards the front of the house in a loop. There was a long porch roof to shade the doorway. From his height Dan could see the house was built with a central courtyard, hacienda style. In the courtyard was a pool with screening hung over much of the space to protect it from the harsh sun. Two fountains splashed and the abundant potted plants gave the courtyard a cool, inviting look. Beyond the courtyard was a flat area of packed dirt with a windsock at one end. *Probably a helipad. If everyone arrives by helicopter this could be a difficult shot.* Still it was nice, he thought, for them to give him a wind gauge. On one side of the hacienda was a tower with a wind mill on top. It probably drove the pump that supplied water to the ranch. A barn stood out back to one side of the helipad. The associated corrals gave evidence that the ranch had housed horses at one time. Now everything seemed empty.

Before the morning cool had completely dissipated, two men came out of the front door. They were armed. Through his binoculars, Dan could see the weapons were military in style but very short. *Most likely MP-5s.* The MP-5 was one of the more popular submachine guns in the world. It was generally fitted with a thirty-round magazine and was reliable, accurate, and very easy to control.

The weapon in the hands of most shooters was good for close up work only—up to one hundred yards at the most. Dan's position was well beyond their range. The ranch was nine hundred feet below the mesa rim and about seven hundred and fifty yards from its base, angling to the east, which gave Dan a shot of eight hundred yards to the front door. It was long but well within his capabilities and the capability of his rifle.

The men walked around the outside of the hacienda, checking the walls and few shrubs growing along their base. They glanced out across the flat land but there was no cover for concealment. Dan could see they were relaxed. No one could sneak up close to the ranch and the surrounding hills were uninhabited and far away. He smiled at the thought. *They never take the sniper into account.* That oversight was going to cost them. A maid came out to sweep the porch and walkway out to the dirt drive. It looked like a futile effort to Dan. *Maybe she just wants to show how industrious she is.*

He went to his backpack and wrestled out the rifle case. He spread out a cloth on the dirt and opened the package. He had chosen a Barrett MRAD firing a .338 Lapua Magnum cartridge. The round could penetrate body armor at one thousand yards and was effective up to nineteen hundred yards. It was more than enough. The MRAD had a twenty-four inch barrel and was equipped with a Steiner scope. A suppressor was screwed on to the end of the barrel. The suppressor would mask the dust signature and the source of his shot. The only thing anyone would hear would be the sonic boom which would give no clue as to the direction the shot came from. At the point of fire, a forceful, squishy *chuff* would be heard followed by the sonic boom. The bullet would arrive at its target in just over eight tenths of a second.

Dan thought the weapon was a bit awkward. The design incorporated a sealed upper receiver, where the bolt retracted when ejecting a cartridge. This design made for a longer than normal receiver. The gun was heavy but Dan expected that from a large caliber, precision rifle. It was not his favorite weapon, he liked the M110 better, but it was the right tool for this job. The M4 felt more comfortable to him and, even with a suppressor mounted, did not create too long a barrel. The weapon could switch from semi-automatic to fully automatic fire. It had a familiar feel, being similar to the M16.

An hour later a woman appeared in the courtyard accompanied by two kids. Dan shifted his position in the dirt and focused his binoculars on her. She was tall and slim with model good looks. She looked and acted like she was the mother of the kids—definitely not the nanny. There was a boy, maybe nine and a girl that looked a bit younger. The woman sat down in a chaise lounge and the kids jumped into the shallow end of the pool to play. A maid brought the woman something to drink, which only reinforced Dan's conclusion that she might be Mendoza's wife. If that was so, these were his kids.

Instead of opening a book or magazine, the woman watched the kids. She seemed to be engaged with them, talking to them as they played. The boy flicked some water at her and she pretended to be shocked. She jumped up from the lounge and ran out of his range. Then she grabbed a cup and dipped it into the pool and threw some water back at the boy who seemed to scream and dove under water. It looked, from Dan's view through the binoculars like the woman was laughing and enjoying her children as they played. Next the two kids began doing jumps off the diving board, twisting around and striking different poses while in the air, all to the delight and applause of the mother.

"Shit," he said out loud. *Why the fuck did he have to bring his family here? This is business for God's sake.* Dan didn't like it. Kids shouldn't be involved in this business; wives maybe but not kids. He knew many of the drug lords and their lieutenants had families but Dan always figured they were kept apart. There was some separation from business in the mafia families he encountered in Brooklyn during his vendetta and Dan assumed there would be even greater separation in this environment which was much more brutal than even the mafia. It seemed like the mafia of the thirties only with more firepower.

Back then they had Tommy guns; the Thompson submachine gun which fired a .45 caliber cartridge. They had a high rate of fire but were hard to keep on target. Now there were many more weapons to choose from. The choices included high-powered rifles, automatic assault weapons that were more accurate, semi-automatic handguns that held seventeen rounds in quick change magazines, grenade launchers, and even rocket launchers. It was a deadlier business now, no place for kids...or wives.

Maybe I'll get lucky and they'll stay inside. Still Dan didn't like having them present. They would see the results of his work first hand. No kid should see that. It didn't matter if they were a drug lord's kids. A sour taste formed in his mouth and his stomach tightened. *What am I going to do? The SOB had to bring them.* He knew Jorge had a mansion with lots of protection in the suburbs of Mexico City. *You should have left them back home.*

Mexico City was off limits to gang violence; drugs were okay but not gang violence. That, Jane had explained, was an unspoken pact between the cartels, the government, and the *Policía Federal.* Keep the violence out of the capital so they could pretend it wasn't happening. Dan snorted. *Fools, you made a pact with the devil. You allow the cartels room to operate, in exchange for what? Your souls and the soul of your country. And you, Jorge, you made your own pact and put your family in harm's way. You should have kept this separate. Did you think you were untouchable? You're not. I'm going to reach out and touch you. Touch you with a .338 Lapua round. You'll never know it happened.*

Chapter 6

Thirty days earlier, after Dan's meeting with Henry and Jane, Henry sat in Jane's small office. "Dan seems to be more than just argumentative. Is he going to be reliable?" he asked.

Jane gave her boss a long, steady look. "Henry, you know how Dan came to our attention, how his family was killed by the mob and he went on a vendetta against them. He is a man who has suffered damage...emotionally, to his psyche. Remember he had no options when I recruited him and we have set him up for a life bordering on insanity."

"So you expect him to flame out in short order?"

"I didn't say that. I think he has a good moral compass, but he's going to have quite a time squaring that with what we ask him to do."

"He'll be taking out the enemy, not innocents—"

"I understand, but there's always collateral damage, you know that. It will weigh heavily on him. I'm going to have to work hard to help him maintain a semblance of balance if I want him to survive. And I *do* want him to survive."

"I detect something personal there."

"Maybe. He's pretty emotionally needy even if he doesn't realize it. It strikes a chord with me." She shifted in her chair, sitting more upright. "But don't worry about me. I'll keep things professional. But he's going to have my full attention."

Just days before the mission to Mexico, Dan sat in Jane's small office with two other members of Jane's team. There was Fred Burke, Jane's researcher. His strength was combing through the data that flowed into the CIA, looking for clues to terrorist activity and identities. With him was Warren Thomas who was Jane's technical guy. He was a master at surveillance technology, as good as anyone in the firm. He was especially good at getting the most out of commercially available devices which couldn't be tracked back to any government agency.

Today Fred laid out a list of equipment he had written up that Dan should take with him. It included a sniper rifle, a tactical carbine, sidearm, grenades, grenade launcher, flash-bang grenades, ammunition, listening devices, a satellite phone, a complete medical kit, a tent, MRE packets, water, extra footwear, and clothing.

Dan went over the list. He looked up at Fred who sat nervously at the side of the desk. "Did you calculate how much this would weigh?"

"It is a bit heavy, but I couldn't see what could be taken out."

"How heavy?"

"Seventy-eight pounds," came the reply. Fred was nervous. He was sitting across from a trained killer. That was a first in his short career with the CIA.

Dan looked over at Jane and shook his head. "Almost eighty pounds. Jane, that isn't going to work. My butt's going to be on the line out there."

Jane was nonplussed. "That's why we're going over all of this with you. We are all on a learning curve. But if we work together, we'll learn quickly. Tell us what the problem is."

Dan took a deep breath and turned, "Okay, Fred, here's the learning curve. We start with the fact that eighty fucking pounds is too much to lug through the desert in the summer for two days. I have to be able to move quickly. So let's walk through the list and see how we can reduce it." Dan looked down at the paper in front of him. "Take this listening gear. I'm not going to be close enough to listen in on conversations, even with this hi-tech equipment. I assume we have the latest in hi-tech here." He turned to Jane.

She looked over at the fourth person in the room. "I'll let Warren answer. He's the expert."

Warren had unstylish, black framed glasses along with a large clump of curly hair that sat unruly on his head and looked like it would never submit to combing. He was dressed in baggy khaki slacks with a checked long sleeve shirt. Dan smiled. He couldn't remember the last time he'd seen a checked shirt. As Jane had explained, Warren could tap into any computer and rarely left any traces. Banks and government officials were no match for his skills. He could tap calls, track calls, generate fake calls and get just about any electronic piece of information you might need.

Warren nodded. "As state of the art as I can get without looking like it came from headquarters."

"What exactly does that mean?" Dan asked.

"It means it's the best you can purchase commercially. If anyone has the knowledge and knows what to buy, this is what they'll buy...if they want the best."

"That's good, but it still won't help me." He turned back to Fred. "Let's get this right."

Dan started lining out items on the list. "Forget the grenades, all types. The sniper rifle needs only half the ammo you listed. After the shot, I don't plan on using it. If I need protection, the M4 is what I'll be using. Skip the .45. I'll take a 9mm. The gun and ammo weigh less. One change of shirt and pants, one change of underwear and socks, and no extra boots. I won't need clean clothes until I get exfiltrated. Bag the tent but put in a reflective blanket. I'll sleep under it." Fred was furiously taking notes as Dan went on. "No MREs. Just some power bars. Let's trim down the medical supplies. If I take a hit and it's not fatal, I need to stop the bleeding, disinfect the wound, bandage it, dull the pain, and give myself a good general antibiotic, preferably in the form of a shot to protect against infection. If I have to treat more than one or two wounds, I'm toast anyway so don't plan for that." He looked over at Fred who appeared to be uncomfortable; perhaps from being in Dan's presence as well as missing the mark so badly.

It was hard not to notice Fred's discomfort. Jane was experienced, but her team was new. She had faith, though that they were smart enough to learn quickly.

"Don't feel bad. You'll get this right. Go with what I said and get this load down to fifty pounds. Can you do that?" Dan asked.

Fred nodded his head vigorously.

Jane indicated that he could leave so Fred quickly got up and rushed out of the office. "He'll get used to this," Jane said after he left.

"I hope so, or you're going to have to do his work for him," Dan responded.

"His real strength is researching, finding the bad guys from money trails, getting information on their habits, travel histories, living arrangements. This is the information you'll need to find them."

"Did he find out about this cartel meeting?" Dan asked.

"No, that was Warren," She said.

"It wasn't hard," Warren said. I learned of something going on from the NSA intercepts. Then I just monitored Mendoza's calls along with his lieutenant, Ortega. It didn't take long to verify our suspicions about a meeting, or to find its location." He paused for a moment before going on. "You have to take the sat phone though. That's how you'll contact us for picking you up."

"Okay, I'll do that. Who am I going to call?"

Jane spoke up. "My number is in the phone and we've got a number for the people who'll extract you. You call it and just let them know you want to be picked up at their earliest convenience. They'll know what to do and where to go."

She pulled out a satellite photograph of the desert north of the target. "You see this road?" Her fingers traced a dirt road, almost a trail running east to west across the mesa. "You'll cross it on your way to the target. It's a day's hike from the canyon rim. After the shot, when you're half a day away from the road, you call the phone. Someone will acknowledge your request and they'll come out to pick you up." She pointed to a mark on the picture. "I'll give you the coordinates. This is where you'll meet."

"This is secure?"

"The phone is, plus your communication will be simple and general. Also the roads not traveled. It dies out twenty miles west of where you are going to meet when it gets to the mesa rim. No one travels it because it doesn't connect with anything. There used to be a few farms to the west, the road serviced them, but they're abandoned now. Twenty-six miles to the east, there's a small crossroads with a gas pump and a few houses about ten miles before you reach the paved north-south road. You'll take that road route north, away from Chihuahua. You'll go north and then west to Hermosillo where a private plane will pick you up and fly you to the U.S."

"And if something gets screwed up? The car doesn't arrive or the plane doesn't arrive?"

"If the car doesn't arrive we have a problem."

"Damn right. I won't have enough water to hike north. And I can't take enough with me."

Jane ignored Dan's response. "If the plane doesn't arrive, you can still be driven north to the border. Either we smuggle you out, like I did in Massachusetts, or you can get out and cross over with all the other illegals who walk into the country."

"Thanks for that." Dan said.

"Sarcasm doesn't become you," Jane replied with a smile on her face.

"Just don't forget who's stuck out there if the connection isn't made."

"Henry assures me that everything is set up. The embassy doesn't have any hint of what is going on. All they know is that they are supposed to send someone to pick you up and drive you to Hermosillo.

"After the shot, the shit will hit the fan, you know that," Dan said.

"Yes, but no one will put you together with the shooting, at least for some time. And the driver will not know anything about what is going on. He'll be pre-positioned and just awaiting the pickup call."

Dan shook his head. "The pickup is the weak link in this adventure. I guess I'll have to take your word that it's all set up, but will you double check that yourself?"

Jane nodded. "I'll go over all of this with Henry again.

Dan remained worried, but as Jane had said over and over, he had to rely mostly on himself. There would be operations where all he was given would be the target's name and last known address and Dan would have to devise a plan all on his own. He decided that if the pickup didn't happen for whatever reason, he'd hike east to the crossroads and improvise from there. He would be about one hundred miles from the Texas border. He'd figure something out. The key was avoiding both the cartels and the federal police. *Piece of cake, right?*

Chapter 7

Tariq slept little that night. He awoke early with anticipation. This was the day. The ship was due to dock at noon. One large hurdle was about to be overcome. He would be reunited with his men by that evening. Mendoza had arranged for a car to pick Tariq up and take him to the docks. They would wait nearby while Mendoza's drivers hooked up to the containers. When they departed Tariq's driver would follow and join the convoy when out of town. From there on, Tariq would be with the trucks. There were orders to stop at night so that the containers could be opened and the men inside get some relief. Then it would be back in the containers; the goal was to drive through the night to reach Chihuahua and the warehouse by late the next day. Once there the men would be able to begin their recovery. Tariq would oversee their activities. They would probably stay a week before moving on to the border. A section of the Arizona border had been selected. It avoided the Rio Grande and the increased focus on the Texas border areas. Once on the U.S. side, the men would be transported by members of the cartel to a safe house outside of Phoenix. After getting some forged documents they would disperse separately to infiltrate the country.

Tariq's plan was to see them off from the warehouse in Chihuahua and then wait to hear they had crossed successfully before departing the country. Although Rashid had encouraged him to kill Mendoza he knew he wouldn't, at least not yet. It was not out of good will. There was still too much business to do, delivering drugs and men to the cartel to be smuggled into the US. Maybe when they were not going to do business any more he could try to satisfy his sponsor.

Tariq checked out of the hotel and went across the street. He was not hungry but knew he should eat something. The restaurant would have nothing that was halal but Allah would not mind since he was in the middle of jihad. He ordered strong coffee and a pastry.

At nine the car arrived. The driver spoke little English and Tariq spoke little Spanish. He was directed to sit in the back seat and they departed for the docks.

Being on the top of the deck stacks, the five containers were off-loaded first. Tariq was anxious. He had to force himself to sit quietly in the back of the car. Within an hour of the start of the unloading process the five containers had been put on trailers, cleared customs, and were on their way through the streets of Veracruz with Tariq's car following. Tariq could only wonder what the men inside were thinking. They would know they are on land and being transported by truck. He had told them that patience at the end of the voyage was important. They couldn't just unload them and open the containers in public. The men had to wait until it was safe to be let out. This evening they would stop and he would be there to greet his mujahedeen, the men who would take the fight to the American people. Tariq smiled as he thought about the future of his plan.

Dan sat patiently as the day grew hotter, grateful for even the limited screening he had arranged with the boulders and netting. He drank carefully, not knowing how long his limited supply of water would have to last. His ankle seemed to have settled down. Still he kept it elevated. He leaned his Barrett MRAD against a niche in the rocks along the rim. It was locked and loaded, ready to fire at the flip of the safety. Alongside the rifle, covered by a cloth, were three more ten-round magazines.

He checked the house at regular intervals. At noon, the maid brought lunch out to the woman and kids in the courtyard. Shortly afterwards he was beginning to doze off when he heard the sound of an engine. Dan quickly took a look through his binoculars. A truck was approaching the house. When it pulled up he could read the name of a caterer. The maid came out and two men exited the cab and opened the rear doors. They started unloading boxes and carried them into the house at the direction of the maid. *Getting ready for guests.*

A dozen boxes and coolers were hauled into the hacienda. Then came flower arrangements. The woman had disappeared from the courtyard, leaving the children alone. Dan assumed she was directing the placement of the flowers. *Putting on quite a show for your guests. I'm sorry but I'm going to have to spoil the party.*

When the delivery van was emptied, the men departed. A gardener came out and began to line the front walk with potted flowers. After putting out nearly two dozen, he disappeared only to return shortly with a hose and proceed to water them. *Going to need a lot of water to keep them alive in that sun. Probably only need them for one day.*

All the activity confirmed the schedule was still set for tomorrow's meeting. The kids had departed from the courtyard pool as the sun climbed higher and the heat rose. He could see shapes moving past windows but could not make them out. Was one of them Mendoza? There were three vehicles, one Mercedes S500 stretch sedan and two Suburbans, all black, along the edge of the drive, to the left of the front entrance. Dan guessed the Mercedes was armored but it wouldn't stop a .338 magnum if he had to shoot it up.

The two guards did their walkabout every two hours. They looked like they were going through the motions. Nothing had changed throughout the day, no one came or went; there was no concealment anywhere near the hacienda. Except for some fleeting shadows noticed inside and the desultory patrols around the house perimeter nothing moved. Dan found himself dozing off a couple of times. *Don't get lazy. You may get an early opportunity.*

The day faded; the shadows lengthened and stretched away eastward towards the hills. The heat lost its strength and for a few hours there was a pleasant interlude from the furnace heat of the day and the coming chill of the desert night. Dan stretched and tried to relax.

Then he heard the thumping of a helicopter. He lurched up from his reclining and looked over the rocks. At first there was nothing to see in the fading light. After a moment he zeroed in on the direction of the sound; it was coming from the south. Dan reached over and grabbed his MRAD. *Are they all coming by air? And tonight?* Plans always had to change when the circumstances dictated. *Got to play it out...be flexible.*

He kept his eyes scanning to the south and soon the running lights of the copter came into view. It was a civilian but it was coming in fast. As it got closer Dan identified it as an Airbus H155. It was capable of around one hundred and eighty knots. It was one of the fastest civilian helicopters made and could carry eight to twelve passengers, depending on cabin configuration. *Expensive machine.*

When the chopper got near the hacienda the pilot slowed and gently eased it down to the helipad. Dust swirled everywhere. Dan aimed his rifle on the area but had trouble seeing through the dust. Then the rotors powered down and the door opened. A figure jumped out and held the door open. A second person stepped out and jogged toward the hacienda. The boy came running out and threw himself into the man's arms. He was followed by the woman and the girl. They were all hugging one another. Jorge Mendoza had arrived.

With no clear shot and the kids in the way, Dan relaxed and sat back. It would be tomorrow. He just hoped for a moment with no kids.

Chapter 8

The truck caravan pulled in to a closed down roadside stop. The sun had just dipped below the mountains to the west. They had been on the road for seven hours. There was a packed dirt area for truck parking behind the abandoned gas station and store. The trucks drove around back, where they were shielded from the road. Men from the cabs posted themselves near the road to keep anyone from pulling off.

Tariq raced around to the rear and watched as the seals were cut off and the doors opened. He heard the men calling out in Pashto. There were sounds of the cloth bales being torn away and soon heads appeared.

"*Salam aleikum*" Tariq called out in greeting. "*Pa khair raghla*", "Thanks be to god you came safe and sound". Several voices responded "*Ao, ao*", "yes, yes". The cartel drivers and guards stood to one side as the containers were dug out from the inside and the sixty gaunt and ragged men began to emerge. They looked to Tariq like men let out of prison, a starvation prison. They had to be helped down from the containers. They all had long ragged beards and the thin, shrunken cheeks; the look of lost men. It was going to take some time to get them into shape. He found Kashun, the leader of the group. They spoke in Pashto.

"Did everyone survive?" Tariq asked.

"I can only speak for my group. I must see about the others." Kashun went to the others coming out of the steel boxes. He spoke quietly with them and then returned to Tariq. "Yes we all survived the journey, *saaqhib*." He used an honorific title meaning "master".

"No, no, 'brother'," Tariq responded.

The men all stood around with a few shuffling their feet in the dirt. They all breathed deeply from the clean desert air. From the insides of the container a foul smell drifted out. The cartel members stepped away from the noisome odor.

A couple of the drivers brought jugs of water and juice from the cabs of the trucks. These were passed around and drunk with relish.

"Have the men go into the scrub to do any business," Tariq pointed to the desert. "And then, I'm sorry, but we have to load you back up. We will be in Chihuahua by tomorrow where you can rest and wash. Do you need food?"

"The water and juice is enough for now. We have eaten so little we should not take much for now. Better to wait."

Tariq smiled. "You will have a good rest and regain your strength. Then we go into the heart of the infidel's country." He gave the man a wolfish smile that was returned in kind.

By noon the next day the caravan arrived in Chihuahua. They drove to a rundown warehouse section on the east side of town. Many of the streets were dirt. The trucks pulled into the compound and backed up to the main warehouse. The property was lined with an eight-foot-high metal panel wall. The containers were opened after the metal gate was closed hiding the yard and building from the street. Again, the men had to be helped out.

Inside, the warehouse was divided up into dorm cubicles housing four men each, a kitchen, communal eating/living space and space for exercising and training. There was a large bathroom with showers at one end of the building. The space was not new or clean but it would work for Tariq.

Hector Ortega, Mendoza's second in command, showed Tariq the facilities.

"This will have to do," Ortega said. He had a sour disposition and seemed unenthusiastic about the project to Tariq.

"It will do," Tariq replied. "Where is *Señor* Mendoza?" he asked. "I called his phone but he doesn't answer."

"He is busy with other issues, so he sent me to take care of things here." Ortega looked around at the men milling about and getting divided into their bunkrooms. "You can't stay too long. People will begin to question what is going on."

Tariq gave the man a disapproving look. "You don't control what is going on around here?"

"We don't want to attract any more attention than necessary."

"But you don't mind killing publically. I assume that attracts a lot of attention."

Ortega looked at him like he was a child. "That is to send a message. I prefer not to send messages having to do with this project."

Tariq gave the man a thin smile. "We will be ready to depart in a week."

Ortega just nodded and walked off, leaving Tariq to direct the men. When he was out of Tariq's hearing, he pulled out his cell phone. "The goods have arrived," Ortega said as Mendoza answered. "We'll repackage them and be able to ship in a week. How are plans for your meeting?"

"Good. This will all work well together. We will establish an organizing council and your work will demonstrate how we can diversify."

"Let's hope so. I don't like dealing with these people. I'll be happy to deliver these goods and be done with this."

Mendoza laughed. "Don't be so negative, *mí amigo.* There will be more opportunities and more new things that we have to adjust to. That is the way of the world, the way of the future."

"I'm not so sure, but I do what you say."

"You do your job, even if you don't approve. You will see. We're on the right path." With that Mendoza hung up.

Dan spent the night sleeping lightly in anticipation of the next day's action. Mendoza would certainly come out of the front door to greet the arrivals. Whether they would come in a caravan or individually, he didn't know. The important thing was that Mendoza would appear out front. That was his shot.

Chapter 9

D an awoke early the next morning. He crawled away from the rim to relieve himself and began to stretch and loosen up. A day and two nights of lying against the boulders of the rim had stiffened him. After fifteen minutes, feeling better, he crawled back to his shooting nest, ate a power bar and drank some water. Then he went over his rifle, checking to be sure his scope settings were still good.

Next he scanned the hacienda with his binoculars. There was no breeze at the moment, but it would come up later as the heat rose. It was that period in the morning, like the evening, the soft period between the chill of the night and the fierce heat of the day. The two guards came out front and again began their casual perimeter check. The maid followed shortly to broom off the walkway. Everything looked the same except for the flowers out front and the helicopter out back.

An hour later he heard the engines to the east. The dust rose from the dirt road as a caravan of three SUVs and two large sedans drove through the hills. *They're all arriving together!* This was better than Dan could have hoped for. He picked up his rifle and, after laying down a cloth on the ground in the niche of the rocks, nudged the barrel through the opening. With the rifle's scope he tracked the caravan on its approach. As it drew close, he switched his focus to the front of the hacienda. The two guards had come out now and were standing more alert, their machine guns held at the low ready position.

The five vehicles stopped along the circle in front of the walkway. The dust cleared and the doors opened. Men spilled out of the vehicles. It was confusing; some were obviously bodyguards, some were lieutenants, and five of them were cartel bosses. Dan had to look closely to see who everyone deferred to in order to guess which ones were the cartel leaders.

The front door opened; Dan turned his rifle back to it. A third guard came out followed by Jorge Mendoza. Immediately behind Mendoza came his wife and children. *Damn!* He waited. There was not a clear shot, but it would come. The guard stood in front of the family with the first two guards on the sides of the path. Mendoza's wife stood by his side with the boy in between the two adults. The little girl went over to her father who scooped her up in his arms.

Dan watched in frustration as he held her while waiting for the other drug lords to exit and walk up the path. It looked like Mendoza was sending a message. "This is a safe place. See, I have my family with me. I don't do violence with my family around so you're safe." He couldn't have played it better and Dan realized he could not take the shot. There were moments where he was sure he could miss the girl and hit his target in the head but he couldn't do it.

You conniving son of a bitch. Using your family as a prop. Dan knew all about Mendoza's ruthlessness. As Jane had outlined it, he was a murderous drug lord who had killed and intimidated his way to the top. The Sinaloa cartel was known for its viciousness throughout its ranks. And here he was putting his family on stage to make the other cartel leaders feel relaxed in order to further his agenda to take over leadership of all of them. Dan didn't have any illusions; Mendoza's push for coordination among the cartels was a tactic for him to gain some level of control over them; to be the "godfather" of the cartels.

The memory of his wife, Rita, and their unborn child, both killed by the mob came rushing to his mind. It was a memory still filled with pain. Now here he was, ready to strike down the father of two children. *Do I let him off just because he has kids, a family? That doesn't stop him from killing others.*

He began arguing with himself as the men walked up the path and shook hands with Mendoza, who turned and led them into the house. The bodyguards were led around back, probably to the kitchen to offer them separate hospitality. Smoke arose from the kitchen area as meal preparation began. Dan pulled his rifle back from the notch. He scowled in frustration. *I'm not going to shoot the father right out from under the daughter. If I have to stay in Mexico another month, I'll find a way to take him down.* Part of him was adamant but another part wondered how that would work. He had no backup plan or support for a lengthy stay. He would have to depend on Jane to arrange things and she might not want to do that since this op was under very deep cover. *This can't just be run out of the embassy.*

In the end he could not give the man a pass and give up on his assignment. *If he didn't bring his kids here, he'd be dead and the kids would have to learn how to deal with it.* He was not worried about the wife; she knew what she was getting into. But she'd have to explain it all to the kids.

He shut off thoughts of Rita and the children. *That was different.*

He sighed and sat back against the rocks, not sure of what to do. *Wait,* he told himself. *Maybe you can catch him alone or at least without his children.* He leaned the rifle against the boulder and picked up his binoculars. It was time to wait; wait and watch. How many times had he done that? The first was in training, then in Iraq, and then in Brooklyn and the woods of western Massachusetts where he had struck back at the mob.

The crowd gathered in the courtyard along with Mendoza's wife and children. She was now dressed in a light, floral print dress, fitting for hot weather. The children were out of their bathing suits and in nice clothes, not ones for playing in the dirt, but ones for family affairs. Drinks were served and finger snacks were set out. Everyone seemed to be in a jovial mood as best Dan could discern through his binoculars. After an hour the men retired and Mendoza's wife and children were left in the courtyard. Smoke was still coming from what Dan assumed was the kitchen area. *Getting the main meal ready. Negotiate, then eat.*

He pulled a power bar out of his pack and began to chew on it, wondering what sumptuous food had been spread before the drug lords. Mendoza's family ate in the courtyard and Dan assumed the guards were being fed in one of the rear rooms near the kitchen. He thought he could smell the aroma of roasted pork and beef but it was probably only his imagination. *When I get back*, he promised himself.

After finishing his Spartan meal, Dan sat back and thought about his life while he watched the hacienda. Was this how it was going to be? Waiting in one shithole after another for a shot that might or might not come? And in between? He'd read the spy novels and watched the Bond movies, but his life was not going to be anything like that. Just what would it be like? To begin with he had to keep in mind he was part of a test program. As such he was disposable. There were no benefits attached even if it worked. And if it didn't, what then? Could he go back to civilian life? Just how well had Jane covered his tracks?

He had led a pretty crappy existence while he had gone on a three-month vendetta against a Brooklyn mob family; a certain capo in the Silvio Palma family who had ordered the firebombing of his restaurant. He and his wife had started the business after he mustered out of the Army. Dan had been a sniper and had done two tours in Iraq. The two of them had worked hard at the restaurant. It had prospered and they had been expecting their first child. The mob kept trying to hit him up for protection money but he and Rita refused to pay. To teach him a lesson they burned his restaurant. What was supposed to be a small fire turned into an inferno and Rita and their unborn child were caught in it and burned to death. The police and fire investigators found no evidence to connect the mob with the blaze and Dan left town shortly afterwards.

With nothing to live for, he had formed a plan to exact his own payback and headed back to Brooklyn to carry it out. Using his sniper skills, his revenge on the mob was devastating, taking down the capo responsible for the fire along with most of his crew.

Jane Tanner had recruited him. Her pitch was that he could channel his skills to go after the enemies of the country, the terrorists along with their helpers and financiers; get to them before they got to us. Jane and her boss, Henry Mason, wanted to go on the offensive against them. It would be a black operation, unknown to only a few in the CIA. With the FBI closing in and no options,

Dan took the offer. He didn't have an exit plan after exacting his revenge and realized that he had no options beyond going to jail or becoming a fugitive for the rest of his life. Jane offered him a lifeline and had shown herself to be honest and committed. In addition he had found himself attracted to her but wondered if that wasn't just a side effect of her ability to rescue him from the trap that was closing in on him.

In any case, he felt this was something Rita might have approved of, at least for a while. She would eventually want him to enjoy being a husband and father. *Maybe someday*, he thought. *But not now.*

The miserable life he led while attacking the mob had been of no concern at the time. Dan had been focused on his revenge he lived an existence solely devoted to that course of action. He had no life other than his mission. Now things were going to be different. He would have to find a way to live a somewhat normal life in between assignments...or he wouldn't survive long. There had to be relief from what he expected would be a series of brutal mission experiences. This realization made him less content with his surroundings. *I'm going to be immersed in what snipers are always involved in: the waiting, the discomfort, the stealth. That all goes with these clandestine operations. But I'll have to create something else along with the way.* Something that maybe even Jane would not know about.

The time passed slowly as Dan ruminated on his new life and the moral balance he was trying to maintain. He recognized people's ability to rationalize any behavior, but he detested hypocrites, especially the ones who weren't even aware of how hypocritical they were. *A kill always affects more than the victim. He is someone's father, husband, son, brother, or cousin. But does that mean I don't act? People make their choices and must reap what comes from them. There is always collateral damage.* His thoughts didn't bring any satisfaction. The question of balance remained open.

In between these thoughts he kept checking the hacienda. The sun was getting dangerously low in the sky. It hung over his shoulder so that wasn't a concern. Dusk and dark concerned Dan. He had his night vision goggles with the monocular intake. He could use them with his scope but that wasn't going to be as accurate as a dedicated night scope. *This is too long a shot to be off, even by a small amount.*

Suddenly the drivers and guards came around the house and headed to the vehicles. Dan dropped the binoculars and grabbed his rifle. He nestled the weapon into position as the door opened. A bodyguard stepped out first followed by another who held the door. The sun was at the rim of the desert; still enough light. Then Mendoza stepped out with another cartel leader next to him. The four others followed in a group. They stood around in a group. Almost surrounding Mendoza, talking, shaking hands, and clapping each other on the back.

There were no kids. Dan noted that fact and then pushed it aside. He slowed his breathing and heart rate. His scope steadied on Mendoza even when he was covered by others. The world shrunk to a narrow corridor between Dan's rifle and Mendoza. Nothing else registered. As the other men stepped towards their waiting vehicles Mendoza was left alone. Dan exhaled part way and he squeezed the trigger. The rifle made a small squishy *whomp* sound and kicked back into his shoulder. Less than a second later Mendoza's head exploded and his body collapsed. Everyone looked around in shock as the crack of the sonic boom hit their ears. Then they saw Mendoza fall to the ground. It only took a second for the group to start charging to their cars. The bodyguards pulled out their handguns and raised their machine guns but there was nothing to see or shoot at and the sound didn't give away the direction of the shot.

The cartel bosses and lieutenants started towards their waiting vehicles but Dan had already shifted his aim. He swung his rifle to another target just beginning to bolt and sent a bullet through his chest. The guards started shooting in Dan's general direction but there was nothing to see. Dan swiftly moved from target to target; each shot striking another fleeing figure. One drug boss was almost in the open door of his SUV when Dan's bullet slammed into his back shoving him inside, most likely dead. The others had reached the partial safety of their vehicles. Dan was able to drop one driver who was trying to get into his car. One of the SUVs sped away spewing dirt behind it. Dan quickly sent four rounds into the back of the machine and it veered off the road and jammed into a ditch with the engine running. Dan struck another guard as he tried to get into an SUV; he couldn't tell whether or not there was a boss inside. Another SUV took off and Dan sent his remaining rounds into the back.

He ejected the empty magazine and slapped a fresh one home. He sent round after round downrange to the target area, dropping men with almost every shot. He could cycle the bolt action quickly enough to engage multiple targets but the action was slower compared to a semi-automatic. The shot-up SUV continued off to the east followed by the armored sedan after another driver had jumped into it. The remaining SUV had headed around to the side of the hacienda. Dan sent some rounds after the sedan and then stopped. His training was not to fire indiscriminately but at defined targets. The field of fire in the front of the hacienda was now empty except for the dead bodies and vehicles. The remaining targets had driven off or were back in the cover of the hacienda.

As Dan surveyed the scene in the lengthening shadows, he saw four figures running out back. He swung the rifle to the rear of the house. It was the wife and the kids along with the pilot. Dan hesitated. *Wife and kids are non-combatants. But what about the pilot?*

He waited. They scrambled up the steps and closed the door. The blades started to turn. *Hot start up, no pre-check. He must have had the chopper ready just in case.* The machine rose from the ground. Still Dan held off. The .338 Lapua rounds could bring the chopper to a stop, especially when near the ground. But the kids inside? It climbed into the sky. *Don't come this way. I can't let you come towards me, even with the kids. Turn away.* Dan stared at the chopper through his scope, willing the pilot to go the other way. At less than fifty feet off the deck, the chopper swung off to the south, tilted forward, and shot away from the mesa rim. Only then did Dan realize he had been holding his breath. *Good choice.* They would live.

Chapter 10

He surveyed the scene out in front of the hacienda. Mendoza was dead. Scattered around him in the area were eight more bodies. There were two shot up vehicles possibly with bodies in them. Inside the hacienda were an unknown number of drivers, guards, and cartel leaders along with a terrified staff. He could spend time taking shots at them if any were stupid enough to venture outside. It didn't seem like a good idea.

It was time to go. He had accomplished his main task and added a few more bodies to the count, which included some cartel leaders. There was no question his actions this day would be a major disruption to the drug smuggling operations in Mexico. Maybe someone in the Mexican government might take advantage of this to go after the cartels while they were off balance. Good thought, but somehow Dan didn't think they would.

He dismantled the MRAD and began gathering and packing up his gear. *Why'd I take all those shots?* He had been pretty far through his second magazine when he had stopped shooting; sixteen rounds in total. Training, Dan thought; training and opportunity. All the bad guys were here. This was a meeting of all the cartel leaders, their lieutenants, and some low-level bodyguards. The hacienda was a target rich environment. None of those present had clean hands except for the servants...and the kids. *Get the most bang for the CIA's buck. Why just take out one leader when for the same price I can take out multiple bosses? Not sure what Jane will think about this, but I was hired to be able to improvise, act on my own.* Dan shrugged. The fallout didn't much matter to him at this point. It was time to rendezvous with his ride and get out of the country. He laced his boots tight and crept back from the rim. When he was clear, he turned his back to the killing field and started hiking north.

The helicopter sped south away from the killing field that had been the front yard of the hacienda. The two children were crying, huddled against their mother. She maneuvered one arm free and pulled her cell phone out. At first she was unsure of who to call; her mother, the family attorney or Jorge's lieutenant, Hector.

It was the first day in the warehouse. Hector had gotten everyone settled in. He was anxious to know about Jorge's meeting with the other leaders. Twice he had called his friend and boss who told him things were going well and to not bother him after lunch as he would be in the middle of his presentation and negotiations. Now it was late in the day; surely the meeting would be over by now.

As Hector was reaching for his phone, it rang. Odd, it was from Jorge's wife, María.

"Hector!" María shouted as he answered the call. "They've shot Jorge and the others. It's so bloody, bodies everywhere."

"What's going on?" Hector shouted back at her. He could hardly hear what she was saying over the noise. Where was she? "What did you say? Jorge's been shot?"

"Someone killed him. Right out front. And some of the others. Some got away."

"Where are you? I can hardly understand you."

"I'm in the helicopter. I have the kids; we're flying back to Mexico City. Hector, who would do such a thing? What will happen to us? This couldn't be the *policía* could it?"

Hector's head was spinning. Shot? How, why? "I don't know who would do this. Get back to the mansion and don't leave. Don't let the kids leave. Tell the staff to be on alert. I'll call for some men to come over and guard you."

"Should I call Eduardo?" Eduardo Murillo was the attorney for the Mendoza family and the interface between the personal activities of the Mendoza's and the cartel business which had its own attorneys.

"*Sí, sí*. Call Eduardo. Tell him I'll call when I can get more information. And remember, don't go out and don't let anyone in. We don't know where this came from and we don't know how the others will react."

There was a pause on the line. "Hector, I'm frightened. What will happen to us? Jorge's gone. I saw him lying on the ground. It was horrible. He was shot in the head. I went and found the children and the pilot. There was so much shooting. Then it stopped and we ran to the helicopter." She started to cry.

"I don't have answers for you, María. But I will find some. You will be fine. I'll see to it. For now, just get to a safe place and stay there. I have to go." He hung up the phone and just stood there looking out into space; thoughts flying in all directions.

His world was beginning to crumble. Who would try to assassinate Jorge and the others? Was it one of the cartel leaders that had escaped? Hector sucked in his breath. He had to act and act quickly but what to do? He wished he knew what had happened.

He turned quickly and headed to his car where his bodyguards were waiting. Along the way Tariq intercepted him. "I want to go into the market and try to find some lamb so we can cook food like at home."

Tariq. He was a hard man. Tough. A fighter for sure, but Hector had no patience for him, nor for babysitting his band of scrawny stowaways that he was supposed to fatten up for their trip across the border.

Tariq grabbed Hector's arm as he was rushing past. Hector turned to him with his eyes blazing. "Do not touch me. You have what you need to eat. It is enough."

"We just want to go into the market. We can pay for our own food."

"No," shouted Hector. The ferocity of his reply caused Tariq to step back and eye the man suspiciously. "You do not leave this compound. I will not have you running about the town, drawing attention to yourselves. You are outsiders and this is Chihuahua, a small town that doesn't see many outsiders. You will bring the *Policía Federal* here. Then you will have real trouble." Hector turned to go.

"What is wrong? I have not offended you. Why do you speak to me this way?"

"I have no time now to talk. Just make sure you do what I say," Hector spoke over his shoulder as he exited the warehouse.

Hector gave orders for his men to spread out around the compound. No one was to leave the warehouse compound, on pain of death. Next he called the hacienda. After a long number of rings, one of the servants answered. She was crying. Hector ordered her to get one of the bodyguards on the phone. He did not want to waste time with her. She located one of the Mendoza bodyguards who had been inside the house when the shooting started.

"Tell me what happened," Hector said when the man picked up the phone.

"Everyone said their goodbyes and went out the front door. There were twenty people altogether. The other bosses were all surrounding *Señor* Mendoza. They looked happy. I was watching from the doorway. The drivers and bodyguards were heading to the vehicles. We had five men outside along with the other guards. When the bosses turned to go to their cars, one shot rang out. *Señor* Mendoza was hit in the head. Everyone then started to run and there was more shooting, men dropping. Three vehicles got away. In the end ten men were killed including García and Lopez."

Hector shuddered. They were cartel leaders. Counting Jorge, three of the six bosses at the meeting had been killed.

"Do you have any idea of who did the shooting? No one can get close to the hacienda. I ordered regular patrols around the property to insure that."

"*Sí*. And that is what we did. It is open for miles in all directions." The guard paused. "There is one thing—"

"What is that?"

"Like I said, the land is open for miles in every direction...except to the north. The mesa rim is about a half mile away. The river runs below it. It's about three hundred meters high and the whole desert from there north is uninhabited."

"You think some group snuck up on the rim and attacked from there?"

"That is the only place where there is any cover."

"But it's so far away."

"*Sí patrón*. But sharpshooters could shoot that far."

It was not lost on Hector that the man called him "boss". He would have to cement that position, for his own security, for the security of the cartel, and for the security of María. Knowing how the attack could have happened still did not make it clear who was responsible. Answering the "why" would yield that knowledge. But who would gain from this? Hector's first suspicions had to center around the three cartel members who remained alive.

Manuel "la Roca" Chacón was head of the Juarez cartel. Juan Escobedo ran the Gulf cartel and Hector Beltran-Leyva headed the namesake organization. Hector pondered the relationships for a while. The Gulf and Juarez clans were close together on the U.S. border, they could only feel strong enough to do something like this if they had joined together. Hector had no inkling of such an alliance. The Beltran-Leyva cartel was already aligned with his Sinaloa organization. They had fought over territory over the years but were now working peacefully alongside each other. No answers jumped out at Hector.

Damage control had to be initiated however, even if he didn't understand the situation. He picked up his phone again and started calling the cartel leaders who had escaped. He talked with each one. All three bosses were both frightened and furious. They blustered and promised retaliation. When Hector pointed out that Jorge, his friend and boss had been the first killed, and further, seemed to be the only one that was specifically targeted, they quieted down. Hector made sure to leave the impression that he was searching for someone who had something to gain from killing his boss and the others. Hector Beltran-Leyva seemed to be the least defensive and promised to work closely with him.

After the calls, Hector felt only slightly better. He contacted the other lieutenants and told them to get men out on the streets to look for answers. Next he ordered some small planes into the air to search the mesa to the north of the hacienda. They were told to take thermal imaging goggles with them and fly day and night. If any group were out there, he would find them.

Chapter 11

Dan hiked through the evening and into the night. When he had started north, he placed a call on the sat phone to Jane.

"The package was successfully delivered earlier this evening."

"Are you headed back now?" Jane asked.

"Yes. I'll call the other number when I'm ready to be picked up."

"Good. That's the only call you'll need to make."

"There is one thing...you got a bonus on this delivery, some extras for the price of one."

"What are you talking about?"

"I'll tell you later, but expect a larger result." That would give her something to think about and when the news broke, she would not be so surprised. He started to shut the call off.

"Wait," Jane said.

"What is it?" Dan asked.

There was silence for a moment. "Just...just be careful...and get back here safely."

"Is that your professional advice?"

There was a pause in conversation. "More personal. Just be careful." With that Jane ended the call.

It was 10 pm when he heard the sound of a single engine plane. There was only one reason for such a plane to be flying in this area. They were looking for him. It was night, so Dan guessed they had thermal imaging goggles. He headed for the nearest rocks, two large boulders. He took off his backpack and pulled out his reflective blanket. He squeezed himself and the pack into the crack between the rocks and then pulled the blanket over him. It would reflect his body heat back to him. It was a survival tool; it kept his body heat from escaping and therefore being seen by thermal imaging. It was about ninety percent effective and Dan hoped the rocks would hide the ten percent that escaped. The rocks gave off heat for many hours through the night.

He lay still, almost holding his breath as the plane made multiple passes. After each pass, Dan peeked out to spot its location from the running lights. The aircraft was working its way north. *Great. I'll just follow it.* In two days he would be at the road and his pickup. *They'll never find me or the gear. I'll leave them a mystery they'll never solve.* He stuffed the blanket back into the top of his pack and headed off again. His left foot hurt and he limped, but the pack was now lighter with his diminished supplies and he felt less burdened. A successful mission buoyed his spirits as well.

After Dan hung up, Jane sat back in thought at her desk. *What the hell did he mean about a bonus on this delivery?* Dan must have included some other drug lords into his targeting and had been effective at eliminating them. She couldn't stop a grin from spreading across her face. She had picked Dan because he was so good at what he did. Killing and disrupting the Brooklyn mob. He had acted on his own, using his own resources. The training he had received had only made him better, more lethal. She thought back about how Dan had shaken up the training staff at the Farm. He broke the rules. He didn't play into their mind games. It was what she wanted from an assassin that was going to have to operate alone without much support. Now it seemed he was showing those traits in the field. *Some people may not like this.* She picked up her phone.

"Henry, can we talk privately?"

The next morning they walked along the towpath on the Chesapeake and Ohio, or C&O canal bordering the Potomac River. The idea of the canal had been promoted by George Washington but construction hadn't started until 1828. It was one hundred eighty-five miles long and used to bring the wealth of the interior, coal, lumber, and farm goods out to the east coast markets. The river was not navigable above Washington, DC as it climbed from the tidal plain into the piedmont. The canal had been in operation for over one hundred years. Now it was a long, narrow national park enjoyed by millions of hikers, joggers and bicycle travelers.

Jane and Henry both eyed the passing traffic, pausing in their conversation as people went by. Occasionally either Henry or Jane would stop to look at something and glance over their shoulder to see if anyone was following. They both had the ability to memorize the clothing of people around them and would spot anyone spending too much time in their wake.

"So you think Dan took out more than Mendoza?"

"I'm sure of it." Jane had arranged to talk with Henry that same afternoon after receiving Dan's call.

"No reports yet?"

Jane shook her head. "The cartels will try to keep this under wraps for as long as possible. It may take a few days for the news to get out."

"The embassy may be shook up. They don't like anything to disturb the status quo. You think the job went down cleanly?"

"No way to tell, but Dan sounded fine when he called. My guess is that no one on the receiving end knows who did this...or how many were involved. They'll be looking at each other pretty hard."

Henry smiled. "That's a good thing."

"If war breaks out among them, there will be lots of bodies. That always makes the Mexican government look bad. It could destabilize the president."

"You mean the president who has cabinet members on the take from the cartels?"

"He may be the best of the options for the Mexican people."

"The government, especially the *Policía Federal*, will let them kill one another so long as it doesn't involve too much civilian collateral."

"It always does, though...in the end."

Henry shrugged as if to say, what can you do? "No one will connect this to the U.S."

"Except for the exfiltration. That's the weak link. Dan called it right away. He has a good sense for those things."

"Someone from the embassy sent to pick up this stranger and take him to the airport in Hermosillo." Henry looked around again, surveying the passing foot traffic. "No one will know who he is or why he's being picked up."

"But they will know he's coming from an area that could be connected to the assassinations. And Dan will have weapons on him."

"If the issue gets too intense, we can always claim we had an asset in place to spy on this meeting. When the attack happened we pulled him out."

Jane looked over at her boss. She admired Henry. He was old enough to be her father; and wise enough to qualify for the position. And she liked that he still had the fight in him, after all the years he'd spent in the agency. "You think anyone will believe us?"

Henry smiled. "It doesn't matter. They'll be no trail to follow any further. All they'll be left with are suspicions. Meanwhile the job will be done, with the effects we want happening." He turned to Jane, now with a serious look on his face. "Get him out cleanly. Don't let there be any contact with others. He's a ghost now and he needs to disappear from Mexico. He went in, he did the job; now let's get him out and all the suspicions in the world won't add up to a damn."

They turned to go back to their cars, both going to work where Jane sat in her office to wait for word on Dan's extraction.

Chapter 12

Dan walked through the night. While he relished the cold, dry air, his left ankle grew ever more painful and his limp increased. Tomorrow was going to be a long, hot day if he was going to keep moving. His instinct was that he had to put miles between him and the shooting site. There was safety in the miles. Three more times the planes came over. The last time, Dan barely made it to some rocks to gain cover. When day came it would be more difficult to continue. He would have to keep close to cover. To be caught out in the open, on the flat pan of the desert would be disastrous. The pans were areas of just sand and small rocks with no brush or trees for cover. A sharpshooter could take him down from a small plane and with nowhere to hide his only defense would be to try to take down the plane. That would only escalate the dangers and ruin his chance of a clandestine escape.

He stopped and took off his backpack. Pulling out a bottle of water, Dan took a long drink. He breathed deeply the cool night air. There were few smells in the desert, especially when the heat of the day burned off any odors. This was not like the eastern woods, which were rich in odor of things growing and decaying. Out here things dried out. Still the night brought subtle scents of cactus along with the alkali smell of the sand and dirt.

Dan's ankle throbbed fiercely. He looked to the east. The black of the night was turning to blue as the sun crept towards the horizon. He would go another two hours and then he had to stop and elevate his ankle. He had some anti-inflammatory pills he could take. Hopefully with those and a few hours of keeping the ankle raised, he would be ready for more hours of hiking. He put the water bottle away, shouldered his pack, and, with a sigh, limped off to the north.

Tariq was fuming. This man, Hector, was now acting like they were prisoners. He could see the armed men standing around the compound. When he had approached, they indicated he could not leave. Most acted like they didn't understand English. The one who would speak to him just said that there was a problem and they had to stay inside the compound. They could not be seen. Something was clearly wrong, but Tariq could not find Hector to learn what it was.

Meanwhile Hector had received a phone call from an informant in the U.S. embassy. The man spoke of a plan to pick someone up on a dirt road that ran north of the mesa. He found a map and saw a dirt road running east and west north of the mesa on it. It went nowhere. Could this be the pickup point? Could this have been the way shooters got to the rim? The road was probably two days hike away from the south rim. Who would set up something like that? He didn't have answers but he didn't have much else to go on. Hector met with some of his men in town.

"Four of you go north on this road," he pointed to a dirt road that ran into the desert. "Here at this crossroad, you go west. You see the road dead ends? You follow it to the end. The shooters may have used it to get close to the hacienda. They could shoot from the mesa rim. If they had gone south or east after the shooting we would have seen them, so I'm guessing they went north." He looked at the men. "They may be meeting someone to get them out of the area. Take automatic weapons. These are dangerous men."

He pointed to the crossroads. "There is a gas station and little store here. Stop and ask if anyone has seen strangers come through the area. Make sure they contact you if they see anything."

He gave them the map. "Call me when you get there and after you've driven the road. Someone or some group shot Jorge and we have to find them. Bring them back alive if you can. I want to find out who sent them and then we have to kill them in a manner that no one will forget."

The thought had occurred to Hector that it could have been a clandestine police or army operation. If so, it required an even stronger response to let those know they must not get out of line. His contacts in the government were going to hear from him next.

Dan stopped just as the sun broke over the rim of the horizon. The problem during the day would not be his heat signature, but being visually hidden. He was in an area of small trees and bushes. Cutting a few bushes and placing them together so they looked natural seemed to be a good way to stay under cover. Hiding under rocky overhangs would work, when there were some nearby. His greatest danger was still going to be the open pans that he had to cross to get to the rendezvous point. For now, he found some large rocks and nestled himself in between them. He stretched his camouflage netting overhead and hoped for the best. He didn't dare unlace his boot for fear of not getting it back on. Instead he propped it up and took four anti-inflammatory pills and lay back to rest.

If his ankle held up, he would be at the pickup point by mid-day tomorrow. That was if he could walk through the night. His thoughts returned to Rita and the life they had lost. A wave of grief followed by anger came over him. Not only had he lost his family, but Rita's parents blamed Dan for their daughter's death. Dan had no family of his own outside of his sister in Montana, and now his in-laws had rejected him.

His plans for revenge had inexorably led him to this point. Jane may have saved him by pulling him away from the grasp of the FBI or the mob, but that act had not resulted in much of a life for him. He snorted in derision at his own follies. He had dealt his payback, but that path had led to him lying here in the Mexican desert with a bum ankle hiding out from spotter planes. He was hot; his clothes were dusty and dirty. He hadn't washed in almost a week. His face was caked with dried dust; his hair thick with it. *Quite a sight,* he thought. *Quite a life.*

"Rita, Rita," he said. "I sure do miss you. Can you forgive me?"

In his mind came the words, "Forgive you for what? We make our bed and we lie in it."

He opened his eyes. *Did I just hear that or is my mind is playing tricks on me? It must be the heat.*

He looked out over the desert. Nothing moved. The day was growing hotter. Then his eye caught sight of the bird. It was large and black. Was it the bird he'd seen days before? The ruffed feathers at its throat confirmed it was a raven. It had a strong black beak. It was perched on the limb of a dead tree, five feet off of the ground and about fifty feet away from where Dan lay. The bird sat there looking directly at him, its head cocked to one side, a dark eye staring straight at him.

Is that bird looking at me? Dan wondered. He called out, "I'm not dead, just resting. No food here for you." The bird watched him without moving on the branch. Dan wondered whether or not the bird would come over and peck him if he went to sleep. "I'm just going to rest my eyes. You stay where you are. Deal?"

Am I getting heat stroke? Talking to a bird? The thought crossed his mind. The raven seemed to nod its head. As Dan was thinking about that gesture that seemed to be more than random, the bird called out. It sounded like "*agua*" but it was not clear. The bird made the sound twice again.

Is my mind playing tricks on me? What the hell? Dan thought. The desert might be getting to him but he had time to pass. He took out a water bottle; one almost finished. He cut away the bottle and left a cup-like bottom with a couple of swallows of water in it. Placing it carefully on the ground, he took the butt end of his carbine and gently pushed the cup towards the raven. The bird watched him and when he had pulled the rifle back, it leapt off the branch and dropped to the ground. It walked to the cup, its head bobbing in time with its feet. The bird kept an eye on Dan. When it got to the cup, it grabbed it in one claw and backed it up a few paces. Then the bird dipped its head to the water and drank. When it was done it squawked, this time with no intelligible words and launched into the air. It circled Dan and then headed off north across the desert.

Dan sat there in silence, wondering at what had just taken place. He had a raven, a scavenger, which seemed to be following him...for days. It seemed to answer the questions he posed to it. And then the bird sounded to Dan like it asked for water. It approached him to take a drink from the cup that was offered and flew off. *My imagination is getting too overactive; that's not good for a sniper and assassin.*

Chapter 13

Hector had his hands full. He put in a harsh call to a mid-level Deputy Minister of Justice, reminding him that Hector expected his cooperation and if he found anything to implicate his department in what happened it would not be healthy for him or his family. A commander in the *Policía Federal* also received a similar call. From both men he got nervous assurances that their departments had nothing to do with the killings. Hector guessed that they would be looking closely into their departments, terrified that someone may be connected to what happened. Next, he concentrated on the other drug gangs.

The three cartels whose leaders were alive were holding back for now. Los Zetos and Tijuana, cartels whose leaders had been killed, had already started attacking some of his Sinaloa members. Hector was frantic to get to whoever was controlling them. His problem was no one was certain who would emerge with control. Right now various elements were acting without control from the top. He expected more to come including raids on his drug warehouses and processing plants.

The planes had not located any sign of men hiking through the desert. Hector told them to keep flying; the shooters had to be out there somewhere. He had men climb up the escarpment to the mesa ridge. Careful exploring uncovered some evidence of human activity, footprints, tamped down dirt, but it was very slight and there were no shell casings to be found anywhere. The distance was so far as to make the site suspect to Hector, but he had nothing else to go on. He realized he was holding out more and more hope for the men checking out the dirt road. But if that was the exit route why had the planes found no evidence of movement in the desert? Nothing added up.

By the second day the papers had the story. It was splashed all across the country; "Drug Lords Shot in Ambush!" "Cartel Leaders Gunned Down; By Whom?" "Major Cartel Summit Ends in Death!" Chihuahua was swarming with reporters and investigators since it was the nearest population center to the hacienda. The *Policía Federal* had taken over the hacienda. They interrogated all the staff that they could round up. Hector talked to the investigators and characterized the meeting as an attempt to bring peace to the cartels in order to stop the killing. He did his best to portray Jorge as a reformer who wanted to do good for his country.

Mexico had always had a soft spot for Robin Hood characters, outlaws who help the poor. It was a nice meme but mostly false. Hector now played upon that mystique to paint Jorge, and himself, in a sympathetic light. Some in the press lapped it up; a few were skeptical, as always. María found herself subject to similar assaults by the press, but by staying inside the family compound, a fortress mansion, in Mexico City, she was able to keep away from the intrusions of the reporters; they could only try to reach her by phone.

Dan set out later that same day. The planes had stopped for some time, probably to go back to refuel in Chihuahua City. He limped along as fast as he could go and when he heard the faint sound of an engine, he headed directly for cover. The planes made two passes while he hid. Then the night came. The hiking was easier in the chill air and his thermal blanket gave him protection from being spotted by thermal imaging. By early the next morning he was closing in on the dirt road.

While he was an hour out, he marked the spot in his GPS where he would meet the driver and then made the call to the number programmed into the satellite phone.

"*Hola*," someone said when they answered the call.

"I'm a half hour out from pickup." He proceeded to give him the coordinates out to the fourth decimal minute. He was asked to repeat the numbers.

"*Sí, sí.* Yes, we'll meet you there. Half hour."

Dan started walking. *That was a Mexican. Why would the embassy send a Mexican to pick me up?* Dan's sense of danger was triggered. *Maybe locals are a good idea. They won't draw attention to themselves...or me.* He argued with himself, but his concern would not go away.

Hector got a second phone call from his man in the American embassy. He was surprised at the news. It was hard to think one man could be responsible for such an attack. Still it was the best news so far and would go a long way in stemming the growing violence. It would also help cement himself as the rightful successor to Jorge Mendoza. The first thing he would do is get these mid-Easterners out of the country and get back to business.

He called his men waiting at the crossroads to inform them.

"Remember, take him alive, however injured he may be keep him alive. I want to question him personally. Take him to the interrogation house outside of Chihuahua."

The house had a basement dug under it. No one could be heard from inside it.

"I'll meet you there with Carlos."

Carlos was used as an interrogator. He was a brutal man who enjoyed inflicting pain. He had become very effective at it over the years and was much feared both in and outside the cartel.

"I'll get the information I need and then he will die in a dramatic and grisly way."

If the man was a gringo and connected to a U.S. agency, Hector would have to be careful. It was dangerous to openly go after DEA agents. Still he would exact his revenge in some manner.

Dan covered the remaining distance as fast as he could. He wanted to be ahead of the pickup. The phone call still didn't sit right with him. He wanted to arrive early so he would have the opportunity to control the situation.

There were two boulders near the dirt road. They were ten feet high and between them, thirty feet across. Twenty yards behind them was a rock outcropping that sloped up from the desert floor elevating it above the dirt road. The boulders had probably split from the outcropping behind them and then had been worn smooth over thousands of years of sand and wind. Dan found a spot in the outcropping behind the boulders and slipped into it. He was shielded from the road and had a clear view of anyone coming around the two large rocks. A plan began to form in his mind. How it would play out he couldn't tell, but it was good enough to start with.

He squeezed himself into the cleft of the outcropping, pulled out his 9mm and screwed on a silencer. Next he picked up his sat phone and called the pickup number.

Chapter 14

The phone rang and a voice said, "Hola."

In Spanish, Dan said he had injured his foot a mile back and could not walk or stand. They would find him lying in the shade, behind the boulders. He needed them to come around and help him to the car.

"How many are with you?" Dan asked. There was a pause. Dan continued, "I need to know because I need to put my foot up. It may be broken and I don't want it to swell too much. What are you driving and is there room?"

"*Sí*, there's room. We have four-door pickup. A big machine. You will have plenty of room to be comfortable. Don't worry."

Dan hung up. *Fat chance of that.* He now faced a dilemma. He had better not kill an embassy employee, but he was becoming more and more convinced this was not an employee. And he was sure the man was not alone. How many would he have to deal with? It would be at least two and no more than four. That made the upcoming encounter tricky to play out.

Dan put away the phone and settled himself in the rocks. He would not be seen right away; that was a positive, but his position was not protected. He would be vulnerable if anyone fired on him. And there was no fall back. He could not retreat further into the cleft; he could only go forward and out which would expose him further to enemy fire. Dan didn't like his position but he had few options.

The minutes passed. He waited patiently, going over and over how the scene would play out. The first thing was to take a moment to identify whether or not these were bad guys. It was dangerous, even fatal to do so, but Dan decided he couldn't afford to kill a friendly. He knew it would not be just as he imagined, but he had to start with a plan and then improvise. *It's what you do well. You got to do it now to stay alive.*

He heard the sound of the engine and saw the dust trail way off to the east. *Coming soon.* He adjusted his position and cradled the 9mm carefully across his arm as he lay in the rocks.

The beat up looking pickup pulled up and stopped on the other side of the boulders. Dan heard two doors slam shut. *"Hola! Amigo!"* a voice called out.

"Hola!" Dan called. "I'm around back, in the shade. I need some help." He would have only a moment to decide whether or not they were friendlies or the enemy.

Two men came around the boulder to Dan's left. They were dressed in jeans and light shirts. They had boots and cowboy hats on and carried what looked like MP-5s. *We don't issue those to embassy employees.* The guns were held at ready, not a friendly sign and the men looked around, not yet seeing him. Decision made; Dan squeezed off one shot. The silenced pistol gave out a muffled *pop* and one of the men collapsed with a hole in his forehead. The second one turned to the rocks and raised his submachine gun. Before he could fire, Dan shot again and he went down with a hole in his forehead, just like the first man.

Two down, how many to go? The sound wouldn't have carried out to the SUV, so Dan waited switching his gaze back and forth to either side of the boulders. There would be more coming.

"Luiz?" a voice called out. "Manuel, *qué pasa*?"

There was no answer. As Dan was looking to the left, a head and submachine gun peaked around the boulders from the other side. The man saw his companions lying dead on the sand; then he saw Dan in the rocks. He brought his weapon up but before he could shoot there was a shriek in the air. A black missile shot down from the sky and strafed the man's head. He instinctively ducked. The sound brought Dan around. Before the man could bring his machine gun back up, Dan shot him. The bullet hit him in the face, below his right eye. His head snapped back. His hand tightened reflexively on the trigger and the machine gun fired off a staccato burst, the rounds flying harmlessly into the air.

Dan shoved himself forward out from the rocks and limped towards the boulders. The object that hurtled down from the sky was sitting on top of one of the boulders. It was a raven. He heard the truck start up. *Can't let him get away.* Dan lurched forward. The raven flew up and towards the vehicle. As Dan came around the boulder the driver was turning around. In the middle of the turn the raven attacked his windshield, grabbing the wiper blade and spreading its wings to block the driver's vision. There was a terrible raucous screeching coming from its throat. The driver flinched and didn't complete the U-turn. He started to back up. By that time, Dan had gotten to the road and let loose three rounds through the passenger window. The driver slumped and the pickup stopped moving. The raven leapt into the sky with an exuberant cry. Dan watched it as it circled the scene and then flew off to the north.

He just stood there, in the road, in the heat and the dust. What had he just witnessed? He was not sure if he could believe what had just happened. But he was alive precisely because of what happened. He carefully reconstructed the events that had just unfolded. It had taken only moments, seconds for each scene to play out, but Dan slowed it down in his mind so he could examine each point of action.

He stood in the middle of the dirt road going over the scene. At great danger to himself, he had waited a moment to determine the men had not come to assist him, but to kill or capture him. He had taken down the first two with quick, accurate shots. That had been part of the original plan. Then things had gone weird. He had to watch both sides of the boulders. He hoped whoever would come around would still not be on full alert. But, that person had been on alert and was ready to attack. The man had suspected an ambush. Dan was looking the wrong way when it happened. Dan shuddered. That glance the wrong way could have cost him his life. Except...for the bird.

Where did it come from? Was it the same one he gave some water to? That dive bomb saved his life. But why would a bird attack a man with a submachine gun? And then, to make things stranger, the bird attacked the driver, keeping him from escaping. Dan looked around but there was no sign of the bird, only silence and the heat. He scanned the sky; it was clear and bright. He scanned the desert, nothing moved. He looked down the road. It shimmered in the heat, seemingly to float and undulate. There was nothing as far as his eye could see.

Shaking his head, Dan turned to the pickup. He pulled the driver out and shut off the motor. Next he went around to the back of the boulders and took the MP-5s from the three men. They were all dead. He unscrewed his suppressor and stuffed it in his vest pocket. He picked up his backpack and threw it along with the weapons in the back seat. There was more ammunition there along with rope and duct tape. The truck was older and beat up but had a winch and reasonable tires on it.

He got into the vehicle and was happy to note that the tank was almost full. There was a map on the passenger floor. Dan spent some time going over it. Going east, the dirt road reached a small crossroads. If he continued straight he would hit a paved highway in another thirty miles. But at the crossroads he could turn north, still on dirt. Pavement meant faster speeds but it also meant more chance of being seen or stopped. He had no cover and the weapons would insure he would be detained. Dan was reluctant to give up his weapons. He didn't want the Barrett sniper rifle to be found and with his exit out of Mexico now being improvised, he wanted to hold on to the M4. The dirt road looked like a better option.

His thoughts turned to what might have happened to his ride. Had he been set up? Questions flew around in Dan's head. These guys had a sat phone. It had his number programmed in. How did they get it? Were they the ones sent from the embassy? Dan didn't think so, but what happened to the embassy team? Whoever sent these men would be looking for them soon. If they didn't check in someone would suspect they had failed and assume that he was now driving the pickup. Would they expect him to head to a paved road and try to get away? Probably, it was the fastest route. But the police and cartels had too many connections for Dan to feel comfortable with that route; too many possibilities of running into a roadblock. The dirt road still looked to be the best option for going north.

He decided to stay out of communication while he tried to figure out what had happened. Right now he didn't know whom to trust. There must have been a security breech and someone had given the cartel the information. And they had gotten the sat phone as well.

It was tempting to call Jane and unload on her. But he held back. Would the call be monitored? Would it give away his position? He didn't know. The CIA could have a tracking device in the phone that was transmitting even if he wasn't using it. If that was so, why did they have to wait for him to call in? Why send planes to search the desert? Just to maintain appearances? Dan went around back and pulled the phone out of his pack. He laid it on the seat next to the one the gang members had used, not sure if he should throw either of them away. *I'll have to get out on my own.* He started the truck and drove off to the east.

Chapter 15

When Dan reached the crossroads, he didn't stop. There was a gas station and little store, but he felt there was too great a chance that information could get back to the cartel. He needed to put miles between him and the recent ambush. He turned north and disappeared down the dusty road. Unbeknownst to Dan an old man was watching from the store. He noticed the pickup which had waited at the store with four men in it. Now it came back with only one man, a gringo, and turned north on a road almost no one used. The old man picked up the phone and made a call as he had been instructed. He didn't want any trouble from the cartel. Dan also didn't see the pickup truck that was stashed behind the station. Nor was he aware of the two bodies that had been dragged off into the desert to be scavenged by the coyotes and ravens.

Hector was in downtown Chihuahua City, in an office used by one of the cartel's attorneys. The office was his command post where he was trying to control the fallout from the shootings. In the middle of trying to control the police and their investigation, reassuring the surviving cartel bosses that he had nothing to do with the attack, and preparing for attacks from the other cartels while doing what he could to placate them, he pulled out his phone and answered a call. He didn't recognize the number and almost canceled the call, being so busy, but decided to answer, hoping that any call might bring more information to help him solve this mystery.

"*Hola*," he said.

"*Señor*," an old man said, "I was told to call this number if I saw anything unusual."

"Who are you?" Hector asked.

"Just an old man. I run the gas and roadside store north of Chihuahua City. It's just a small crossroad junction in the desert."

Hector recognized the crossroads where he had sent his men. "So you talked to my men? Are they there?" He wondered why they hadn't called him as instructed.

"*Sí*. I did talk to them. They found two men waiting in a pickup. They took them into the desert to question them. I do not know what happened—"

"I know what happened. Where are my men now?"

"They drove off on the road going west. It goes nowhere."

"Did they say anything to you?"

"They told me to call this number, to call you, if I saw anything unusual."

"They haven't come back? So, what did you see? Why are you calling? Quickly. I do not have much time."

"The men...your men waited for three hours. Then they drove off, all four of them, as I said, west on the road that goes nowhere. An hour later their truck came back. It had only one person in it...a gringo."

"*Maldita sea!* Damn it!" Hector swore. "Where are my men?"

"I do not know, *Señor*. But they did not come back."

"Which way did the truck go?"

"North, *Señor*. It turned north without stopping. That road goes bad many miles into the desert. The driver, he cannot get through and if he goes too far, he cannot get out."

Hector sat at his desk, his mind running over the possibilities of what had happened.

"*Señor?*" the old man interrupted his thoughts.

"*Gracias.* You have been helpful. I will remember this. Say nothing to anyone and call me again if the gringo comes back. Do not fail me."

"*Sí, Señor.* I want no trouble. I will watch."

Hector ended the call. He slammed his fist on the desk. One man? One gringo did all of this? Shot up the meeting and killed all four of his men? He didn't doubt they were dead. That is the only way the gringo would be driving their truck. He tried to settle his anger in order to go through what he had learned.

Someone had traveled, probably from the dead-end road, to the mesa rim. By foot? That someone had shot Jorge and two other cartel leaders along with other lieutenants and bodyguards. But he had not shot the helicopter that had taken María and the kids away. Now that one man had hiked back to the road avoiding all the air patrols he had set up. And there were two men, also gringos, waiting at the crossroads to get a call to pick him up. This man had also been able to kill four of his armed men.

Hector had the pieces but still couldn't figure it out. This was a well-planned operation. It involved a serious assassin and many people to get him in and out of his target area. But who would do this? And why? Was there a connection to María? He had let her escape. Hector shook his head. There were so many possibilities and none of them made sense...yet. If the goal was to disrupt the cartels, make them war, it was close to being successful. Now the question was who would gain from such an action?

He picked up his phone. Ramón was one of the men Hector had brought from Mexico City. He was ruthless, like many, but showed himself to be smarter, able to think as well as kill.

"I want you to get two pickups ready for the desert," Hector said when Ramón picked up. "Get ten men together. The assassin is heading north on the dirt road, the one from the crossroads with the gas station. It goes into the heart of the desert. But the road does not go through. He will not make it. Catch up with him and capture him, if you can. He must not get away."

"Ten men? For one man?"

"Do not be a fool. He killed more than ten at the hacienda and just killed four more of our soldiers and took their pickup. He is dangerous."

"*Madre de Dios*. One man did all of that? How did he get to the mesa rim?"

"I do not know. But it doesn't matter. What matters is that you find him and stop him. If we are to keep a war from breaking out, we need to give the others this man's head. Hopefully after we have emptied it of what he knows."

"*Sí, patrón*. I will find him."

"I am '*patrón*' for now, but not for long if you don't find this man."

"It will happen. I will take my hardest men."

"Take Rodrigo as well. Rodrigo was the lieutenant in charge of Chihuahua. I am counting on the two of you, Ramón. There is much reward for success in this mission." Hector hung up. There was much reward, but only if he could solve the mystery of what had happened and show his leadership. With that he would be able to settle the others down, especially with a united front formed by him, Escobedo, Chacón, and Beltran-Leyva. The other two cartels would back off if he gave them the killer's head so that their honor was assuaged. And with success, he would consolidate his leadership of the Sinaloa cartel. And he could inherit María. Where else would she find protection and continuation of her lifestyle?

Ramón said goodbye to his wife and jumped into his pickup. He called one of his men and told them to round up two trucks and eight more men. They were to take extra gas and weapons. The trucks should be ones with good tires; they were going deep into the desert.

Tariq was standing in the yard outside of the warehouse. The cartel guards did not let the men out, but didn't stop Tariq. He watched as the man, Ramón, drove into the compound. Tariq knew that Ramón was a trusted underling to Hector. He got out and stood around impatiently waiting for something. Soon Rodrigo, who seemed to be another important man in the gang, showed up.

In a half hour two more pickups stopped outside and the sheet metal gate was opened for them. Each truck had four doors and was four-wheel drive. One had a cab mount that held an M60 machine gun. The other pickup had been modified with armor plating bolted to its sides. There was plating bolted over the door windows and windshield which had small slits in the metal for driving. It had a roof vent so a shooter could stand up inside the protected cab and fire. Both trucks had aggressive tread, off-road tires.

The men climbed out; Tariq counted twelve including Ramón and Rodrigo. The men all wore armored vests. As they stood around, Ramón inspected their weapons. Most of the men carried AK-47s. This was a familiar weapon; Tariq and his men used them. The rifle shot a 7.62mm round which was much larger than the 5.65mm round used by the U.S. military in their M16 and M4 rifles. One man carried a shotgun, probably 12-gauge Tariq thought. It was equipped with a large magazine. Some of the AKs had grenade tubes attached below the barrels. There was also a rocket launcher.

These men are going into battle. Tariq could see the signs. There was nervous laughter, rough gestures and friendly scuffles among them. He had seen it before. *Nervous energy. Even experienced fighters need to burn it off.* Ramón was talking to Rodrigo. Tariq edged closer to try to overhear what was being said.

"*Don* Hector wants me to lead this chase. I have picked the men. You will be under my command. Do you understand?"

"If Don Hector wants it that way, I'm okay with it. Do you know what you are doing?" Rodrigo asked.

Ramón looked at Rodrigo with disdain. "Of course I do. Just do as I say."

"How many are we going after?" one of the men asked Ramón.

"Just one," he replied. The man looked at him with a quizzical expression on his face.

"One man? We have enough to take on fifty men."

"*Sí*, but this man has killed almost twenty men so far. He is not to be underestimated."

The man nodded, but looked unconvinced.

"Be happy I'm taking so many men. You are safer for it." Ramón said dismissing him.

Tariq watched the assemblage load up and then head out. He wondered if they had anything to do with Hector's keeping his men bottled up in the warehouse. Hector had seemed very distracted. Something had gone wrong in their world and this looked like their response. He quietly watched and kept to himself. No one would tell him anything; he would just have to make himself and his men ready to deal with whatever came up. Tariq had little trust in Hector. It was Jorge whom he had negotiated with. He wished he could talk to him now. He had sensed from the beginning that Hector did not like this operation. Tariq would be happy when his men were across the border and he could head back to the middle-east.

Chapter 16

The road was getting worse. Dan's pace was reduced to a crawl. Better to make progress slowly than to break the truck. What made the travel more difficult was that the tires, while suitable for some off-roading, were not really strong enough for the full desert. As the road deteriorated, they showed their deficiencies in how easily they spun and how they flexed over the uneven terrain. Dan worried about tire failure as much as getting stuck. At times he stopped and walked ahead to use the pickup's jack to pry a large rock out of the way so it wouldn't damage the suspension or undercarriage.

He labored on as the afternoon waned. When it got too dark to see the road, he finally stopped and grabbed some power bars and water. It was dark now and Dan realized that he needed some rest. It was not prudent to drive in the dark; the headlights were inadequate for lighting the path enough to avoid boulders and soft sand. He would have to take a chance and stay put until it was light. There could be pursuit. It might be happening already and Dan would be finished if his vehicle died on him. The further he got into the desert the more he realized that he was on a one-way trip. Sometime tomorrow there would be no going back. The only way out would be to get across this uninhabited expanse to another road and some level of civilization. He could only hope his pursuers would have to stop at night as well.

By late afternoon the two pursuing trucks reached the end of what passed for a graded road and now were on the unimproved two-track. As dusk approached Ramón realized that the armored truck was a poor choice for the desert. It was so heavy that it kept getting bogged down and had to be pushed often. Still, he couldn't abandon it. If he put all the men into one pickup, it would be overloaded and have the same trouble. In addition, he didn't think he could fit all of the weapons in one vehicle. No, he would have to labor on with both trucks. He knew the truck they chased was not any better adapted to the desert so there was a good chance the assassin was having problems as well. When the night got dark, Ramón finally called a halt. He would push hard tomorrow and close up on his quarry, but for now, he needed to wait for light in order to not damage the trucks.

Dan woke as the black sky of night turned blue in the east. As the darkness faded away, he set out, even before the sunrise. He drove slowly but kept the truck moving forward. Sometimes there was no sign of a track. He pushed forward and was relieved each time the faint trace of the two-track reappeared. He was still on the right path; one that would eventually get him to a real road.

He came to a hill studded with rocks of various sizes. Slowly, in low gear, he made his way forward. Here the path was easier to see. The two-track wound its way upward in a circuitous manner, never attacking the slope directly. Dan stopped numerous times to lever larger rocks out of the path.

The pickup lurched its way forward on the loose surface. The engine got hot under the load and Dan feared it would overheat before he got to the top. Who knew what lay on the other side, but gravity would be an ally then, not an enemy. After many painful minutes of lurching forward with the wheels searching for traction, each one slipping or grabbing as the gravel-laden dirt shifted under them, he drove over the summit and stopped just beyond the peak.

Dan shut off the engine and climbed out with his binoculars. He walked back up to the top and lay down. He scanned the terrain over which he had come that morning. Nothing moved except dust from the winds that stirred the desert floor. There was no sign of any pursuers.

They must be coming. He lay and watched for ten minutes. Finally he got up and scrambled back to the truck. *They're coming. I'm just lucky they're still far behind. I might make it yet.* He got in and started the engine.

The sun burned down. The pickup was black which didn't help Dan's situation. The motor ran hotter and hotter. He turned off the air conditioning in order to ease the strain on the engine. He wasn't sweating. The dry air blew through the cab sucking the moisture from him immediately. His lips began to develop cracks from the dry heat. He could not swallow; there was not enough moisture in his mouth. He suppressed the gag reflex and tried to not think about swallowing. He would wait until he let himself drink from his diminishing supply of water. The truck groaned on, bouncing forward as if in a drunken stumble. The day wore on and still the horizon ahead showed nothing but more desert. Hills rose around him on all sides. The two-track trail, ever faint, still went north, threading its way around the largest of the hills.

That afternoon Dan stopped almost by instinct. The ground ahead looked different. Gone were the rocks of different sizes from pebbles to ones large enough to threaten the pickup. What lay ahead looked too smooth, too easy. He got out and walked forward. Within two steps of getting into the smooth sand, his feet sank up to his ankles. He dragged them out and stepped forward. Again they sank. This was a sand hole; soft and unstable. If he drove into it, the truck would be stuck deep over its axles and never get out.

Dan turned and plodded back to the stony ground. His heart was racing. How easy it would have been to have just driven into the sand? He caught his breath as he thought about his close call. *Listen to your instincts.* Something had caused him to suspect the terrain and to stop. *I can't make that mistake or I'll never get out of here alive.*

He calmed down and looked for a way around the sand hole. He could skirt it to his right by driving along a slope that dropped into the sand. It didn't look too steep but it sloped down to the sinkhole. *Hope the truck holds and doesn't slide down.* He set out, inching forward. If he spun the tires they would slip sideways taking the truck down towards the trap. Slowly, slowly he moved along the cross slope, his front wheels cocked to the right, pointing uphill. After a tense fifteen minutes he passed the sand hole and was able to turn back to the track. He went forward again, only this time with increased vigilance.

That night he stopped on the north side of a small rise. The truck and his flashlight would be hidden from any pursuers. After eating the last of his power bars and drinking more of his water than was prudent, he scanned the ground to the south of him for any sign of pursuit. At one point he thought he saw a light far off in the distance but he couldn't be sure and it only showed once.

The water ran out the next day. The danger of dying had increased, but there was nothing to do but continue. The day passed in the same, slow manner as the previous ones. The next day, the second one without water, Dan sucked on a pebble to try to get his saliva going and lubricate his mouth.

How many days could he go without water? He had to find water soon. Dan knew the average was three days. *We're sixty-five percent water so we can't afford to lose too much. Circulation and organ functions depend on it.* Dan guessed he had two, maybe three days left before his body would give out. *Keep going. The weak perish, the strong survive.*

The third day without water Dan's reflexes were slowing. His attention wandered and the truck was hitting more rocks. It was increasingly hard for Dan to keep locked on the subtle marks of the two-track. It appeared that there had been no vehicles on it for years and it was fading in the desert from the wind erosion. That afternoon he hit a rock with his front tire and it burst.

He slumped back in the cab. His options were closing down, not expanding. That was not a good sign. He sat in the cab for ten minutes, not able to move. Then, gathering his strength he got out and went to the back of the pickup. The spare would be in a carriage under the rear. He could do this. He could get it out, jack up the front tire and change the flat. He would continue on.

The spare was held in a cradle under the gas tank. The cradle was bolted closed and the bolt was rusted tight. Dan looked around for a wrench but couldn't find one. He hammered the bolt with a rock to no avail. After twenty minutes of work, Dan sank to the ground defeated. *Options closing down.*

After mentally cursing the pickup's dead owner, Dan got up. He would walk. He went to the back of the truck. *What to take?* There were a few power bars left. He couldn't imagine trying to get them down now but he could use them if he found water. He put them in his pocket. He studied the weapons: the Barrett, the M4, his Beretta M9, the ammunition. He felt some affection for these weapons. They all had been modified for him to be the best examples of their kind. He had relied on them for his survival. Now, however, they would only slow him down and could make the difference between getting out of the desert alive or not. He grabbed the M9 and a spare magazine, his binoculars, and a small compass. There didn't seem to be anything else worth carrying.

If I make it out, what shape will I be in and what resources will I need? The question bore considering. He would still be in Mexico, which he had to treat as hostile territory. He still had to find a way out and across the border. He reached into the pack and grabbed his fake ID and a handful of cash. *This isn't heavy and if I make it I'll need the cash to get north.*

With a last look around, Dan put on his brimmed hat and trudged off. He headed towards some hills just following the faint two-track trail.

Chapter 17

Ramón chaffed under the slow pace, but it was the only way to keep going. The armored truck went first. If it got stuck, the second truck could sometimes just push and get the two going again. If it couldn't he would have it drive around, hook a tow strap to the heavier truck and, with six or more men pushing, pull the truck forward until it was free.

He could see the track of the pickup they were pursuing. He was confident of his route, but he needed to close the gap. Somewhere up ahead this miserable trail would intersect a graded or paved road. He had to catch this assassin before he reached that point.

After another stop during the night, Ramón decided he had to drive, even in the dark. They were not traveling fast enough to close the gap. He had extra drivers, the assassin did not. He would use that to his advantage.

"Everyone up," he shouted just after midnight. "Enough sleep. We drive in shifts and we don't stop until we catch this man."

The men grumbled but gathered their pads and blankets and loaded themselves into the trucks. The ones in the cab leaned against the doors and went back to sleep.

The ones in the rear lay down and tried their best to sleep in spite of the bouncing against the metal bed.

Three hours later, before the sun could lighten the eastern sky, the armored pickup drove into the sand trap that had almost captured Dan. The driver gunned the motor and spun the wheels deep into the sand. He tried forward and reverse until Ramón reached over from the back seat and grabbed him.

"Stop! You'll only dig us deeper in." Ramón opened the door. It scrapped against the sand. The truck was buried up to the cab. "*Chingado!*" Fuck! He exclaimed after shining his flashlight on the truck. Ramón roused the other men and had them attach the tow strap to the back of the truck. The second truck pulled in reverse and the men pushed the armored truck but it went nowhere.

"Dig out the tires," Ramón instructed. The men grumbled but began to dig. They had no shovels so they had to work with their hands. After ten minutes of digging, he had them try the pulling while the other men pushed. This time the pulling truck allowed the strap go slack and when it snapped tight, it broke with a loud report.

"You idiot," shouted Ramón.

The driver jumped out. "You drive if you think you can do better. I can't see the damn strap. How was I to know it was slack?"

"Never mind," Ramón said. "Knot it together and we dig more and try again."

They tried two more times, digging in between each pull. The problem was that with each try, the armored truck spun its wheels and created deeper holes beneath them. And then when the body was fully resting on the sand, the wheels just spun futilely as the truck sat grounded on its frame. It was going nowhere. They would need metal ramps and much more digging to free the truck body enough to move.

With the sky getting light, Ramón called a halt to their efforts. He had the men off-load as many weapons as they could into the second pickup. Now they would cram five men into the cab and seven into the bed of the truck.

There was little room for weapons or supplies. Ramón left the M60 and the rocket launcher along with the ammunition for both weapons. He didn't want to but there was no room. He would rely on the submachine guns and rifles the men carried. After all there were ten of them. He didn't like losing those two valuable weapons, but they were of no use to him at this point.

When it was light enough, Rodrigo, who had deferred to Ramón's leadership on this chase, scouted how the assassin had made it around the sand trap. He found the track on the side slope. With everyone out, the pickup carefully worked its way across the slope and joined the trail on the other side. The men climbed in and the truck lumbered off. It swayed heavily as it lurched over the rocks and ruts.

They drove through the day. The men in the back grumbled. Ramón had to rotate some into the cab so they could get out of the sun. There was little food and the men had only the water they had brought with them. By the end of the day the water was gone.

Now Ramón began to worry. He had to catch this shooter soon. His men would not last many days without water and he was already two days into this empty part of the desert. He pressed on through the night.

The next morning he looked at the men. They were covered with dust, lethargic and could only talk in whispers. Still he drove them forward. He could not go back to Hector in failure. Even if he lost men, he had to capture or kill this man he was chasing. Ramón spoke little. The men spoke little. They lay in the bed of the truck or, if they were fortunate, had some time in the cab. It was no cooler inside. Ramón had ordered the air conditioning to be turned off as the motor was running dangerously hot, but inside there was some relief from the sun's fearsome rays.

Late that day they stopped to rest from the bouncing and to change drivers and seats. One of the men took a cup, stepped away from the others, and peed into it. He held his breath and drank the urine. Those who saw him told him he was going to poison himself.

"How long have you been doing that?" one of them asked.

"Two days," the man replied.

"It will kill you," another said.

The man shook his head. "At least I won't die of thirst."

Two hours after they set out the man began to spasm with stomach cramps. He could not talk and just curled up and moaned or cried out when the truck bounced and caused more spasms. By that evening he was unconscious and barely breathing.

No one spoke. Ramón ordered him unloaded from the truck and set him aside on the sand. He could not afford to carry a comatose man who would never recover. There were no shovels. Ramón said a few words and commended his spirit to Santa Muerte. They left him lying on the ground. No one had any energy to even put rocks over his body. Ramón ordered the men back into the pickup. They filled the cab and crawled in the back. The truck set out again.

He drove the men through the night. Without the large, desert tires and beefed up suspension, the truck would have already broken down under the load. As it was the suspension was challenged to handle the weight.

Another man died during the night. Now the men were voicing complaints even with their limited ability to talk.

"We are too far into this desert to go back," Ramón told them. "And do you want to face Hector and tell him you could not go far enough to capture this gringo? Do you want to face Carlos? He would like to make you feel some pain for your failure." The men backed off their demands. No one wanted to be in the hands of Carlos.

"We are going day and night. This gringo cannot do that. He is not some super hero, *el superhombre*. He does not have super powers. He is a man like us and thirsts like us. Let's catch him, kill him and take his water." It was as much of a speech as Ramón could muster. The men got back in the truck and they set out.

The next day another man died.

On the third day three men said they would go no further.

"Do you want me to shoot you?" Ramón asked.

"You can try. Or maybe we shoot you?" came the surly reply.

"You will die without the truck."

"We will die with the truck. We are going west with what strength we have left." One of the men pointed to the foothills that loomed miles away to the west. "There may be water there. You can see things growing on the hills."

"You will never make it," Ramón declared.

"Maybe, maybe not, but it is better to try than to continue north. North, there is nothing but death."

The three stood looking at Ramón. Each man held a weapon at ready. Ramón thought for a moment. It was useless to shoot them. He would have to kill all of them and might be killed himself. They were of no use any more and as good as dead.

"Go then. You are all dogs, not worth saving. You are dead men. But if you make it out, watch for me. I will be coming for you."

"If you make it out yourself, fool." The men turned and walked into the desert.

Ramón was down to six men. One man died before evening. As the sun was going down, another man said he was heading west, after the others. Ramón did not even try to talk him out of it. He had no energy and talking was too hard.

There were only four of them left now. The truck rode much better and they made better time. Ramón drove hard through the night. *We will catch him soon.* The thought encouraged him. But in the back of his mind was the question of what he would do after that. How would he get out of this empty desert?

When Ramón could drive no further, he changed with one of the other men and slumped against the door, trying to sleep. Sleep would not come in the bouncing cab, but he forced his eyes to close. The truck bounced along, faster now with the lightened load. Ramón cursed the men who had left. He could have brought the extra weapons if he knew they were going to desert him. Now it was too late.

The men drove on through the day. Ramón was glad he had brought along the extra gas cans. He was also glad he had hidden some extra water under the seat. It was not enough for everyone, but it would be enough to keep Ramón and a few close comrades alive.

Chapter 18

Within an hour of setting out, Dan's ankle was throbbing. His limp became more and more pronounced as the night wore on. *Have to make progress while it's dark so I can hole up somewhere during the hottest part of the day.* He still worried about the pursuit he knew was somewhere behind him. He was rationing his water, drinking just enough to keep him going but not nearly enough to slake his thirst. That was the only way to stretch out his trek to where he, hopefully, would find water.

His mind began to wander as he stumbled along. He kept his eye on the North Star, low on the horizon at this latitude. If not careful, he could easily start walking in a circle; he'd read many stories about people lost in the desert. One foot, one leg, one side of the body is dominant and when your focus faltered, you started walking in a slow circle, going nowhere. Dan shivered in the cold of the desert night. *Don't need that to happen. Gonna be tough enough to get out as it is.* There were low hills on the horizon. He kept his eyes on them. If they held any water he'd make it. If he found no water, he wouldn't. His mind kept coming to that inescapable conclusion. His options had closed down to one final, binary outcome; an outcome which he didn't control.

Visions of Rita kept coming and going, floating before him, hazy and indistinct, but unmistakably her. *Not a very good end is it?* He thought as he gazed at her. *Not quite the heroic warrior, fighting against terrorism. Just the killer of a drug lord, dying in the desert.* A wave of regret washed over him. But where else could he have gone? He didn't know. But he told himself he hadn't screwed up this first assignment. He'd done what he set out to do. The challenge was to not make this one his first and last.

Keep walking. Don't ever quit. The words came through the clear night air. Dan wasn't sure that he didn't hear them spoken out loud, as if Rita were speaking to him. But of course she couldn't. It had to be his mind playing tricks on him. Still it was encouraging. He kept shuffling forward, favoring his left ankle.

As the sun lit the sky, Dan limped ever more slowly. His ankle throbbed with pain. He looked for a place to stop; a place to get out of the sun and rest his ankle. His lips were cracked and swollen. He could not swallow. There was no more saliva so it was useless to try to eat anything. Besides, he had no appetite, only a raging thirst. The visage of Rita that had accompanied him on and off through the night, encouraging him, was replaced by visions of flowing water, waterfalls and clear, bubbling water flowing over clean stones. They promised refreshment and replenishment to his body. But the reality around him was only dust, sand, and rocks, burned by the ever-relentless sun.

Dan shuffled over to a large boulder and dropped to the ground in its shade. As the sun moved across the sky, he would slide around the rock, keeping to the meager shade it could provide. *Just rest for now. I'll be able to walk again later in the afternoon.*

Just before dawn after driving all night with just the four of them, Ramón's headlights picked out Dan's truck. He shoved the man next to him and told him to wake the two in the back. They pulled up, weapons ready. They got out and slowly approached the pickup. Ramón was careful, but he had already concluded the gringo was not there.

He tried to smile but with his cracked and burned lips it came out as a vicious smirk.

"The gringo is on foot. Today we will catch up to him."

There was no response from the others except to nod in agreement. Most figured the chase was now almost over. But how they would escape the desert was a question that still lurked in the back of their minds.

"*Vámonos.*" Ramón got into the truck. He drove faster now. He was tired and it was still dark but he was closing in and the hunter in him wanted to catch his quarry. Hector would be proud and they would deal harshly with those sons of bitches who had abandoned the chase. They would not spare their families either. All would die, painfully. A strong message needed to be delivered: there could be no defection in the ranks.

He pushed the truck ever faster, slamming into the rocks when he couldn't avoid them. The other men bounced around in the cab and held on as best they could. Dust blew through the truck, almost blinding everyone, including Ramón. The four-wheel drive machine with its large desert tires flew across the ground seemingly impervious to the rocks and uneven terrain. Ramón hunched himself over the steering wheel, now driven by a newfound energy.

The ground rose slowly without slowing the truck. Ramón kept his eyes focused on signs of the two-track. He didn't want to lose the trail in the night and have to retrace his route. As the truck skidded around a curve, the inside front wheel hit a large boulder half buried in the sand. It tipped up on its side. Ramón was slow to counter steer to get the center of gravity back under the frame. The truck went higher and higher. Ramón let off the accelerator and touched the brakes. This caused the outside front wheel to tuck under, sending the truck into a roll. Over it went and down the slope, tumbling over and over. A door flew open and a body flew out only to be crushed by the truck. Gas cans and weapons flew out from the bed of the pickup. When it stopped rolling it lay on its right side, crushing open a gas can that had been thrown out of the back. The gasoline spread under the overheated engine. There was danger of it catching fire.

Inside Ramón was slumped over the center console. The front passenger was not there, having been thrown to his death during the rolls. One of the men in the back, Rodrigo, lay against the right side of the truck, jammed up against another man whose head was tilted at an unnatural angle. Rodrigo could smell the gasoline spreading underneath the truck. He had to get out. He reached up and pushed against the left rear door. It would not budge. Thankfully the window was down. He began to crawl out. When he was halfway free of the truck he remembered what Ramón had said about having extra water stashed under the seat.

Was it worth going back into the cab? Could he retrieve the water before the truck started to burn? He would probably die without the water, so he decided to try. He slid back inside and dug under the seat in front of him. With the truck on its side he had to stand on the body of the man that had been sitting next to him. Rodrigo tried not to think about his feet crunching against the man's chest and face. He dug under the seat and pulled six plastic bottles free, tossing them through the open window. There were more, but he could not free them. There was a sharp *whomp* as the gasoline ignited. He had to go. Rodrigo climbed back out of the window out and let himself down to the ground. He quickly gathered the six bottles and staggered uphill a safe distance away.

His head was spinning and he felt bruised all over. He sat down as the fire flashed and filled the truck. Rodrigo didn't know if Ramón was alive, but it didn't matter now. What mattered was that he was alive, but alone and lost in the desert. He gathered the precious water bottles and pulled them to his chest. He sat on the hillside and watched the truck burn. His mind was numbed from the shock of the accident; he could only sit and stare at the fiery coffin below him.

When the sun cleared the hills to the east, Rodrigo stood up. He put the water bottles in his pockets. He had no weapons except for the .45 pistol in a holster at his side. Slowly he climbed back up the slope and stood on the trail. It still went north. Did the gringo go north? If he ran into him would he be killed? This phantom gringo that no one had seen and lived to tell about was out there ahead of him. Rodrigo dropped the thought. It was useless. The gringo could walk as fast as he and had a head start. They would never run into each other. His decision had to be which way to go, west or north.

He figured that if he drank a bottle a day it would keep him alive and he would have six days to find his way out of this cursed desert. At the top of the rise, he scanned the horizon. The hills to the north looked closer than those to the west. And to Rodrigo's way of thinking, following a trail, no matter how faint, was better off than heading further into the trackless wilderness to the west. A trail, no matter how old, generally went somewhere, came out somewhere. He would rely on that assumption. He would walk north.

He had no family except for his sister and her ten-year-old daughter. Rodrigo knew he had to get back for her sake. Carlos, the torturer, had had his eye on Miranda for some time. She was twenty-six and pretty. Carlos wouldn't try anything while Rodrigo was around. Rodrigo had been a *sicario*, a hitman, who had risen through the ranks. He was in charge of Chihuahua area, directing the *falcones*, the eyes and ears on the streets. Hector knew who he was and Rodrigo knew Carlos had to respect his rank and not cross him directly. But if Rodrigo died in the desert, Miranda would have no one to protect her. Carlos would move in, forcefully even, and take her even as he would try to take over control of Chihuahua. Rodrigo shuddered at the thought. And his niece, Solana? Carlos was not above taking her as well.

Chapter 19

The boulder offered only a stingy amount of shade. Dan sat with his legs stretched out in front of him. There was no way to elevate his ankle, but just taking his weight off of it helped. He tried to sleep but sleep wouldn't come. A part of him feared going to sleep. Would it be the same as going to sleep when caught out in the cold? You might never wake up? He didn't know and his mind could not process the question.

At one point he did drop off to sleep but a raucous cry startled him awake. There, on a rock, ten yards away from where he sat was a raven. Dan stared at it. His mind, now dull with dehydration and heat struggled to understand what he was seeing. The thought finally came again. Was the bird looking to see if he was carrion, ready to be picked over? The bird was definitely watching him. It turned its head from one side to the other. It had one black eye, gleaming like a dark jewel, and one red eye.

Red eye! The first raven had one red eye. The one he had given some water to. Did all ravens have multicolored eyes? Dan's mind struggled with the thought. This could not be the same bird. He was a good eighty miles away from where he had seen the previous one.

The sun had slipped lower in the sky. Dan was not in the shade anymore but the worst of the day's heat was past. Suddenly the raven leapt up and flew towards Dan. He ducked and threw out his hands to ward it off. It had a wing span of over four feet and long, sharp claws. The bird swooped close to Dan and then up to the top of the boulder he was sitting against. It began to squawk at him. Dan looked up and the bird acted as if it was going to attack him again. Dan cringed away to protect his face.

The raven flew down to the ground. It started to walk towards Dan. Along the way it jumped into the air in a flurry of wings. Dan finally concluded that the bird was going to give him no peace. He slowly got to his feet. His head was spinning. He leaned against the rock to steady himself.

Now the bird flew off to the north, the direction Dan had been walking. It went only a dozen yards and stopped. It looked back at Dan and flew another couple of yards, then looked back again. A thought formed in Dan's muddled mind. *Is this bird telling me to get up and go...in that direction?* The thought seemed outrageous. He must be delirious. Still it seemed to be urging action. *Walk*, he finally said to himself. The words from Rita the previous night came back to him. *Don't ever quit.* He limped forward. When he started moving the raven gave a loud cry and flew off, to the north.

Dan plodded through the night. His mind wandered but he made himself check his orientation to the North Star regularly. His path wasn't straight, but he hadn't started wandering in circles. His limp increased as the pain increased but he kept shuffling one foot after the other. Occasionally he stumbled on a rock and fell to the ground. It took long minutes for him to get back up. The temptation grew to just lie there; the night was cool, even chilly but the sand gave back a little warmth. Rita's voice kept coming back to him with the same message. *Don't ever quit.*

He forced himself up against a growing desire to stop and started forward again. To move was to survive, to live. To stop was to give in and die. Dan figured he would die trying; that was the least he could do. Or was it the best he could do now? His confused thoughts could not make sense of things. Only that he had completed his task and then failed to escape.

Jane'll have to find another assassin. Made a mess of it.

The night wore on, the limp increased, the shuffling slowed. Dan's breath came in harsh rasps. His cracked lips could form no words. There was no moisture to wet them anymore. His face, what he could sense of it, felt like leather; dry and dust covered. With each stumble, now coming more frequently, it took longer to get back on his feet. Finally the sky lightened in the east.

Can stop soon. The thought gave him some relief. In the back of his mind though, a certainty grew that he might not get back up after this day.

He came upon some rock outcroppings. The land was now hillier, lumpier. He was out of the flat pan of the desert floor. Still, he saw no vegetation that might signal water. He was at a slight rise. The ground sloped gradually away to the north and where it flattened out. These hills didn't fulfill the hoped-for promise. He looked out over the flat expanse further out in front of him and would have cried if he had enough moisture for tears. Instead he limped over to a rock that promised some shade and slumped to the ground. He could go no farther. While one part of his mind kept repeating the mantra to not quit, another part slipped into acquiescence of his fate. He did not have the ability to walk across that looming expanse to the north. He would die here.

The light grew but did not improve the scene nor Dan's situation. There was no water and he had an even more barren, dry landscape in front of him. There was nothing in retreat and nothing in going forward.

If you're gonna die, die out there, not here. The voice in his mind; Rita's, his, he couldn't tell anymore; it began to speak over and over against his fatigue and thirst. *What's the use? Who cares?* He answered back.

Dan sat and stared out at his death; the looming expanse in front of him. The slight rise he had navigated continued to his west but showed no sign of water. It became even more rocky and difficult to traverse. To the north and now, to the east it just gradually sloped away to another flat pan. There was no other way to go.

The sun was now full in the east. With it came the raven. It did not surprise Dan. Somehow he thought the bird might return. Nothing made sense now in this heat and emptiness, so why should it be odd to have a raven come along to witness his death? But the bird was not sitting to witness. It flew at Dan with its harsh cry. Over and over until Dan turned over on his hands and knees and slowly levered himself upright.

You want me to go out there and die? Maybe die faster for you? What was the bird's purpose? Dan didn't have the energy to think it through. He started forward. Immediately the bird stopped dive-bombing him. It flew ahead and perched on a rock as Dan stumbled forward, now aided by the subtle push of gravity. He had no more strength to climb but he could give in to gravity. As Dan got closer, the bird again flew forward and stopped as if waiting for him. By now Dan had no doubt it wanted him to go forward, but he had no idea why.

By that afternoon Dan's legs gave out. He collapsed to the ground. The bird, after a few moments, flew back and began to dive bomb him with its screeching. Dan didn't respond. He looked up. The bird was standing ten feet away from him watching. Suddenly Dan saw a large four-footed animal approach. It was a coyote. The raven didn't fly away. Even in Dan's depleted state, he thought that was odd.

The coyote stopped also about ten feet from Dan and sat down. Its large jaws were open, panting in the heat. It almost looked like it was grinning at him. *Maybe I should shoot it and drink its blood.* The coyote stirred as if reading Dan's thoughts. It got up and walked around to Dan's rear. Then it approached. Dan felt a nip at his leg. He pulled his legs up to get away from those powerful jaws. *Is it going to eat me alive?* The thought gave him a surge of energy. *Not eaten alive.* He kicked out and got to his hands and knees. The coyote again moved forward. Dan lashed out his foot again. The animal easily dodged it and nipped his leg again. He didn't break the skin but Dan could feel the teeth through his pants. He lurched to his feet, bringing a rock up with him. Turning, he flung it at the coyote but missed. Now it sat back on its haunches, its tongue lolling out of its mouth, panting, almost smiling. The raven now flew up and gave a call. Dan turned. The bird flew ahead and then stopped and looked back.

Was it leading again? Why?

He was now on his feet and the part of him that didn't want to quit, that wanted to die trying, told him to go forward. Whatever had just taken place, he was at least on his feet again. He lurched onward. The raven kept flying forward and then alighted on the ground as if to wait.

When Dan looked back the coyote was following but not threatening.

An hour later Dan was off the slope and facing the flat pan. He caught his foot and fell forward. There was no strength to rise. The coyote again began to nip at his legs, but Dan could not pull himself up.

"Why the hell should I get up for you?" he said in a hoarse voice. A stupid question, especially to put to an animal. But the coyote persisted, aided by the raven. Finally Dan got to his hands and knees and began to crawl.

He crawled for a half hour. Then a dry wash appeared in front of him. It was about eight feet deep with steep sides. He noticed it as the raven flew up ahead of him and disappeared out of sight. A moment later it came up, out of the wash into the air in front of Dan.

I go down in there, I'm not coming out. The bird seemed to want Dan to go forward. Dan resisted, seeing the wash and the cliffs on either side, easily scrambled up by a healthy person, but in his state, impassable.

"No," he said as loudly as he could. Whatever insanity was going on he would not go down there.

The raven squawked loudly and flew at him. The coyote now nipped at his rear end. Dan felt the sharpness of the teeth that now bit into him. Instinctively he went forward on his hands and knees. One last nip caused Dan to lurch forward and he slipped over the lip of the ravine. He flung his hands out in vain to stop himself. It was too late. He had no strength left. He rolled over three times and lay on the dirt.

The coyote scrambled down after him and started growling at him, threatening him. Meanwhile the raven hopped and flew forward, away from the threatening animal, encouraging him to follow.

Dan crawled forward. Each time he stopped the coyote attacked him, nipping at him, but not injuring him. After ten minutes Dan collapsed. His face lay against the dirt. For a moment he didn't move. Then he sensed a hint of moisture; it could have been a hallucination. There seemed to be some moisture in the ground. He took his hand and dug his fingers through the dry top surface and below it he felt a cool moist texture. He looked up. The gully bent around to the left, heading into the rocks above from where he had just crawled. The raven hopped and flew forward.

Chapter 20

Dan gathered up what little energy he had left. If he had been in a rational state, he would have questioned more of what was going on. Now he just responded to what he saw. The bird and the coyote wanted him to go forward. He had come upon a hint of moisture. He would go forward, maybe there would be more. Maybe he would not die. Dan began to crawl.

When he got around the turn, he could smell it: water. Ten minutes of crawling later and he could hear it. Ten more minutes brought him to a small pool, fed by a flow coming out of the rocks above. The pool was small and clear. It disappeared underground after a few meters. It had the smell of life. Dan breathed great gasping breaths as he crawled to the pool. The air was filled with moisture which soothed his throat. Reaching the pool he dropped his head into the cool water and started sucking it in. He had never experienced such a sweet taste. It was the taste of life, of living. Not dying.

He would not die here in the desert. The thought slammed into his brain. Suddenly a hand grabbed the back of his shirt and pulled his face out of the pool. Dan rolled over and looked up.

An apparition looked down, lost in the glare of the sun. Dan moved his head. Was it a demon? Now he saw a face as it blocked the sun; the sun's rays were bursting out around the visage like a medieval icon of a saint. It was a man; an Indian. He had long black hair coming out from an old, floppy brimmed hat. His face was dark brown, deeply lined, and appeared tough as tanned leather. It was an ancient face as if belonging to a different time. He was medium height and his body evidenced what was once a powerful build, now diminished with age. He wore a white shirt over leather breeches. His eyes shone with a fierce light. One was deep black and the other one was a deep red. They burned into Dan as the man stared at him.

"Too much and you get sick." The man spoke with a strange accent, but Dan could understand the Spanish.

"Who are you?"

The man stared at him. "Later. Come now." He reached to help Dan on his feet.

"One more," Dan mumbled and turned over to the pool. He pulled in a deep draught and then turned back. The stranger helped him to his feet and half carried, half dragged him forward. To one side of the spring, there was a hut, framed with sticks and covered with tarps, built up against the rock wall. The canyon was deeper here and the spring well hidden. Dan's head spun and he passed out as he was pulled into the hut.

When Dan awoke he lay on a pallet of blankets. There was a soothing salve on his face. He felt thirsty but his throat was not dry and choked as before. From the low light and long shadows outside, he guessed the sun was low in the sky. He stared at the roof of the hut. It had a hole to vent smoke from a central fire pit. He rolled over and on the other side of the hut was a wooden pole with a

"T" top. On it perched the raven. Lying next to the pole was the coyote looking very relaxed, not like it was going to attack him. Its jaw hung open, the large teeth gleaming in the low light, the tongue lolling at the side of the mouth. It appeared to Dan to be grinning at him. Next to the raven's pole a bed was laid out on the ground. To the rear were shelves with wooden and clay bowls and pots holding various items which Dan assumed were for cooking.

Dan rolled back and stared at the ceiling. *I should move*, he thought, but he had no strength. And where would he go? He wondered where the man had gone. Was this all just a hallucination? No, he was lying in a hut; somebody made the hut; somebody lives here. And, it seemed to Dan as he started to think more clearly, these animals live here as well.

I'm missing something. Dan tried to think, He was missing some clarifying clue. There was something that tied this together in some weird way. What was it? He forced his mind to run through the events of the day. He was near his end. He couldn't go on, but he thought he should die trying rather than give up in the rocks above the desert pan. Then there was the raven and the coyote. It had not been his imagination. He had not been delirious. They had forced him forward. Even when he had to crawl, they wouldn't let him rest. *Why?* And what was the connection that seemed missing in his mind?

Dan rolled back over to his right and looked across to the raven and coyote. They both looked back at him. The raven turned its head and then he saw it; the one red eye. Ravens have black eyes. This one had one black and one red. That was somehow significant. Dan's mind wrestled with the thought and then the image of the Indian came back to him, almost blinding, framed by the sun. The man had one red eye and one black eye.

What rabbit hole have I dropped into?

He propped himself up and called out, "*Hola*. Anyone here?"

The two animals stirred but didn't move from where they were. There was no answer.

Shortly he heard a soft footstep outside. The entrance went dark as the man blocked the light. He stooped and came into the hut. He had two rabbits, skinned and cleaned in one hand and some greens bunched in the other hand. They looked like pieces of cactus and other desert plants. The coyote and the raven looked attentively at the man. Saliva dripped from the coyote's mouth. He spoke to them in a language Dan did not understand and the coyote lunged for the door with the raven flying out just behind him.

Dan watched as the man laid the rabbits on a board. He started a fire in the central pit, poured water from a pitcher into a pot and set the pot over the fire. Next, he chopped up the greens and the cut the rabbit carcasses into small pieces. He left them on the board, waiting for the water to boil. Dan now noticed his hat had many feathers bristling out from the band.

"Who are you?" Dan asked in Spanish.

The man ignored him.

"How long have I been out?" Dan asked.

"One night, one day," came the reply. The man turned to him. His face was leathery. A fierce scowl was etched into his mouth. His eyes riveted him. They seemed to burn through him, seeing everything in his mind. "You spoke much. You spoke to your wife, Rita."

Dan felt a surge of adrenalin go through him. "What did I say?"

The man turned back to preparing the meat and greens. "Many things. You wanted forgiveness. She does not blame you. She told you 'don't give up, never quit'."

"You heard her speak? Are you a medium? You can talk to the dead?"

The man shook his head. "I do not consult the dead. But she spoke loudly. She has a strong spirit."

"She's dead." Dan almost choked on the words. "How can she speak? Are you playing with me? Who are you and why am I here?"

"There is much to tell you, but first you must drink and eat. You must get strong and we don't have much time."

He reached over to Dan and handed him a cup. It was filled with an aromatic liquid. "Drink."

"What's in it?"

"Water and juice from the cactus. Soothe throat and mouth. You drink many cups."

Dan took the cup and drank. He was in the man's hands. This old Indian had rescued him, somehow, from dying. Dan had no reason to worry about the concoction he offered.

The water boiled and the meat and pieces of cactus were put in the pot. Some flour and salt was sprinkled into the pot as well and the man placed a lid on it.

He turned back to Dan, "You have many questions. I will try to answer."

Dan's mind swirled. The questions came so fast he didn't know where to begin. Why had he saved him? How did he find him? How did the raven and coyote come into this? What was their relationship? What did he want? He stopped himself and tried to focus.

The man stared at him. "Your mind is still confused. You asked me 'who am I'? Your first question. I am a shaman as my father and grandfather, for seven generations. I saw you.

I knew you were coming, that you would fall out of the sky, like a comet. I found you after you fell to earth."

"That's impossible!" Dan exclaimed, interrupting the shaman.

The shaman stared at him with his glowing eyes, one red, one black. "But you are here."

Dan had no answer. "The raven I saw...when I was hiking south, was that the same bird as this one? Your bird?"

"Not my bird, my friend. *Sí*, same bird. That is how I found you."

"What do you mean, 'how I found you'?"

"You ask foolish questions. It is a white man's trait. You try to make everything fit your mind, even when it does not. There are more important questions."

Dan sat up now. "Maybe, but I need to understand how this all fits together. Help me out."

"I am Tlayolotl. In your language, 'Heart of the Earth'. I knew you were coming...someone was coming—falling out of the sky—to strike the darkness. Raven and I set out to find you. And we did."

"But how—"

The shaman held up his hand. His face grew sharp and his eyes seemed to glow in the dim light of the hut. "Listen, not speak. Your questions are like dust devils that swirl around in confusion and blow away to nothing."

He turned to stir the pot and then refocused on Dan. "I told you I do not speak with the dead. Some shamans do, I do not. I have great power and can heal or strike one dead. But I do not. I am a Watcher. I have been called to this."

"What is a 'Watcher'?"

Again, the man held up his hand. "I see things. I see darkness and light, the forces of good and evil."

"I don't understand."

"You will. I had dreams. They kept coming back for many weeks. I didn't know what they meant but I could not ignore them. The dreams were of someone coming, from the north, a gringo. To fight the darkness that has been growing, strike a blow. So Raven and I went to look. We went to look for this darkness and then we looked for you. And we found you. We tested you. You gave us water, so we knew your heart was right."

"How did you know that?"

"Do not be foolish with your questions. I was there, with Raven. That is how I know."

Dan held himself in check as more questions surged into his mind. The Indian, or shaman, was one hundred percent right about the water. He thought he had heard the bird call "*agua*" and decided (why had he thought of it?) to cut the plastic water bottle, make a cup out of the bottom and give it to the bird.

The shaman continued, his eyes never leaving Dan. "Then we waited for you. We knew you would come back north after you completed your task. But you were in danger. We could see, Raven and I. Bad men had taken over your escape plan.

"The bird...that was you?"

"Raven and me. We attacked."

"That attack saved my life. How did you—"

"We watched. We could see what was happening."

"Could you see I would get stuck in the desert?"

"We don't see the future. One can only guess at it. We see what is happening."

"So you and the bird and the coyote came to keep me from dying back there?"

"Raven and Coyote came by themselves. I was not there but they knew what to do."

"They wouldn't let me rest, not let me quit. You sent them?"

The shaman nodded.

"I thought of shooting the coyote...for his blood. But I had no strength."

The man's face flickered dark and dangerous. "You would not have been able to hit Coyote. He is the trickster. He can deceive men."

"This all seems unreal. It doesn't seem possible."

"To the white man's mind. But you are here."

Dan took a deep breath and exhaled slowly. His head still felt light, either from what he had been through or what he had just listened to. He lay back on his pallet. The shaman watched him carefully. He told him to take off his left boot. When Dan did so, he went over to him and examined Dan's swollen ankle. He put his hands on it, around it, massaging and squeezing, as if to feel the insides.

He grunted. "It is not broken. I will wrap it to heal quick."

Tlayolotl went to the back of the hut and dug around in the assembled stores. He took a bowl and went out to the spring. He returned with water and mixed in powders until there was a paste-like consistency. Then he rubbed the paste over Dan's ankle. Dan could feel the mixture sinking into his skin.

"What's in this?"

"Healing. From plants. It will take away your swelling and give you strength there."

"What herbs did you use? I can really feel them going into my ankle."

Tlayolotl did not answer him. After coating his ankle, he wrapped it in a cloth and tied it tight. "That is good for tonight. Tomorrow you will be able to walk."

The shaman turned back to the pot and stirred it. The smell awakened a fresh hunger in Dan. His thirst had been slaked and now he felt the pangs of not eating for days. Tlayolotl ladled some of the stew into a wooden bowl and offered it to Dan.

"It is hot."

Dan blew on it and forced himself to be patient. He did not want to burn his mouth on top of the cracked, sore lips he had from the dehydration. They ate in silence. Dan savored the stew, enjoying the chunks of meat and the broth, almost sweet with the cactus greens boiled in it.

Night fell as they ate. Tlayolotl lit some candles. The coyote and raven returned and took up their positions.

Chapter 21

D an tried a new tack with the shaman. "Okay, somehow you knew I was coming, you saved me twice and now I'm here. You have a strange connection to the bird and coyote. Somehow you see things that are physically far away. That is hard to believe, but that seems to be what happened."

He leaned forward towards Tlayolotl. "Tell me why you have done this? Done what seems impossible."

"Now you begin to ask the right questions."

"And you can answer them? You did not do this for no reason."

"I told you I am a Watcher, one of many. We have a gift to see the spirit world. You white people think there is nothing beyond what you can see. Yet you believe in atoms and things you can't see. What you don't accept is what is right in front of you if you had sight for it."

"What is that?"

"The spirit world. There is the world of things you can touch and feel and there is the world of spirits. You can't touch or feel this world but it is not less real. I will tell you it is more real than the world we sit in."

The shaman put the eating bowls aside and pulled the pot off the fire. He settled down to get more comfortable.

"There is a battle between the forces of darkness and the forces of light. It is between good and evil. The spirits play out this battle here in our world. We are in the middle of a battle. We are part of it."

"There are enemies out there, bad men who want to hurt people, who want to destroy society. I know that."

Tlayolotl shook his head. "It is more than that. It is driven by the darkness. This darkness has grown in Mexico. It has infested Chihuahua City. You have come to fight the darkness."

Dan interrupted. "I came to assassinate a drug lord. And I did that. If you want to call it fighting darkness that is fine with me."

The shaman shook his head. "I hoped you could understand."

"I see you are trying to make some cosmic thing out of what I am doing...what I did. I'm an assassin, that's all." This last he said with some force.

Tlayolotl just stared at him, his eyes burning deep in his face.

"But you cannot dismiss how you came to be here." His voice grew sharper, the words biting into Dan. "You were dead twice. Because of me you are not dead. In my world you owe me your life—two lives. You have a debt to pay to me."

"I'm grateful for you saving me. And I don't understand how it happened, but I don't have a debt to pay to you."

Tlayolotl stood up. His voice boomed in the hut. The coyote rose and started to growl. "You owe me your life, twice! If you can't or won't accept that, I can take it back, twice!"

The coyote inched forward. Dan recoiled on the pad from the shaman's intensity.

"I should turn you out to die in the desert. I thought you were the one. Maybe I am old and don't see so well." He pointed a finger at Dan. "But you are the one who doesn't see well. You are blind. You try to remain blind while I try to give you sight."

He stepped out of the hut into the night. The coyote followed after a last growl in Dan's direction. The raven clung to its perch and looked down at Dan.

I've done it now. Pissed him off. He rescued me and if he turns me out, I'll probably die. The man was old but Dan had no doubts that, with the coyote, he could be driven away without much hope of survival. He made a decision and got up and walked out of the hut.

Tlayolotl was standing near the pool of water looking up at the sky. The night sky was filled with stars, bright like diamonds. They alone lit the clear air enough to cast shadows. The coyote sat beside him.

Dan approached slowly. The coyote turned to watch him carefully. "Tlayolotl, I am sorry to speak to you with no respect and no thankfulness. You *have* saved my life, given it back to me when it would have been lost. I am ready to listen."

The shaman stared upward without responding.

Dan continued. "You have some reason for doing this and I need to hear it. Please tell me what you have to say."

Slowly the shaman turned. In the dark, Dan could still see his eyes glowing, like coals in a fire. "I am old. Ancient. Older than you can imagine. But my power is still great and I still see what a Watcher needs to see." He pointed to the hut. "Go back in. Maybe it is not too late for you to learn."

Dan walked back into the hut and the shaman followed a few minutes later. He sat down on a stool.

"A woman has called you to battle. I saw it in my dreams. I sense her heart is good but I do not see her clearly. I do not think she knows what she battles. You are important. More than you know. More than this woman knows, although she suspects there is more." He pointed to Dan, "She wants you to be the warrior. Much will depend on you, but you must not fight blind. You must understand the battle.

"I brought you here to show you the battle you fight. To help you to see. If you open your mind and accept my words, you will see and understand. It will make you a stronger warrior."

The shaman looked at Dan for some time. "You must learn to still the chatter in your mind. It is like the squirrel busying about, here and there."

"You can read my mind?"

Tlayolotl shook his head. "No, but I can sense how busy your mind is. It keeps you from hearing and understanding."

"If this is a spiritual battle, like you say. And you say it has to be fought here, in the physical world. I don't see how that changes things."

"It is better for you to know more than less. It will keep you safe in the future. A warrior's mind can go bad from fighting if he doesn't know his role—the part he plays and how he helps. It will all seem to be too much killing after some time." Tlayolotl pointed to Dan. "What I will show you will keep you safe. You will see. Tomorrow night. Tonight you must rest and I must go looking, watching. Tomorrow I will prepare you to see. Are you willing to see?"

His eyes bore into Dan as he asked the question. There was no turning away from him.

"Yes."

Chapter 22

That night Tlayolotl took out some pieces of cactus from a jar; they looked like small buds or buttons taken from a larger section. He lit a small piece of brush and the smoke filled the hut. It was pungent, not unpleasant. Taking a large feather, Dan guessed it was from an eagle, Tlayolotl began to waft the aromatic smoke around as he chanted, softly, rhythmically. The coyote relaxed on the ground, his eyes fastened intently on the old shaman. The raven began to pace back and forth on his perch, always watching the man. Tlayolotl brushed his arms, torso and face with the feather.

After what seemed like a half hour, Tlayolotl began to eat the cactus pieces, chewing them and swallowing the pieces. He kept chanting and singing in a language Dan didn't understand, but what seemed to be prayers or enchantments, in between bites. After consuming eight pieces he stopped and sat still. Dan watched him closely as his breathing grew softer and slower. It looked like he was going into a trance.

Then the raven squawked. It startled Dan. The bird jumped off its perch and flew through the opening of the hut. Tlayolotl didn't stir. The coyote did not move except to glance at Dan now and then.

After an hour or more, Dan wasn't sure; he got up to check on Tlayolotl. When he stepped forward the coyote growled and moved forward, putting himself in between Dan and the shaman. Dan stopped. He rethought his idea of checking up on Tlayolotl. He had no desire to be attacked by the animal that showed an enormous loyalty to the shaman as well as an amazing awareness of what was going on between the two humans. He stepped back and turned to go outside of the hut. The coyote did not follow.

The night air was clear and chilly. The stars were stunning in their brilliance. They hung in the sky, closer and sharper than he had ever seen them up north. The hills came into dim view as he looked up out of the depths of the ravine. It was a well-chosen place. You would not see this from above. You would have to climb into the nearly impassable rocks that overhung the spring behind where he was standing to be able to see the pool of water. You would still not see the hut. And the creek draining the pool sank underground before it went around the curve in the gulch. As a result, in crossing through the gulch farther down, where the slope let you descend into and climb out the other side, you would never know this oasis was just around the bend.

How long had he lived here? Dan wondered. Did he sustain himself on rabbits and cactus plants? Did any other humans visit or even know he was here? The questions were flying around in his mind. "Busy as a squirrel." Dan remembered his words. These were not the important questions. It would not matter if he never got the answers to them. He was beginning to understand.

But what are the important questions?

Why am I here? And what do you want of me? These were the ones he needed to ask. Tlayolotl was in a trance.

He could do nothing about that. Dan guessed the pieces of cactus were peyote and that Tlayolotl was on a hallucinogenic trip. The coyote would protect him during that time and Dan would have to wait. *How long would that be?*

He turned back to the hut. *He said to rest and tomorrow he would show me. Show me what?* Dan didn't know, but he was ready to rest. He went into the hut and lay down on his pallet.

Tlayolotl flew with Raven across the desert. They winged south towards Chihuahua City. As they approached he saw the dark. It was not a cloud so much as the absence of light. There was no substance to it; it was nothingness, nothing emanated from it...and nothing penetrated it. Raven flew around it, not getting too close. Tlayolotl was old and experienced. He would not risk an encounter. The darkness could engulf and snare him. He was a Watcher and it was best to just watch.

Raven alighted on a roof. When Tlayolotl had noted the source of the darkness, the bird took wing and they headed back north, out over the desert. Tlayolotl needed to find someone. A gang member lost in the desert. He would help Dan. The pieces were falling in place.

Tariq looked up as Raven flew off. But he only saw a flash of dark wings. Tariq thought it odd for a bird—it looked like a crow or raven to him—to be out at night.

As they flew closer to Tlayolotl's hut the bird began to fly a crisscross pattern across the desert. Hour after hour they flew, searching. Finally, Tlayolotl spotted a figure staggering along. The man was close to collapse. The shaman could see he had been going in circles for most of the night. He hoped the man had one or two days in him. He would be needed for Tlayolotl's plans. They watched him for a while and started back to the hut.

Hector was concerned. The men he had sent into the desert to chase down the shooter had not reported back to him. He was blind to what might have happened. He sensed there was trouble; that the plan had not gone well. After the men departed, he gave orders that no one was to leave the warehouse while the police were all over Chihuahua City. He was assured by the high-level officers of the local police that none of his senior men would be arrested, but they would lie low and wait for the *Federals* to go. It was strongly suggested that Hector needed to get control over the gang war that threatened to explode since the shooting. There were many outbreaks of violence and he was struggling to contain the fighting. The press was still in sensational mode with lurid headlines and pictures. Inter-cartel violence would only keep them engaged and fuel the killing.

Tariq had not liked the delay nor the orders that no one was to leave the compound, which included himself. Hector didn't care. He would have liked to just kill them all, but it was not possible in the city now with all the activity. He didn't care about killing Jorge's plan for diversification, but the loss of the heroin source gave him some pause. Still, if Tariq irritated him too much...he would enjoy killing him. Hector had no interest in Tariq's hatred of the U.S. The U.S. was simply a market to him.

Now with nothing more to do for the moment, Hector had flown back to Mexico City. He needed to place himself in the center of action, the center of power of the Sinaloa cartel. That place was Jorge Mendoza's compound. María would have to understand his need to dispense direction and orders from this location. She needed to understand that he was the one who could keep her safe and allow her to keep her lifestyle intact.

The cartel lawyer also had to acknowledge Hector. He would do so because it was in his interests. Any other man trying to assume leadership would be challenged. Now was the time to establish Hector as the leader. María's family lawyer had to be brought on board as well. Some quiet words from the cartel lawyer and some veiled threats from Hector about how the man needed to protect his own family as well as María's would do the trick. He arranged for the two men to be at the Mendoza compound.

"You want to stay here, in the house?" María asked. She was talking with Hector in the front living room after he had landed in his helicopter at the compound.

"It is necessary," Hector replied. "I am the only one who can keep the cartel together and who can avoid war with other cartels. Two other leaders were killed along with Jorge and many blame us. They want revenge."

María's face fell at the mention of Jorge's killing. "I would like to be alone."

Hector smiled at her. "It is not possible. Not now. I have to be here and so do you. Your presence will give approval to my position." Hector wanted all the signs to point to him as the leader. He reached out to touch her arm. "I am the only one who can keep you safe. You are a beautiful woman, María. Jorge, may God have mercy on him, did not fully appreciate you or what you could be. If you stay by my side, I can assure you no harm will come to you or your children. You must talk with your lawyer. He will agree. I will have him talk to you later."

"Hector, what is it you want?"

"To keep the cartel intact and to keep us dominant."

"What is it you want...of me?"

Hector took her arm and walked her back towards the study. "Just your support, nothing more. We can talk of more, later when you are ready."

She looked sideways at him as they walked. Hector could see her trying to discern just what price she would have to pay. He didn't say more. She would do what was necessary. She had not been deeply in love with Jorge and he had not asked for more; just children, a glamorous partner, and one who quietly let him do his whoring as he wished. With her children, she now had more motivation to work the current situation to her advantage. Hector smiled inside. That calculation would lead to him taking not only the reins of the cartel, but also the beautiful wife of the cartel's now dead leader.

"I have followed Jorge all through his rise in the cartel. I am the one behind his power. Now I can inherit that power and use it to protect you."

María slipped her free hand over Hector's hand that still gripped her arm. It was as if she had made a decision. She squeezed his hand gently, and then slid her fingers off sending a chill down Hector's spine. "Thank you." She smiled at him and then disengaged herself and turned towards her own rooms.

Dan awoke with a start as the raven swooped into the hut with a flurry of wings. It hooked onto the perch and looked around, ruffling and flapping its wings as it got itself comfortable. Suddenly Tlayolotl stirred and looked up. He saw Dan looking at him from his pallet.

"You stay awake? You need to rest. There is much to do tomorrow."

"The bird woke me. It flew off when you went into a trance. That is what you did, isn't it?"

"Raven and me went to see. To prepare for tomorrow." He held up his hand in anticipation of a question from Dan. "No foolish questions now. No time for that. There are still hours left in the night. You sleep. Raven sleeps. Raven has much work to do tomorrow."

The raven had already tucked its head to one side and was fast asleep. Dan looked over at the coyote; it was now asleep. Tlayolotl drank some water and he too lay down on his pallet to sleep.

Dan yawned and lay back. *Tomorrow would bring the answers, as Tlayolotl said.*

Chapter 23

Jane sat in Henry's office. It was not much larger than her own. Henry's tie was loose and his hair ruffled. He had a scowl on his face rather than the usual easy going professorial look. *Something's bothering him.*

Henry sat at his desk; there was a manila folder in front of him. "Have you heard from Dan?"

"Not since he checked in five days ago. His phone battery may have died."

Henry pointed for Jane to sit in the chair in front of the desk. "He had a sat phone?"

"Yes but he hasn't used it since checking in."

"So you don't know what has happened?"

"Only that Dan said we got a bonus on the job. I'm not quite sure I know what he means by that. What's up? Did you hear anything?"

Henry tapped the folder. "We got a cable from the embassy in Mexico City. The place is in an uproar."

"The city or the embassy?"

"Both, actually. It seems he not only killed Mendoza but two other cartel leaders along with some lieutenants. It was quite a shootout. On top of that, the men sent to pull Dan out may have been ambushed. They're missing as is the vehicle they used. We have to presume they're dead.

The embassy is raising hell and asking what this was all about. They want to know if their pickup instructions had anything to do with these shootings."

That's what he meant about an added bonus. Jane looked over at Henry. "We've got to maintain the cover that we sent a man in to do some reconnaissance and they were to pull him out."

Henry shook his head. "That's going to be hard to do. The connection will be made. The police have found the shooting site. It's just where we would send a man to do recon but it's also where we would send a sniper."

"Did they find anything?"

"No, Dan cleaned it up."

"Then they still can't prove any connection—"

"Unless they catch Dan. And you haven't heard from him. How are we to get in touch and get him out of there?"

Jane shook her head. "I don't know. If he doesn't turn on the sat phone...we can only wait until we hear from him."

"Meanwhile we're in some deep shit."

Jane looked at Henry quizzically.

"Roger Abrams, my boss, wants to talk with us. This morning."

"But he's your friend. He'll work with us, won't he?"

"He wants the full story and then I may have to talk to the DDO, Garrett Easton."

"Holy shit," Jane exclaimed. Everyone will know about this before the day ends. Henry, this will get taken down before we get off the ground. All our hard work for nothing."

"Maybe, maybe not. It's certainly not a good start, but not impossible to patch over. Roger's not happy but he's going to be on our side. He just wants future missions to not impact the State Department. He thinks he can convince Garrett to let us ride this out. Garrett's an old Soviet hand, worked with Roger over there. Roger says he still understands what needs to be done."

Jane just shook her head. This was not the way she imagined; the first mission blowing up into a media storm and one of our embassies raising hell. She realized the program could be sacrificed to make peace between State and the CIA.

"When do we meet with everyone?"

"Roger will be down here momentarily. I wanted to prep you. After we three talk, I'll go up to see Garrett."

The sun slanted into the hut waking Dan. It was already pretty high in the sky. Tlayolotl was up and making an herb drink. Dan got up, stretched and went outside to relieve himself and splash water from the pond on his face.

"Your ankle?" Tlayolotl asked as he came back in.

Dan hadn't even thought about it when he walked outside. "It's fine. I didn't notice it. What you put on it worked. You could make a lot of money from that poultice."

Tlayolotl ignored the comment. He handed Dan a cup of the herb brew. "Drink this, it will strengthen you." He then started cooking some flat corn meal cakes on the fire. When they were done he handed one to Dan with some honey spread on it. Dan accepted the food and ate the cake hungrily. All the while Tlayolotl watched him.

When they were done eating, Tlayolotl spoke. "There is much to tell you today and much to show you. Your mind will want to put up barriers to what you see. It will raise questions like before. Questions that serve no purpose but to let you put what you learn into a box. You can't put aside what you will learn today. If you do you will be no help."

"I am willing to listen and to learn...to try to understand. Just like I told you yesterday."

"You may not understand even if you hear and learn. Can you accept that?" Tlayolotl's eyes burned into him.

"How can I help if I do not understand?"

"You will see if you are willing."

After a long moment of silence, Dan answered, "Okay, I'm willing." He didn't know where all this would lead, but he felt he had already jumped down the rabbit hole and following this old shaman's plan was the only way out.

Tlayolotl began. "You accept the fact that you are here. You accept the fact that I saw you coming, falling out of the sky, that Raven and I found you and saved your life twice. I heard Rita speak to you. You did not tell me any of this, yet I know it. You can't understand how but you believe because you are here and not dead somewhere in the desert."

Dan stared hard back at the shaman who seemed to be waiting for an answer.

"Yes," he finally said.

"Good. Now last night I ate the peyote. I went into a trance and Raven left. You saw that. What you didn't see is that I left with Raven."

Dan felt the obvious question arise in him even as the shaman put up his hand, anticipating it.

"Don't ask. Hear and learn", he said. "My spirit went flying with Raven. We located the darkness. We also located the man you will need to help you in your mission." Again, he raised his hand to keep Dan silent.

"I am a Watcher. I told you that before. There are many of us around the world. We can see the battles going on in the spirit world, battles using humans for their purposes. We see what is behind what you see with your eyes.

"You have a different role to play. You were hired by the lady up north to fight enemies. She was correct in choosing you, but she does not fully understand your role and the full dimension of the battle. This is my task. To show you the full importance of what you do. And to provide you with what help I can.

"But what am I to do? I completed my assignment from Jane. I even killed more bad men than she directed. I'm on my way home now."

The shaman shook his head as he looked down at the dying embers of the cooking fire. "I told you, she doesn't see the full extent of the battle. This battle between good and evil between the forces of dark and light must be played out. I watch. I guide. Jane, the lady you talk of, she directs against the foe she doesn't fully understand.

"You," he leaned forward and pointed his finger at Dan. His eyes lit up as though a fire burned behind them. "You are the tip of the spear in this battle, the sharp end that thrusts into the enemy. You are the warrior who delivers the blows in this world that push back the spread of the evil."

Dan stared, riveted by the shaman's eyes and the force of his voice.

"That is why you must experience what most gringos cannot handle. You must come with me to see. Your mission here is not yet over. You must strike again at the darkness I found."

"So I'm not going home? Will I ever get back home?"

Tlayolotl shook his head. "I told you I don't read the future. If you are smart, yes. Much depends on how well you learn."

Chapter 24

Back at the CIA headquarters Roger opened the door to Henry's office without knocking. He looked like there was a storm brewing in him. Henry got up and waved him in and to a seat across from Henry's desk. Jane sat in a similar seat near the other corner of the desk.

"Good to see you Roger," Henry said, shaking Roger's hand. "You know Jane Tanner. She's been instrumental in getting this project off the ground and picking our first operative." Roger sat down without shaking hands.

"So, give it to me straight, from the top. I've got to talk to the DDO later. I kept you out of it. I'll handle that conversation but I need to know everything. I can decide what to tell Garrett, we can have that candid a conversation. But", he leaned forward towards Henry, "I can't get blindsided by this."

"Understood," Henry replied. He turned to Jane. "Fill Roger in on how you found Dan." He turned back to Roger, "You might as well get the beginning of the story as well."

Jane went through the narrative of how she became aware of Dan and the steps she took to connect with him and help extricate him from the trap he had found himself in. Roger said nothing but occasionally snorted at some of Jane's more egregious actions.

"Jesus, you played things pretty loose there," He said after Jane was done talking. "Are you always so dismissive of rules and regulations?"

Jane shook her head. "No sir, but Dan seemed like an extraordinary find and I needed to take some risks to get him out of his situation."

"Henry, did you know all of this as it was going on?"

Henry paused. He had been kept in the dark, but he didn't want to compound Jane's transgressions any further. "Yes. She kept me informed along the way." Jane gave him a grateful look.

"So, you approved her actions," Roger said.

"I never disapproved them, to be more exact. Jane knew what she was doing and had her end of the situation under control. We could bail out and withdraw at any moment without a trace."

"Except for the FBI agent," Roger said.

"We had him compromised. He would never turn us in," Jane said.

Roger turned to her. "That's another stepping over the line by you. Just what kind of a cowboy are you?" Roger replied. He turned back to Henry, "Henry, you can't run a black ops this fast and loose. Damn it, you'll get us all burned.

Henry gave Jane a sharp look to keep her from responding.

"All right," Roger continued, "tell me about this Mexican caper and how it turned into a shit storm."

"It was to be one man, Jorge Mendoza, the head of the Sinaloa cartel. We targeted him because he was working to organize the other cartels and make peace with them. We felt this would only increase their effectiveness at compromising the Mexican government and would increase the flow of narcotics to the US. In addition, we learned that Mendoza was linking to al Qaeda, possibly to smuggle operatives into the US along with increasing his drug supply connections. Al Qaeda has been involved in drug smuggling for funds and we know how the Soviets worked for decades to smuggle drugs into the US."

"I'm aware of what went on with the Soviets through their satellites," Roger said.

"Anyway, that was our tipping point. Why we set up the assassination of Mendoza as our first operation." Jane went over how they dropped Dan into the desert and how he had hiked to the mesa rim and completed his mission.

"Somehow the exfiltration went wrong. It got compromised and I'm afraid the people sent to collect Dan may have been killed. They haven't been heard from since they left to pick him up."

"So Dan is sent to do a single assassination, a surgical strike. And he turns that into a massacre of some other drug dealers, causing a major upset in the government and maybe starting a war between the cartels. And now his extraction handlers are MIA."

"That's about it, sir," Jane replied. "He has the ability to improvise and for the missions we'll send him on that's a necessary trait. I think he saw the opportunity to take out more of the drug leaders to create more havoc."

"He certainly seemed to have done that. But you don't know how the exfiltration got botched." Roger said.

"We don't know. We suspect there may have been a leak. We did have to tell the embassy to arrange the pickup but they didn't know why. We don't yet know what happened. Only that the two men sent to retrieve Dan and take him to an airport are missing, as is Dan. For all we know he could be killed or captured."

"Let's hope not the latter," Roger said. Jane gave him a quizzical look. "He would tell what he knows. Everyone does eventually under torture. And the cartels know how to torture people. If he's dead, his secrets die with him." Roger looked straight at Jane. "He'd be dead either way."

"But he could still be alive," Jane said.

"Why hasn't he called in, used the satellite phone?"

"Battery dead, or he suspects a leak, a compromise, and thinks he can be found if he turns on the phone? There are many possibilities," Henry offered.

"Fruitless to pursue while we know so little. And the embassy knows nothing?"

Jane responded. "Only that we needed an operative picked up at a certain point and delivered to the airport in Hermasillo."

"So what are you going to tell Garrett?" Henry asked after a long pause.

"As little as I can. He's got the Office of General Counsel nosing about. The man has to respond to the State Department which has their panties in a wad. They've lost two men who worked for them. At this point we can stonewall since we really don't know much. But," Roger put his hand on Henry's desk, "we'll have to acknowledge some kind of operation in Mexico."

"Information gathering?" Jane offered.

"Hard to maintain that position since they claim to have found where the shooter hid. It definitely had the stamp of a sniper assassination," Roger said.

"But the site was clean of any clear evidence of shooting," Jane said.

"Roger let's stick with the information story for now and buy some time until we know more about what's happened to Dan," Henry said.

Roger sighed and stood up. "I'll try. You know Garrett and I have a long history. I'll try to keep him and the OGC off your backs." He got up from his chair. "But if this gets over to Inspector General's office, you're fucked. Let me know when you hear any more." With that he turned and left.

Chapter 25

Y ou are going to have to eat the peyote buttons. Most gringos cannot do this, it makes them sick." Tlayolotl was preparing the cactus buttons and heating a liquid over the fire. "You will drink something that will help you keep the peyote down." He turned to Dan. "Can you do it?"

Dan nodded. "I'll try."

"You must do more than try, you must do it. To go on a spirit journey and get sick or lose your nerve is bad. You might not get back and you make danger for Raven and me." He held Dan's gaze in his glowing eyes.

The shaman was more animated now, his movements quick and sharp. He seemed to lose years as Dan watched him in his preparations.

"We will be on Raven, you will feel the bird. His strength will carry us far. You must not panic or you will fall and be lost. You are safe on the bird. He will get you back. Without Raven, you will be lost to wander forever seeking the body you left. That is what it means to go on a spiritual journey."

Dan's face must have betrayed his dismay, for Tlayolotl added, "I will help you to not fall, but you must look and learn from what you see."

Tlayolotl lit the brush and the aromatic odor began to fill the hut. He took his eagle feather and wafted it through the smoke and over his body. He then began a series of chants and incantations. It was the same set of actions he had done before. After he finished, he began to chant over Dan, waving the feather over him, pushing the pungent smoke over him. Tlayolotl then took some of the water from the spring and wiped Dan's head and face as well as his hands. When he was done, he had Dan drink the strong liquid. Dan almost threw it up but managed to control his gag reflex. After drinking the concoction, Dan felt a numbness spread over the mid-section of his body.

"It will help keep the peyote down," Tlayolotl said when Dan gave him a quizzical look.

By afternoon Tlayolotl had completed his preparations. "Are you ready?" he asked.

Dan just nodded.

"Good. Now come, sit up on the mat." Tlayolotl reached down and picked up the bowl full of peyote buttons. He handed one to Dan. "You break them apart and chew and swallow them." Next Tlayolotl picked a button and broke off some. He put one in his mouth and chewed it quickly, swallowing it before Dan swallowed his piece. "Don't take time, chew and swallow. Let the peyote get into you, cleanse you and give you the vision. Drink from your cup if your mouth gets dry."

The procedure was repeated over and over. Dan worked to control his gag reflex. The peyote was the worst thing he had ever tasted. It had an overpowering bitter taste that lasted long after the cactus was swallowed. The active ingredient in the peyote was mescaline, a psychedelic alkaloid similar to LSD. The native Indians in Mexico have used it for over five thousand years.

Finally Tlayolotl sat back and closed his eyes. He began to chant again, his body rocking back and forth. Dan sat watching, waiting for something to happen. How would he know when Tlayolotl went on his raven flight? How would he go with him? Did he have to do anything? Worry crept in and he fought it back. *Don't go paranoid now.* He sensed that could be disastrous.

Dan looked over at Raven who now stirred on his perch. The room began to move, almost undulate. Suddenly he was looking down at his body from above. He saw himself sitting next to Tlayolotl. Dan fought down a sense of a panic. He was not acrophobic but this was different. He felt separated from his body. He sensed the shaman floating next to him.

Dan heard him say, he couldn't tell if it was out loud or in his mind, "Climb on Raven's back."

There was a pull and then he felt himself swoop out of the hut and into the afternoon sky. His panic now increased. He could feel the strong muscles of the bird propelling the wings. They thrust them through the air. He felt a strong hand gripping him.

"Hold tight." Tlayolotl's voice came into his head, clear and strong. As they gained altitude, Dan began to settle down with the shaman's strong grip supporting him. He began to feel connected to the bird. He could now understand how they moved so quickly through the air. He could feel the forward thrust of the wings that propelled the bird forward as well as gave it lift. He could feel the energy of it pulsing through him. He sensed the bird's mastery of the sky.

At a couple of hundred feet Raven began to glide, seeking out updrafts to maintain altitude. Dan began to feel giddy with delight as his fear abated. The bird began to course back and forth, as if on a survey, looking for something or someone.

"Look sharp," Tlayolotl said.

Dan focused on the ground. Under a rock overhang he saw a man sprawled on the ground. He looked to be dead or near dying. Raven circled and dipped lower until they were only fifty feet above the figure. The man finally looked up as Raven's shadow passed over him.

"You will save this man from dying. He will owe you his life, as you owe me yours. He is going to help you on your mission."

"How can I find him again?"

"Raven will lead you. Tomorrow you will depart."

"So what am I to do?"

"I will show you," Tlayolotl answered and immediately Raven stroked his powerful wings and gained altitude. He then glided off to the south.

"Where are we going?"

"Chihuahua City."

Dan "sat" on Raven as the bird played the air currents, using its wings only when necessary, and kept gliding south. They ate up the miles. Dan's mind was overwhelmed with the wonder of what he was experiencing. Was he still back in the hut? Was this just a hallucinogenic dream? He couldn't tell. The feeling was so real—so immediate. There was nothing to connect him back to the hut. He could tell nothing beyond the fact that he seemed to be on the back of the raven with Tlayolotl's presence and grip still holding him. The desert skimmed below them. As he accepted what his senses told him, he relaxed and drifted off. Suddenly Tlayolotl's grip tightened and he was pulled up and jerked back to the present, to being on the back of the bird. He had almost fallen off, as if he had gone to sleep.

"Stay alert, don't let your mind wander or you will fall and be lost." Tlayolotl's stern voice broke through his reverie.

Looking ahead, Dan could see Chihuahua City coming into view. He had stopped wondering how this was all happening and just accepted the sensory inputs as real. Later, he promised himself, he would apply some critical analysis to try to explain how the impossible was happening.

The bird navigated without hesitation to a warehouse area on the east side of the city. It alighted on a wall across the dirt street from a walled compound. The compound and the warehouse inside of it were enveloped in a darkness that was almost impenetrable. Dan could make out figures walking in the compound.

Tlayolotl pointed towards one figure, more shrouded than the others. "That is the leader who brought this darkness to Chihuahua."

"What is the darkness?"

"Evil. Evil intent, evil purposes, evil minds and plans."

"Is it something in the warehouse?"

"Many evil men are in the building. They are headed for your country. They must be stopped."

"So that is my mission? I'm to stop a group of men who are going to sneak into the US?"

"*Sí*. The cartel is doing this. It has been interrupted by your assassination but it will proceed unless you stop it. The man in the desert is one of the cartel, but he will help you."

"How? If he is part of them, he will not help."

"We will talk more later. Mark where this is, mark the leader, watch out for him. This is where you must strike."

"Does the man in the desert know about this?"

"*Sí*." Tlayolotl spoke something to Raven in a language Dan didn't understand. The bird took off and gained altitude. "We will go back now, but you have another task. Hector Ortega has replaced the man you killed. Hector must also be killed or what you intended will not happen. He will just take command and all will be as it was."

"I can't keep eliminating Sinaloa leaders. I have to end my mission down here and return."

"It will be done when this darkness is eliminated and Hector is killed."

"How do you know all this?"

"I told you, I am a Watcher. There are other Watchers. They have told me. We will talk when we return to the canyon."

Tlayolotl didn't speak again as Raven steadily drove them through the sky with his powerful wings. The bird beat its wings in powerful thrusts, working harder as the evening had killed the heat thermals. The bird flew on relentlessly without hesitation. Dan marveled at the bird's strength and endurance. Finally Raven swooped down into the canyon and into the hut.

The next thing Dan knew he was back in his body and "waking" up. *But I haven't really been asleep.* Now the questions and confusion began to crowd his mind. It had been eight hours since he had eaten the peyote.

Tlayolotl turned to him and told him to lie down and let his mind rest; to sleep if possible. Dan crawled back to his pallet and lay back. His mind was spinning. Slowly he relaxed, and sleep finally came.

Chapter 26

The next morning, Dan awoke. He felt light, relaxed, and hungry. Tlayolotl had some corn cakes cooking over the fire. He handed Dan a cup of some hot liquid. Dan sipped the liquid and then went out to the pool to splash water on his face. He came back in and sat down.

"How do you feel?" Tlayolotl asked.

"I feel fine, very relaxed. I don't have a hangover if that is what you're asking."

"Peyote does not give you hangover. It cleanses and changes your mind."

"Yes, well I do have questions about yesterday."

"Not foolish ones. No time for those."

"Just tell me what happened. I know what I felt, but was that all hallucinating? Was I always here in the hut, imagining all that going on?"

"What did you feel...see?"

Dan sat for a moment to collect his thoughts. "Sitting on the bird," he nodded towards Raven. Either I was smaller or the bird was larger. I felt being on the bird as well as saw it. I saw being in the air. I could feel the bird working its wings, how powerful they were. It gave me a better understanding of how birds fly. I saw the man dying in the desert. Then I saw Chihuahua City and the warehouse compound all shrouded in dark."

"That was not hallucination."

"But...how?"

"Spirit journey. You don't understand that you have spirit and body. Your body stayed here, your spirit went with me and Raven."

"How is that possible?"

Tlayolotl didn't answer. He just stared back at Dan.

"Okay, that was a foolish question. But this is so foreign to me and my world."

"You must grow your understanding of the world...of reality." Tlayolotl turned back to the corn cakes and pulled them from the pan. "Your understanding is too limited. You can't have victory without understanding."

"I'm fighting against the enemies of my country, against terrorists and criminals. So in a sense I'm fighting against evil. I understand that." Dan looked over at Tlayolotl. "Isn't that what this is all about? You just have another explanation for what I'm doing."

Tlayolotl just shook his head. "You see too small. I show you the battle is much larger." He handed Dan a rolled-up corn cake with some meat in a sauce inside. "You are slow to learn." With a sigh, Tlayolotl said, "I will start again. I know you are the one, but you make it hard for yourself." He pointed at Dan and said in a fierce voice, "Listen and turn off the chatter in your mind. Turn off the squirrel chatter.

He continued, "You are the tip of the spear. You are the warrior who is to strike the heart of the enemy. The enemy is the darkness of evil that is working to cover the world. Humans carry out the evil plans but they are driven by the darkness, the spirit forces of evil. That is what you must understand. You are the sharp point of the spirit forces of good. If you don't recognize that you cut yourself off from the spirit help and you will not prevail.

"I am a Watcher," he continued. "I see the spirit battle. I am not alone. There are Watchers all over the world. If you learn and accept, they can help you and guide you because they see where you cannot see. With their help, your strikes will be more effective, more deadly.

"That is what I have done. Take you on the spirit trip so you can understand and see. Your task here is not finished. That is how Watchers help."

"Who are these 'Watchers'?"

"Ones who have a special sight as I told you before. Watchers can see the spirit forces at war. We can help those who fight the dark aim their blows more effectively. We are guides."

"So, I'm to take out the men waiting in the warehouse. Who are they?"

Tlayolotl looked steadily at Dan as he spoke, his deeply etched face displaying his intensity. "You would call them terrorists. I heard her use that word."

"Jane?"

Tlayolotl nodded.

Dan continued, "And then you want me to take out the second in command to Mendoza, this Hector Ortega." Tlayolotl's eyes never moved from Dan. "Then my task will be done?"

Tlayolotl nodded again.

"Where do I find this Ortega?"

"You will find him in Mexico City. He will be at Mendoza's mansion. He is taking over all that was Mendoza's, including the wife."

"And you know—?"

"A Watcher, in Mexico City. There is an old woman there. She is very old and very wise. She is a Watcher like me. She will find you and help you."

"How?"

Tlayolotl ignored his question. "She knows about Ortega. She will tell you what you need to know. Listen to her. She is powerful and can see much. She can see the future in a way I cannot."

"Will she predict how my mission will end?"

Tlayolotl shrugged. "Maybe, maybe not. She will tell you what she wants. It may not be what you want, but if you are wise, you will listen to her."

"How will I find her?"

Tlayolotl shook his head. "She will find you."

It didn't look to Dan like he was going to get any more about the old woman out of Tlayolotl.

"And you think this drug guy, the guy in the desert is going to help me?"

"You will save his life. He will help because he will owe you his life."

"I don't know. There's very little honor among criminals."

Tlayolotl leaned forward and his countenance grew dark. His eyes burned bright—red and black. "He will help." The words now came out slow and deep, like far off thunder. "I have the power to take his life from him and cause his soul to wander without peace if he refuses."

Dan felt a shiver go through him. Tlayolotl was a dangerous man, not fully tame or civilized.

"I will give you water and food for the desert. You must set out tonight. You need to reach him tomorrow." Before Dan could ask, Tlayolotl added. "Raven and Coyote will help you find him."

Chapter 27

That afternoon, Dan loaded his backpack with gifts from Tlayolotl: two five liter skins of water, a salve for burned skin, a jar with an herb drink to give the man energy, and some dried food. His ankle felt completely healed thanks to Tlayolotl's poultice. Before leaving the hut, Tlayolotl had Dan strip to the waist. The shaman lit a fire in the central pit. He took some sprigs of a bush and dipped them in water and brushed them over Dan's head and torso, chanting something incomprehensible to Dan. Next he stuck the sprigs into the fire. They were wet so didn't ignite, but they started smoking, filling the hut with an aromatic odor Dan remembered from the day before. Tlayolotl wafted the smoke over Dan, brushing it onto him with the large feather he used before, all the while chanting over him.

Finally, he stopped. "You are cleansed. Now get dressed. You must go quickly."

Outside the hut Dan put on his backpack. The coyote and raven had followed them out of the hut and waited to one side. Tlayolotl stood facing him. His eyes burned into Dan's. His dark, deeply etched face, burned by so much desert sun, showed no emotion, only an intense, almost fierce interest in him.

"You will accept what I have shown you? You will use it and carry out your tasks?"

Dan nodded. "I don't fully understand but I accept. I can't deny what I experienced."

"That is good. You will prevail if you are careful and smart. I have done my job. Raven and Coyote will now help you start your mission." He grabbed Dan by the shoulders. His grip was sharp. His strong fingers dug into Dan's flesh. "Do not get misled. There are many ways to go wrong. Remember, you are the warrior. Remember your mission."

With that he let Dan go.

"Thank you for saving my life—twice."

"You will repay me with these tasks. Now go."

With that the shaman turned away and shuffled back into his hut. Dan stood for a moment looking after him but there was nothing left to do or say. Would he ever see this strange man again? *I doubt it*, he told himself. He turned away and started walking down the ravine towards where he had fallen into it three days ago. Coyote trotted ahead of him and the raven flew past.

They were an odd group, hiking the desert in the late afternoon, the white man, a coyote and a raven flying ahead and waiting. When night came Dan relied on the coyote and guessed the animal was relying on the raven. His rational mind kept trying to interject and tell him how crazy this all appeared to be but he kept it repressed. It would do no good. He had seen too much and now his life was in the hands of these two animals. He hiked on.

Deep into the night Dan sat down to rest. The raven squawked at him but finally perched on a rock and settled down. He poured some water into the coyote's mouth and set out a cup for the raven. Lying back, Dan closed his eyes and tried to sleep but the events of the past three days kept crowding into his thoughts. Still his body rested, even if his mind wouldn't settle down.

Before the sky lightened in the east with another dawn, the coyote was pushing at Dan with his muzzle and the raven began to squawk. Dan awoke. He stretched and then got some water for himself and the two animals. He set out some of the dried meat that the coyote and raven hungrily devoured. Hoisting the backpack, he looked to the raven, and they set out again, heading south.

Rodrigo sat under the rock overhang. He had stopped that night. He could go no further. His breath came in rough gasps through his parched and dusty throat. There was no moisture to help him swallow. There was nothing to swallow. His saliva had dried up. Only half aware, he watched the sun break over the east horizon. He had no strength to go on. There was nothing to do. He dimly remembered realizing during the previous night that he had walked in circles. For how long he didn't know, but that knowledge took all the fight out of him. He parked himself under the limited shelter of the rock. He was done.

I will die here. The thought became a reality in his mind. Being a member of the cartel, Rodrigo had no illusions about living a long life. He had joined to get out of the poverty he had been mired in. His parents had been killed by a rival gang that had attacked his home looking to kill Rodrigo. Now all he had in life was his sister, Miranda, and her daughter. He lived to protect her and, hopefully, to allow his niece to grow up to a better life. Her name was Solana, sunshine.

Without him, Rodrigo knew that Carlos, the torturer, would take Miranda and Solana. He had eyes for Miranda and only kept his distance because of Rodrigo. Now there would be no stopping him and he would ruin her, Rodrigo thought bitterly. He would even take and ruin Solana. Rodrigo had heard stories of Carlos going after young girls. It was not unheard of for girls as young as twelve or thirteen to be given to older men; "married" but in reality it was sexual servitude and they wound up as sex slaves servicing the gang members. Solana was getting close to the age where this could happen. Her future would be lost. Rodrigo would have wept, but he had no tears. He was too dried up and dying.

He went over his life and the steps that led him to this desert to die. Nowhere could he see how it could have been different. It was as if his decisions meant little in the face of larger events taking place around him. Life seemed to have its own force and imposed it on poor people like Rodrigo. He closed his eyes hoping sleep would come and take away his bitterness. He had no strength for anger. Maybe he could sleep and the end would come without him choking on his dried throat.

Chapter 28

Mid-day a shadow fell over Rodrigo. He opened his eyes to peer up. There was a figure, a man, standing before him. Next to the man was a coyote. Rodrigo reached out his hand in supplication, but he couldn't speak. The man sat down next to him and took what looked like a water skin from his back pack. He poured some over Rodrigo's face and head. Rodrigo ran his hands through the water and held them to his face. The man then put his arm behind Rodrigo's head and tipped some water into his mouth.

Rodrigo started to choke. He saw the man pull back. He took a rag from his pocket and wet it with the water and gave it to Rodrigo. He wiped his face and sucked on the rag, letting small amounts of the moisture trickle into his mouth and throat. The man repeated the process three times for Rodrigo. Finally, he sat more upright and looked at the man.

"*Quién es usted?*" Who are you? Rodrigo asked.

"I am the man you were chasing," came the reply.

"E*stá aquí?*" Why are you here? Rodrigo asked. "Are you going to kill me?"

"I'm here to save your life. Can you drink now?"

Rodrigo nodded and the man gave him the water skin. "Only a little so you don't get sick. You can have more later."

Rodrigo took a big swallow and began to cough.

"Small sips. Don't waste the water."

After a few minutes the man took the flask back. Rodrigo didn't protest. He adjusted himself to sit more upright. He looked at the man. He was burned darker than most gringos, *from the desert sun*, Rodrigo guessed. *But why would he come to save me?* There was no obvious answer and the question could wait. Rodrigo knew he had been at death's door and now that door was closed. He was going to live. For how long he didn't know, but it was enough for now.

The stranger took a jar of salve from his backpack and spread some on Rodrigo's face and mouth. Rodrigo started to turn away but the man said no.

"This is for the burning on your face and lips. They will heal quickly." He handed Rodrigo the jar. "Spread it yourself. When you're done, I have something else for you to drink. It will help you recover quickly."

Rodrigo looked at him suspiciously. The stranger spoke fluent Spanish, not like any gringos he had encountered before. He handed Rodrigo the jar containing the herb drink.

"Drink this. It will give you strength. We do not have much time. We have to move quickly to get out of the desert. Do you speak English?"

"A little. Where are we going?"

"Chihuahua City."

Rodrigo looked up at the man. "Are you loco? There are people there who will kill you."

The man just stared back at Rodrigo with an implacable expression on his face. He had the cold eyes of a killer.

"It is necessary."

"Do you want me to guide you out of the desert? Is that why you have come to save me?"

"You will help me in what I have to do."

"How did you find me? How did you know I was here?" Rodrigo now was thinking about the salve and the herb drink he sipped. It seemed as though the man came prepared.

"I saw you in the desert. Yesterday. And Raven and Coyote led me to you."

Rodrigo saw then, for the first time, the raven perched on a rock to one side. The bird was staring at him intently. It had one black and one red eye. *Play along. This makes no sense but the gringo is here and with him he might yet live to get out of the desert and back to his sister and niece.*

"Can you stand?"

"Give me a few moments, *por favor*. He handed the jar back to Dan.

"What is your name?" the stranger asked.

"Rodrigo."

"Okay Rodrigo, my name is Steve," Dan said using his alias.

"*Señor* Steve, I have been wandering in circles. I don't know the way out. Do you know which way to go?" Rodrigo used a formal*"usted"*. *Play up to the gringo.* He would deal with him when the desert was behind them. If the man was foolish enough to go back to those who wanted him dead, well, that was on him.

"Raven and Coyote will lead us to my truck. There are more supplies there. And then we can follow the truck tracks."

"Your truck has a flat tire. We can't use it and we can't walk all the way back."

"There is a spare tire. I could not get it out or change it. With your help we will do it and drive out of the desert. We will go as soon as you can walk."

Rodrigo took a deep breath. He could feel strength returning to his body from the herb drink. "Okay, then, *vámonos*," he said.

Dan held out his hand and helped yank him upright. When he was standing, Dan reached out and took the pistol out of Rodrigo's holster.

"I'll carry this for now," he said.

He turned to the bird. The raven leapt into the air and flew off. The coyote trotted after the bird and Dan and Rodrigo followed.

That same afternoon, Carlos showed up at Miranda's house. When he banged on the door she came out to meet him rather than let him in the house.

"Rodrigo and the others have not come back from chasing the gringo into the desert. Hector thinks they are lost. I'm afraid the desert or the gringo has claimed them."

Miranda stifled a cry. She did not want to seem weak. She distrusted Carlos. She had noticed how he ogled her and guessed the worst about his intentions.

"With Rodrigo gone, you will need someone to protect you. I can take care of you and Solana. I can keep you safe and make sure you have what you need."

"We will be okay on our own. You don't need to do anything for us."

Carlos shook his head. "I know what the others think. You're attractive. They will take you. I can prevent that from happening."

"I can take care of myself...and Solana."

Carlos reached out to her and stroked her hair at the side of her face. "It is for your own good. You are so pretty.

I don't want to see anything happen to you or your daughter. I will watch over you." He smiled and turned to go. "I'll stop by every day to check on you," he called out over his shoulder.

Miranda shuddered.

David Nees

Chapter 29

W hen are you going to send my men to the border?" Tariq asked Hector. They were standing in the dusty courtyard outside of the warehouse building. It was late afternoon.

"In a couple more days. Be patient. I have to let things quiet down here. A convoy now leaving the city would attract the *federals* and they have to be seen as doing something."

"Why? What happened to cause all this attention?"

"It's cartel business, not yours. I will get your men over the border when I am ready."

"I want to talk to Jorge. Where is he?"

"You ask too many questions. I am in charge of this operation. *Señor* Mendoza is not available for you to talk to."

Tariq sensed something was amiss. "Is something wrong? I need to know. We have an agreement to supply you with drugs." Tariq stepped up close to Hector. "But if you are out of control, perhaps we can't do business with you."

Hector resisted the urge to step back and protect his space. *He wants to intimidate, but he is out of his element. I hold the leverage here.* "Do not threaten me. You are on my territory. If you wish to see your homeland you will do as I say. You are well paid for the drugs and we know how to deal with what is going on. It is our business, not yours. Without your drugs, this smuggling operation is nothing to me, so be glad I'm completing my end of the bargain. Don't tempt me to end it." Hector stared back at the terrorist. In the end he knew Tariq had no card to play and had to accede to his authority.

"Two days? Will you commit to that?" Tariq asked.

"I will give you twenty-four hour notice. That is what I will commit to. In the meantime you stay in the compound. My men will bring you any supplies you need." Hector didn't wait for an answer but turned to go, dismissing Tariq with his back.

The strange procession proceeded through the day for three hours: the two men led by a coyote and a raven. When Rodrigo began to stumble, Dan called a halt. They sat down in the shade of some rocks. Dan parceled out some water for the coyote and raven as Rodrigo watched in fascination.

"These are wild animals yet they act tame around you. What is going on?"

Dan smiled. "You have questions? Believe me I had questions and still do."

"So?"

"Do you know of a shaman, one who lives in this desert? His name is Tlayolotl."

Rodrigo stared at Dan. "I have heard of him. But he is a myth, not real. How do you know of him?"

"He is real. I have met him. He saved my life. The raven and coyote are his companions."

"It is said he is a wild man. One who is dangerous, one who can take your life with a curse or spell."

"He is wild and I believe he can take a life if he chooses, but he saved mine." Dan pointed a finger at Rodrigo, "And he found you and directed me to save your life."

"Why would he do that? What are we to him?"

"I will tell you as we go. I have a mission and you are to help me complete it."

Rodrigo didn't respond. He did not think he would help this man. In fact he thought he might kill him and win the approval of Hector, especially since Ramón had failed and was dead. But he would wait until they were out of the grip of the desert.

"You are not interested in the mission?" Dan asked.

"You will tell me when you are ready," Rodrigo replied.

As the sun waned in the sky, the odd procession started out again. This time the coyote was not with them. He turned back north. The two men were left with the raven to guide them. It was close to dawn when they reached Dan's abandoned pickup truck.

Rodrigo sighed, plopped to the ground, and leaned back against the truck. "I need to rest. I'm worn out."

Dan sat down next to him. "We'll rest for now. As soon as it's light, we need to work on the spare and get the truck running again." He took out some dried meat and set it out for the raven along with a cup of water. The bird hopped over and took a look at the offering. Then it looked up at both men before it gobbled down the meat and drank the water.

"Damn. That bird looks tame," Rodrigo said.

"Only for Tlayolotl."

"You really met him?"

"I found you, didn't I?" Dan used the same line that Tlayolotl used on him. It was hard to argue with the evidence.

"What is he like?"

"Take a look at the bird. What is odd about it?"

Rodrigo looked at the raven as it drank the water. When it was done, the bird looked back, first with one eye cocked towards him, then the other. "He's got one red eye and one black eye. Don't ravens have black eyes?"

"They do. Tlayolotl also has one red and one black eye. There's a connection between them."

Rodrigo looked at Dan for a long moment. "I don't believe that!"

"I saw that...and more." Dan proceeded to recount his encounters with the raven, the coyote and, finally, Tlayolotl himself.

Rodrigo stared as Dan told his tale. When he was done, he said, "I don't believe you. And why would you tell me about the shooting and then killing the men who came for you? They are my gang brothers."

"Are they really? You know better than that. They would sell you out if told to do so. They have no loyalty. You know that."

Rodrigo paused. "It is a hard story to believe."

"And yet I found you and saved your life."

"What do you want for that?"

"Your help. I still have a task to do."

"More killing?"

"The men in the warehouse."

"How do you know about them?"

"Tlayolotl told me after we visited Chihuahua City. He told me I have to kill them."

"You visited Chihuahua? How?"

"We went on the raven. He flew us there and back. That is when we saw you dying in the desert. That is how Raven could lead me back to you."

Rodrigo put his hands to his head. "I can't believe all this. And I can't help you. Helping you will get me killed."

Dan gripped Rodrigo's shoulder hard. Rodrigo stared at him. "You owe me your life, so you will do what I ask."

Rodrigo shook his head.

"If you don't, you can be sure Tlayolotl will pluck your life from you. He has that power."

The raven leapt into the air screaming and flew at Rodrigo who immediately ducked. The bird swooped up and turned in the air, perching on a nearby rock. It stared at the man.

"I would not trifle with a shaman of his power. He can harness the wild animals, he can transport himself long distances, and he can see what is happening from far away. You cannot hide from him."

Rodrigo's eyes grew large but he did not speak.

"The shaman made it clear. I owe him my life, two times. And now you owe me your life. Or to be more correct, you owe Tlayolotl your life because he found you and led me to you. He also made it clear that he could and would snatch back a life he saved if the person didn't do what he wanted them to do."

Rodrigo slumped. "Then I am a dead man. If I help you, the cartel will kill me in a horrible way. I've seen it. If I don't, the shaman will kill me—"

"And damn your soul. Which is worse?"

Rodrigo just shook his head as he stared at the ground.

Dan stood up. The sky had begun to grow lighter. "Let's get this tire changed. We need to get moving."

They walked to the rear of the truck and looked underneath.

"It's bolted into the carrier. There is no wrench to unbolt it. We'll have to hammer it out."

Rodrigo looked. "There's a tool kit somewhere. Did you look under the front seats?"

Dan swore and got up to look. He came back a moment later with a leather pouch. Inside was a set of hand wrenches and a pair of pliers. "Damn. I could have fixed it myself."

Rodrigo unbolted the carrier and pulled out the spare tire. "There's no jack," he said.

Dan thought a moment. "We'll block the axle with rocks and dig out from under the wheel until we have enough clearance to put on the spare."

"That's a lot of work."

"You have a better idea? Walk maybe? It's the only way to do this." He grabbed a shovel and went forward.

Two hours later, they had dug a depression deep enough to change the tire. When they were done the two men sat down in the shade of the truck. It was early afternoon. There were extra supplies in the truck, water and food that Dan hadn't been able to pack and take with him. There were also the additional weapons that he had left behind.

Dan noticed Rodrigo eying the weapons as they rummaged for some water before sitting down.

"I wouldn't get any clever ideas. First, I'm a trained killer and you will find it hard to best me. Second, do you think Tlayolotl will let you get out of the desert alive if you kill me? What I promised you will happen. Remember how he helped defeat the four men sent to kill me at the rendezvous. You should not mess with the shaman."

Chapter 30

An hour later they were ready to drive off. The raven flew to the passenger window. Rodrigo leaned away from the bird. It was large and could easily pluck out an eye. The bird perched there and stared at Rodrigo.

"He's letting you know he's watching you. He's warning you to do what I tell you and save your soul. Listen to him."

The bird nodded its head, let out a loud squawk and flew up into the sky. Rodrigo cringed away from the sound. Shortly the bird was a black shadow on the harsh sky, circling higher and higher. Finally it started gliding north, banking and turning to find the thermals to gain more lift. Both men watched in silence as the raven shrank into a black dot and was lost from view.

"We have the truck now. Let's go", Dan said. He maneuvered the pickup out of the hole and turned it around. He put the extra weapons into a bag and dropped them in the bed of the truck. *No sense in tempting fate.* "Where are the trucks you used to follow me? We can siphon gas from them."

"We must have passed one during the night while we were walking. It rolled off the road and burned. I was the only one to escape alive. The other truck is stuck in quicksand. It is up ahead."

Dan grunted. "I know the place. I almost got stuck there myself."

"It was too heavy to get out so we had to leave many weapons behind. There is extra fuel as well."

Dan drove in silence. He didn't rush; no one was chasing them and he wanted to protect the tires.

"We need to drive at least part way through the night. We're three days out from the quicksand and two more days from getting back to paved roads. We need to cut that time down."

Dan turned to Rodrigo. "Do you believe me about Tlayolotl?"

"*Sí*," Rodrigo answered after a moment.

"Do you believe that he can get to you if you don't help me?"

Rodrigo hesitated. "I think so. But helping you will get me killed for sure."

Dan took a breath. *Patience.* He had been over this with Rodrigo once, but it seemed he still needed convincing.

"Not helping me will get you killed as well. Tlayolotl said he could not only kill you but cause your spirit to wander forever without rest. Do you believe that?"

Rodrigo shook his head. "I don't know what to believe."

"You need to believe what I just told you. I experienced his power. He found me, saved me, healed me, and he found you. I believe he is a wild man, one connected to the spirit world, and I believe he can do what he said."

"But the cartel—"

"What if I can save you from them?"

Rodrigo looked over at Dan with new interest. "How can you do that?"

"I have connections. I can get you into the US, with a new identity. The cartel won't be able to reach you."

"I have a sister and niece. I need to protect them as well."

Dan smiled at Rodrigo. "In for a dime, in for a dollar."

"You can do this? For sure?"

"I have the power to do it." Dan wasn't sure if that was true but he needed Rodrigo to believe him, enough to cooperate and trust him. To cover the miles they would have to drive day and night which meant sharing the driving.

"Okay. I will help."

"Save your soul...and your family. Good decision."

Dan stopped the pickup. "You drive. I'm going to sleep and then I'll drive all night. We should have enough gas with what's in the back to make it back to the truck."

Near the end of the second day, after driving all day and night, they came to the armored pickup that was stuck in the quick sand.

"Let's get what we need while there's still daylight. We need to keep moving," Dan said.

They pulled the full jerry cans from the back of the armored truck, and tied them in the bed of the pickup. When they were done, Dan took some empty cans and a hose from their supply. He siphoned the gas from the tank of the stranded truck. He filled two cans and shouted for Rodrigo to bring a third. When they were done, they had a full tank of gas and enough in the cans to refill the pickup's tank twice.

"This will take care of us all the way to Chihuahua City," Dan said. He was pleased. Things were now going well and they would soon be out of the desert and on paved roads.

"When we get on the roads, we have to be careful of the *policía*."

"I'm expecting you can talk your way through them."

Rodrigo looked at Dan. "How do I do that?"

"Pretend you're taking me in. Who did you say was in charge now?"

"Hector Ortega."

"Use his name. The police will recognize it."

There was no extra water or food to take with them. They would have to do with what they carried and it would have to get them to Chihuahua City. He went through the weapons that were left behind. The heavy machine gun was of no use. Dan had pondered the rocket launcher, going over in his mind how he could use the weapon; what situation might call for it. He was comfortable with his M4 and his sniper rifle. He had suppressors for both the M4 and his 9mm pistol. His work was going to be stealthy in nature rather than frontal assaults or open gun battles. In the end he decided to leave the rocket launcher behind. It was too crude a weapon. He would rely on his sniper instincts and do his work in a more subtle fashion.

They drove off leaving the heavy armored truck stuck in the sand. *Someone will find it decades from now and wonder what the hell it was doing out here in the desert.* Dan smiled at the thought that would give archeologists something to ponder. He settled back down to grab some rest before he had to drive.

When night fell, Dan awoke and drove through the dark and into the dawn. He was exhausted when he finally stopped and handed off the driving to Rodrigo.

"We should get to pavement today. When we do, you wake me. We have to agree on how we'll play things out if the police stop us."

"Should I call Hector?"

"No. I want to deal with the terrorists before you contact Hector."

"And what will I tell Hector?"

Rodrigo waited but Dan didn't respond. *Time enough to figure that out later.*

"I need to see if my sister is okay," Rodrigo finally said.

"We can do that, but does she talk to other cartel members?"

"No. She doesn't want to have anything to do with them. But one member, Carlos, has eyes for her. He may have taken her if he thinks I'm dead."

"Okay. We'll make sure she's fine then we have work to do."

"Do you have a plan?"

"Not yet, but I will." Dan gave him a tight smile and leaned his head against the window.

The pickup bounced at a steady pace over the rough track. The trail actually improved as they got closer to the pavement. Rodrigo increased his speed. Finally they were out of the dirt and on the pavement. Dan awoke. Rodrigo was now banging along at sixty miles an hour and the pavement was not all that good. He was hammering the pickup through the potholes.

"Slow down! You're going to break the suspension or have a flat. For God's sake, drive around the potholes, don't go through them."

Rodrigo looked over at Dan, his face grim. "I'm just eager to get back to Chihuahua to see my sister."

"She's the first place we'll stop, but slow down, damn it. We don't have a spare."

Rodrigo reluctantly dropped his speed back and tried to dodge the holes in the road.

"Now, if we get stopped, you act like you're bringing me to Chihuahua on Hector's orders and you shouldn't be messed with. Tell any police that it won't go well for them if Hector hears they interfered with your mission." Dan looked over at Rodrigo. "Will that work?"

Rodrigo thought for a moment. "*Sí*. It should work. The police know who Hector is, if not I can explain it to them and how he is in charge now that Jorge is dead."

"I'll have my hands behind my back with some line around them to make it seem as if I'm tied up. If we're uncovered, or if the police don't go for your story, we shoot them. I'll have a pistol under my leg."

"What about me?"

"What about you?"

"They'll need to see me armed."

Dan paused; this was a chance he would have to take. "Okay, I'll give you a pistol. I have to trust you. You try to cross me I'll shoot both you and the cop." After a moment he added, "And don't forget what I said about Tlayolotl, your life depends on it."

Rodrigo looked over at Dan who met him with a cold stare.

"You do not want to test me on this," said Dan. "Now pull over and let's get everything arranged."

"What do we do if you are driving?" Rodrigo asked.

"You have your pistol on your lap and explain that you're tired of driving so you made me do it."

After getting the guns and piece of rope, they set out again. As the road improved, Rodrigo went faster. They would be in Chihuahua by sunset.

Chapter 31

An hour out of Chihuahua Dan and Rodrigo were pulled over by a member of the Chihuahua State Police. The officer sauntered up to the pickup.

"You were speeding. That is going to cost you," the cop announced through the rolled down window. "Give me your license."

Rodrigo looked up at him. "I'm on my way to meet *Don* Hector Ortega. He is in charge now that *Don* Mendoza has been killed. You know who he is. You are paid to know who he is and what our business is, so don't interfere and don't try to shake me down. *Don* Ortega will not appreciate it."

The cop straightened up. A look of fear flashed across his face and then was hidden. But not before Rodrigo saw it.

"You can't push me around. I don't know Hector Ortega. And who is this gringo next to you?"

"You may not know him, but you know who he is. You will do what I tell you to do. This gringo is none of your business. What you need to know is that *Don* Ortega very much wants to talk with this person. That is why I am driving fast." Rodrigo leaned out of the window, now more confident. "Amado Gonzales." He read his name badge. "I can let *Don* Ortega know how helpful you were...or how unhelpful." Rodrigo smiled at the cop who was now fully on the defensive. Rodrigo knew he had expected an easy bribe and now faced a serious situation. "It is your call, Officer Gonzales."

The cop gave Rodrigo a nervous smile, "You go ahead. You will not be bothered."

Rodrigo nodded and put the truck in gear and drove off.

"That went well. Are all the cops on the payroll?"

"Many of them. It was a good bet. We go to my sister's house first. We can sleep there."

Miranda lived north east of the *Zona Central*. On their way they drove through a neighborhood called *Campestre Lomas*. The area looked so nice that Dan thought it could be a transplant from a middle class San Diego neighborhood.

"I would like to have enough money to move here," Rodrigo said, "but we have to make do with a less fancy part of the city. Still it is fairly safe, which is important."

No thanks to you, Dan thought.

Miranda's neighborhood had aimed for middle class status but money or commitment had run out. There were unfinished buildings and dirt streets. The houses that were completed showed the owners trying to maintain a semblance of quality amid the roughness of incomplete construction and neglect. They pulled up to a blue house with a white iron fence across the small front yard. There was a single car garage that looked like no car had entered it for many years. A small, Nissan sedan was parked in the drive in front of the garage. The neighborhood was on a slope. The roof of the garage served as an upper deck, opening up to the second floor of the house. It was small, but well kept.

Rodrigo parked around the corner on a dirt street. The houses along this street were not finished. They walked around to the front and Rodrigo opened the gate with his key.

"Miranda!" he called out as they walked to the door. It opened and a good-looking woman in her mid-twenties stepped out.

"Rodrigo," she shouted and ran to him. She threw herself into his arms and hugged him tight. "They told me you had died in the desert. I felt so lost." She pulled back. "You have been burned by the sun, but you're alive. Thank God!" She grabbed him again.

Dan watched from the side.

"How did you get back? What happened to you?" Miranda's questions tumbled out over one another. Finally she stepped back and looked over at Dan. "Who is this?"

"This man saved my life...in the desert."

Miranda stared hard at Dan. He was obviously not Mexican.

"Is this the man you were sent to find?" She turned back to Rodrigo. "I don't understand."

"I'll explain. Let's go inside."

They entered the house. When Solana saw them she shouted and ran to Rodrigo. "*Tío!* You're alive! They told us you were dead. We were so sad. But now you're alive."

After giving Solana some huge hugs and twirling her around, Rodrigo put her down. He turned to Miranda. "Who told you I was dead?"

"Carlos. He's come around twice." Miranda shuddered visibly. "Solana, please go up to your room, I need to talk to *Tío* Rodrigo privately for a moment."

"Mama, Uncle Rodrigo just got here. Don't make me leave."

Miranda patted her daughter's head. "Just for a few minutes, I promise. I'll call you when we're done."

"It's okay," said Rodrigo grabbing her hand. "I don't have any presents for you today, but I have a lot of hugs to catch up on."

Solana smiled at him and ran down the hall.

Miranda led them upstairs to the main floor. They went to the kitchen and sat at the table. She took three beers from the fridge and set them out.

"Tell me about Carlos," Rodrigo said after opening his beer.

"He wants me, you know that. Now he thinks you're dead, he will take me...me and Solana. She doesn't notice his looks, but I do. He has bad thoughts about me and about Solana. He says he'll take care of us. Keep us safe from other gang members. I don't know how to keep him away."

"*Hijo de perra!*" Son of a bitch! Rodrigo growled through clenched teeth. "I will kill him."

"No." Miranda put her hand on his arm. "It's enough that you are back. He won't try anything with you around." She turned to Dan. "But what are you going to do with this gringo? If he is the man you were chasing, why were the two of you traveling together? It's not right. The others will think it's wrong as well."

Rodrigo scowled. "That is going to be a problem." He looked over at Dan.

Dan spoke for the first time. He used his Spanish not knowing if Miranda could speak English. "For now, no one can know I'm alive. We will make up a story of how Rodrigo got out of the desert. He found my pickup, changed the flat tire where I couldn't, and drove back by himself. It's the story of what happened, only leaving me out of it."

"But why did you save my brother? He was sent to kill you?"

Dan smiled at her and stretched himself out on the seat. The fatigue from the trip showed. "It is a long, complicated story. For now let us say I was told to rescue Rodrigo. There is something we have to do together."

"Who told you to save Rodrigo?"

"A shaman named Tlayolotl. He led me to your brother."

Now a look of fear crossed Miranda's face. She turned to Rodrigo, "You will get killed if you help this man. This is the man all of you were sent to find. That is what you said and that is what Carlos said. He killed *Señor* Mendoza."

"Yes, but things have changed and for now we need to hide him." Rodrigo said.

"Not here. You risk me and Solana. You can't keep him here."

"I risk us all if he's found no matter where I keep him. He can't have gotten back here without me. No one would believe that."

Miranda put her head in her hands. "*Madre de Dios*, what are we to do?" After a moment she looked up, her eyes bright with anger, a decision made. "He can't stay here. You have to put him somewhere else."

Rodrigo looked at his sister. He knew she would not budge. "Okay, I'll put him in the garage, the one up the hill. I can park the pickup there as well.

Halfway up the side street, amid the unfinished houses was one that had a completed garage. Rodrigo had secured it with a solid door and locks. It was a safe place that the neighborhood thugs knew enough to leave alone.

The two men stood up. Miranda just eyed them warily, especially Dan. He was the largest threat to them. Without

Dan, Rodrigo could tell his story and no one would know any better. With Dan, Rodrigo's life would be at risk. Miranda had been around enough to hear the stories. Loyalty was prized, but as soon as someone became suspect, the bosses got rid of them. They didn't wait, they didn't mess around. Self-preservation was the rule in the cartel, especially among the higher ups.

Rodrigo and Dan pulled into the garage.

"If we empty the truck of weapons and it will look just like I drove it out of the desert," Rodrigo said.

Dan looked around the space. "I don't mind sleeping here. I've slept in worse places."

"*Bueno*," Rodrigo replied.

Chapter 32

After stashing the pickup, Dan and Rodrigo unloaded it and rolled the weapons in a tarp and hid them in a corner of the garage under some wood planks and other construction debris. It was now fully dark outside.

"You probably need to report to someone. If you had made it out on your own, what would you do?" Dan asked.

Rodrigo thought for a moment. "I'd try to get in touch with *Don* Hector. I don't know where he is, but that would be the first move."

"Where would you go to find him?"

"First the warehouse. He has spent much time there since the infiltrators were stashed there."

"That is the warehouse on the southeast side of the *Zona Central*?"

Rodrigo's eyes widened as he looked at Dan.

Dan smiled. "Tlayolotl. Remember the story I told you."

Rodrigo shook his head. "This is too much for me. I'm a simple man."

"It's not too much for you. You are a drug cartel member, pretty high up, if I'm correct. This Carlos respects you and Miranda thinks he won't bother her and Solana with you around. Don't play the simple man. You're not. You are a criminal, a gang member. Your problem is that a desert shaman has chosen you to help me complete my mission. That could be dangerous for you. You could get killed by the cartel or by Tlayolotl, but if you play your cards right, you will survive all of this...you and your family."

"And what if I just tell *Don* Hector where you are? Then I'll be done with you."

Dan stepped up close to Rodrigo. His cold eyes bore into the gang member. "First, you won't. If you were going to do that you wouldn't have told me. Second, you would still come under Hector's suspicions and you know what could happen to you then. And if Hector decides to whack you, what happens to Miranda...and Solana? Remember, Hector has got to be feeling pretty vulnerable right now. He will lash out at any perceived threat."

"Maybe, maybe not."

"And don't forget Tlayolotl. He will come after you if I haven't killed you already. You have heard me talk about his power and you have seen it."

Rodrigo shrank back. "*Madre de Dios.* There is no way out."

"Help me. Do what I tell you to do. That is the only way out...for you, and for Miranda and Solana."

Dan grabbed Rodrigo by the shoulders. "You go find whoever you need to find. "I'm going to rest. And when you come back I will tell you what we are going to do."

He pushed Rodrigo towards the side door of the garage.

Rodrigo walked back down the hill and entered the house.

"This is madness! Are you really going to help this gringo?" Miranda said when Rodrigo entered.

"Yes. There is no other way. Now give me the keys to the car. I need to find Hector. Carlos shouldn't come by tonight, but if he does, tell him I am back and he must leave you alone."

Miranda just stood there, a mix of anger and fear on her face as Rodrigo went into his room and retrieved a .45 semi-automatic pistol.

In twenty minutes Rodrigo was at the warehouse. He parked outside and went to the metal gate. One of the guards recognized him.

"Rodrigo is that you? Carlos said you were dead."

"I'm not a ghost, so Carlos is wrong. Let me in."

The gate swung open and Rodrigo went into the compound.

"I need to find *Don* Hector. Is he here?"

"He's in Mexico City. He's taking over *Don* Jorge's mansion there. He's trying to keep everyone from starting a war. It is dangerous to be out on the streets."

"Here? In Chihuahua?"

The guard shook his head. "Not so much here, but down in Tamaulipas there are ambushes.

"Also Durango," said another guard walking up.

"When will *Don* Hector be back?"

"A couple of days. He wants to get rid of these Arab dogs. He has much on his hands right now."

"So who is in charge?"

"It should be you, but we all thought you were dead. Carlos has taken over and is throwing his weight around."

"Where do I find Carlos?"

The guard shrugged. "I don't know. He just comes and goes."

"Are these Arabs ready to go?"

"*Sí*. They are ready, the trucks are fueled and sitting there." He pointed to a corner of the warehouse compound where the five panel trucks were parked in a row against the sheet metal fencing.

A wave of fatigue came over Rodrigo but he suppressed it. He had been going nearly non-stop for twenty-four hours but he had to deal with Carlos. He needed to head off his challenge if he was to remain the local lieutenant. Before the fiasco in the desert, Rodrigo had ambitions to become a small time *Reyes*, a local kingpin with his own territory to control. Then all the dirty work would be done by others. Jorge's assassination and now his own presumed death left all those plans in doubt. The key was *Don* Hector, but Rodrigo couldn't wait for him to return. He had to stop Carlos from taking over. He had to assert his rightful position.

"I'll be back tomorrow. Hopefully *Don* Hector will be back soon and get all this straight. For now, I'm going to rest."

Rodrigo left the compound. He didn't drive back to his house. His position was dangerous, especially for the next day or two. He cruised through the neighborhoods that Carlos might frequent. He knew where the gang members collected to drink and party with women.

Pulling up to a large, nondescript house, Rodrigo sat in the car for a moment. He would have the element of surprise on his hands, but he needed to avoid a shootout. The first instinct of the men around Carlos would be to defend him. Rodrigo needed to assert his presence and give the men something to think about. They had been loyal to him before he was declared dead by Carlos. Rodrigo hoped they would again come back to him. But they would be cautious. If they picked the wrong side, the side *Don* Hector did not support, they were all dead men.

Rodrigo stepped out of the car. He put the .45 in the back of his pants, covered by his untucked shirt and approached the house. No one was outside. The door was not locked; which seemed foolish during this unsettled time. He quietly opened the door and entered the house. The living room was towards the rear of the house and he could hear the raucous sounds of drunken men.

Rodrigo took a deep breath and strode down the hall. He entered the room and glanced quickly around, looking for Carlos. Only a few of the men noticed him at first but the noise level quickly dropped as more and more recognized the man standing in the entrance to the room as the man they thought was dead.

Rodrigo held out his hands and smiled, "I am back from the dead. The desert cannot claim me."

Some of the men cheered drunkenly and raised their drinks. Some questions were shouted out: "How did you get back? We thought everyone had died. What happened to the others? Did you get the gringo?"

"I'll tell you all about it, but first, where is Carlos?"

Someone pointed back out of the room. "He's down the hall with his favorite fox. I don't think he wants to be interrupted."

"He will want to see me," Rodrigo said with a smile. "Save a *cerveza* for me. I'll be right back."

He turned and left the room. Going down the hall, he listened at each doorway until he heard the familiar sounds of lovemaking, the grunting and panting.

Pushing open the door he announced himself. "Carlos, it's me, Rodrigo, back from the dead."

"What?" Carlos shouted as he rolled off of the woman and grabbed his pistol from the side table.

Rodrigo smiled and put out his hands. "Carlos, it's me. I'm not here to kill you. I'm here to tell you I'm back. I think you would welcome seeing your lieutenant alive again."

Rodrigo kept his smile firm while Carlos scowled; his gun never wavered.

"Put your gun down Carlos. You don't want to kill me. The others know I'm back and are happy. *Don* Hector will not be pleased if you shoot me."

Finally Carlos lowered the gun. "How did you get back?" He shoved the girl in bed away from him and swung his legs to the floor. He pulled on his pants. "After a week in the desert, we heard nothing from you or Ramón and figured everyone had died. Hell, if the gringo didn't kill you we thought the desert did."

"That is what happened to the others. The desert killed them, but I managed to retrace my steps and get out. I am too tough for the desert."

"And none of the others got out with you? How did that happen?" Rodrigo could see the suspicion in Carlos's face. It would be the tactic Carlos would take to try to discredit him.

"As I told you, I am tougher than the desert. I will tell you all about it tomorrow, after the party."

"I am in charge now. Someone had to take over since you were gone and thought dead. I have been talking with *Don* Hector. You are not the lieutenant any more. Do you understand that?"

"I understand that I am back and nothing has changed. A week away doesn't mean I have resigned. I will let *Don* Hector decide."

"The men take orders from me now, not you. Understand *amigo*?"

"Tonight, yes. But we shall see. It is good to see you, Carlos. But you should stay with what you are good at, torturing people until they talk. That is what *Don* Jorge and *Don* Hector saw in you. Don't try to run things. It won't go well. We will talk again tomorrow."

"There is nothing to talk about." Carlos stood up and grabbed his shirt, sticking his pistol in the waistband. "I will see you out now. You must be tired from your journey."

He escorted Rodrigo down the hall to the front door, not letting him mix with the others in the living room.

"If you know what's good for you, you won't try to interfere with me now that I'm in charge."

Rodrigo just stared back at him. Then he walked off to his car. His back itched as if waiting for a bullet, but none came.

When Rodrigo got back, he went up the hill to find Dan. He entered the garage to find him lying on some of the tarps in a corner with his jacket rolled up as a pillow.

"You don't look very comfortable," Rodrigo remarked.

"I'm used to sleeping in odd places. What did you learn at the warehouse?"

"The men we are to smuggle into the U.S. are still at the warehouse. Everything is ready for them to be transported. They are waiting for *Don* Hector's signal."

"Where is Hector?"

"He's in Mexico City, at *Don* Jorge's mansion. He is supposed to return in a couple of days according to the guards."

"We don't have much time then."

"What are you planning to do?"

Dan gave Rodrigo a long, cold look. "Those men will not get to the border. They will not get into the U.S."

"You are going to stop them? You alone?"

"If I have my way, they will not leave the warehouse alive."

"And how will you do that? It is impossible. They are under guard twenty-four hours a day."

"It is not impossible and you are going to help me."

"I can't do that. It would be going to war against my cartel. It will get me killed in a terrible way."

"No one will know you helped me and, remember, I told you I would get you and your family into my country."

Rodrigo shook his head. "No, no. *Es imposible.*"

Dan stood and walked up to Rodrigo. He stepped up to his face. Rodrigo looked nervous but didn't back down.

"No. You must continue on your own. I helped you to get here into town and to hide you. Now you take the pickup and go do what you have to do. I will tell no one, but I will not be a part of this. It is suicide."

Just then a dark shadow descended into the garage, down the stairs that came from the open, unfinished second floor. There was a great flapping of wings. The bird alighted on the steps and let out a loud squawk.

Rodrigo flinched and turned. It was the raven. It could barely be seen in the night's gloom.

"Tlayolotl," said Dan. "He knows where to find you."

"*Qué demonios!*" What the hell! Rodrigo swore. "How does he find me?"

"He probably followed us. Raven carries him far and wide when necessary. Raven carried the two of us here and back."

"Will I never be rid of him?"

"If you help me, he will help you, I will help you. If you don't, he will take your life. I told you he is not to be bargained with. He is not a normal man."

"Yes, but—"

"Be glad you didn't meet him in person. He follows his own rules."

"And so you do his bidding."

"He saved my life. Now I owe him this." Dan paused. "And it will complete my mission."

"Then he will let you go?"

Dan nodded.

"What about me?"

"As I told you, he will help you."

Rodrigo sat down on the floor with a sigh. "I am tired. I saw Carlos tonight. He is trying to take over my position here in Chihuahua. If *Don* Hector does not come back quickly, it will be dangerous for me. I could be in a battle for my life. What is your plan? What do you want from me?"

"You are already in a battle for your life. Now sit down and let me tell what we are going to do."

Rodrigo sat down with Dan on some boxes.

"How many trucks are there for transporting?"

"Five."

"Tomorrow I'm going to get ten cell phones and some wire. I want you to get me twelve bricks of C-4 explosives with detonators."

"*Conyo.*" Damn, breathed Rodrigo.

"Now you understand what I'm going to do. We don't have much time, so you have to do this right away...tomorrow."

"*Pobre de mí,*" Rodrigo said holding his head in his hands. "I am lost."

"Go to your room. Get some sleep. Tomorrow we will get everything ready."

Dan got up and pulled Rodrigo to his feet. We have much to do, go. Rest." He shoved him towards the door.

Chapter 33

Carlos went into the living room after making sure Rodrigo had left the house. He took out a bag of cocaine and spread it out on the table. Next he brought out more bottles of tequila and whiskey.

"Let's enjoy the night. We have much to do tomorrow. *Don* Hector will be back in a few days and I want him to see we have everything under control."

"What about Rodrigo?" someone asked.

"What about Rodrigo? He's back but he has much to explain. What happened to Ramón and the others? How did he alone get back from the trip? What happened to the gringo?" Carlos paused as the noise died down. "I have my suspicions about Rodrigo's return. It doesn't smell right to me."

Mumblings began as the men reached for the liquor and drugs. Carlos grabbed two men who were close to him, men he could count on in a challenge between himself and Rodrigo, and led them to another back room.

"I'm going to dig into how Rodrigo got back. There is something fishy here and I want *Don* Hector to know about it. You talk with the men. Make sure they begin to question Rodrigo's return. He may have abandoned the others. Maybe he killed them to save his own life, who knows? But I'm not giving control back to him."

The men nodded and returned to the party. Carlos retired to his bedroom to think about this challenge. Not only was his new status in jeopardy, but getting Miranda and her daughter was not looking so promising right now. Maybe he should attend to that first. If he could secure Miranda and her daughter, he could use them as a bargaining chip against Rodrigo.

The next morning, Dan awoke and walked down to Rodrigo's house. He knocked on the front door. Miranda opened it with a frown on her face.

"You should not be standing outside during the day. If someone sees you, it will be bad for us." Miranda stood aside. "Come inside."

"If I knew a back entrance I would use it. I'd like to wash up before I head out."

"You are leaving us?" There was a hopeful tone in her voice.

"I have to get some things to complete my mission. I'm not leaving today, but I will be soon."

"Quicker the better," came the reply.

She led Dan up to the second floor. "There is a bathroom down the hall to your left. You can use a towel from the closet."

Dan thanked her and went off to clean up as best he could. He was dusty and dirty and he smelled bad. He had been sleeping in his clothes for over a week. They were stained with the grime of sweat and dirt.

When he came out, Rodrigo was in the kitchen eating. Dan sat down and Miranda served him a tamale with eggs and sausage in it. He thanked her and wolfed it down along with some water. Then he sat back with a cup of coffee.

"You can get what I need?" Dan asked.

Rodrigo nodded. "We have a storehouse, but I have to make sure no one is there. Questions will be raised if I do this. And afterwards everyone will connect me to what will happen."

Dan looked at his cup. "You're right about that. We can't let what I'm doing be traced back to you."

"What are you planning?" Miranda asked.

Dan looked over at Rodrigo who shook his head. "It's not for you to know."

"But it will put me and Solana in danger, won't it?"

"Only if things go wrong."

Miranda snorted. "Only if things go wrong."

"That's the way it's always been," Rodrigo said, his voice now getting louder. "Do you think we live in a normal world? It is to help Solana live normally that I do this. I don't live in a normal world and neither do you. If Solana can grow up to be a doctor or lawyer, it is enough." He was shouting now.

"I know you want what is best for us, for Solana, but why did you bring this man here? It makes things worse."

"My name is Steve," Dan said. He turned to Rodrigo, "Perhaps I should tell her what happened to me and to you in the desert."

"She won't believe you. I didn't at first."

"Tell me," Miranda said. She crossed her arms and looked at Dan with a challenging expression on her face.

Dan recounted his trek through the desert after the pickup broke down, how he almost died and how the raven and the coyote led him to the shaman. Dan also told her about his encounters with the raven earlier and how the bird had saved his life. He spoke of Tlayolotl and his powers to see beyond his camp, of his power to fly on the back of the raven to travel great distances, and of the peyote ceremony where Dan found himself on the bird with Tlayolotl traveling to Chihuahua and then back to find Rodrigo. Dan recounted how he was charged to save Rodrigo's life from certain death and how Rodrigo had to help him in exchange.

"That is a fantastic story. Maybe good for simple peasants and illiterate people, but I don't believe it," said Miranda.

"Yet I was led to Tlayolotl and was saved. And I found Rodrigo and saved him. And the raven and coyote led us to the pickup. We never would have found that on our own."

"There have been stories about a desert shaman for years. My grandmother told me stories."

"Did she use the name, Tlayolotl?" Dan asked.

Miranda looked at him sharply. "Yes, that was the name she used." She turned to Rodrigo, "But that isn't possible. He would be ancient by now. It is impossible to live so long."

"Maybe, unless one is a shaman," Dan said.

Now Rodrigo spoke up. "And last night the raven came to the garage."

"Are you sure? It was not just some bird you woke?"

"It was the raven. It didn't wake. It flew down the stairs. What bird does that at night? It knows where I am."

"Tlayolotl is not an ordinary man. He is wild and powerful. He promised to snatch Rodrigo's life away from him if he doesn't help. Not only take his life, but cause his soul to wander alone forever."

Miranda shuddered and crossed herself. "*Dios mío.* Can such a person really exist?"

"You must know the stories better than me," Dan said. "There is a long history of shamans throughout the world. And they are well known here in Mexico. I have seen

Tlayolotl's power. I don't understand it but I don't doubt it. He would take my life as well if I don't complete my mission."

"And what is that?"

"No, no. You can't know," Rodrigo said.

"Is there a way out in the end? For us?" Miranda asked.

"I think Tlayolotl will help. But I can offer help as well. If you want, the three of you can come to the U.S. and get new identities. Live there, away from the cartels, from the drug dealing and killing. Solana will have a new life where she can be anything she wants."

"You can do this?" Miranda asked.

Dan nodded his head. "It may be the best solution for you when I'm done. The three of you just disappear." He stood up. "I'd better get going. I hope my explanation helps."

Rodrigo stood as well. "I have to see what I can do about the supplies you need. You take the pickup. I'll take the Nissan.

Dan spent most of the morning hunting down and purchasing burner phones, wire, connections, and solder. The next step would be to open up five of the phones and rewire them. An incoming call would trigger an electrical current to activate the phone's vibrator. Dan would direct that current into the detonators that would be imbedded into the C-4 explosives. He was going to have a busy night.

Meanwhile Rodrigo drove to a small warehouse where the gang kept much of their arsenal. He was hoping the party last night at Carlos' place would mean no one would be guarding the building. It was locked. Rodrigo had lost his key but he knew how to get in.

As he hoped, there was no one at the front of the building. He drove around back. No one was watching at the rear. Rodrigo climbed a fence. Once inside the small lot, he climbed onto an overturned trash can and was able to jimmy open a window and squeeze through. There were no cameras. He dropped down inside and crouched in a corner. No sound came from the building. After a couple of minutes, Rodrigo determined no one was guarding it and quickly went to find the C-4 and detonators. Speed was critical; he needed to find what he came for and get out before anyone came. The missing explosives would not be noticed for some time and when they were, no one would be able to tie him to their disappearance.

Ten minutes later, Rodrigo was back in his car and driving out of the alley. On the way back to his house, he stopped at the warehouse. One of the guards recognized Rodrigo and let him in the compound.

"Carlos came by an hour ago. He said we're not to take orders from you. He's in charge, not you." The guard was friendly but the information was ominous. "What the hell are we supposed to do?" he asked.

"For now, nothing," Rodrigo replied. "I will fix this with Carlos."

"You better do it quickly. No one knows who's boss. *Don* Hector will not like it."

Rodrigo nodded and drove off.

Carlos had gotten up that morning, a little worse for the wear. After driving by the warehouse to give the guards instructions, he decided he would go to Rodrigo's house. If Rodrigo was not there, he would take Miranda and hide her away. He could pick up Solana later, when she came back from school.

Chapter 34

Carlos pulled up to the blue house on the corner. He sat there for a moment. There would be no subtleties; his intention would be clear. If he was going to kidnap Miranda and her daughter, he had to do it quickly and without hesitation. There was no car in the driveway. That was a good sign. Rodrigo must be out. *Probably trying to round up support.* Carlos would change that equation by taking Miranda.

He would use her and Solana to convince Rodrigo to step down and acknowledge his authority. Then he'd have him killed. There was enough suspicion about how he survived the desert to justify doing away with him. After, he would use threats to Solana to get Miranda's cooperation and become his woman. He'd use her as he wished and when she was broken, he'd take Solana.

He got out and approached the gate. It was locked. Putting his shoulder to it, he lunged and broke the shackle holding the deadbolt.

Carlos banged on the front door. "Miranda, open the door. I need to talk to you," he shouted. He could see Miranda in the hallway.

"Go away. Rodrigo is back. You must not come around anymore."

"It's too late now. You have to come with me. Open the door."

"I'm not going anywhere with you. Go away."

Carlos lunged against the door and broke it open. Miranda screamed and ran up the stairs with Carlos chasing her. She went into a bedroom and grabbed for a gun in the closet. Before she could pull it out and aim it, Carlos was upon her.

"No you don't," he said as he grabbed her, knocking the gun out of her hand.

"Let me go," Miranda shouted. "Rodrigo will kill you!"

"No he won't."

Carlos had one arm around her waist and the other fending off her wild swings at his face. He lifted her up and started down the hall. He'd throw her in the trunk when he got to the car.

Rodrigo saw Carlos's car as he drove down the street. A cold chill surged through him. *Why would he be here?* Carlos knew Rodrigo didn't want him around Miranda. He was up to no good. He pulled up behind the car and jumped out with his .45 in his hand. He noticed the broken gate as he entered the yard.

Just then Carlos came out of the front door. He had Miranda in a choke hold and his gun pointed at her head.

"Put down your gun or she will die," he shouted to Rodrigo.

"Let her go and I'll let you live," Rodrigo replied, trying to remain calm.

Carlos laughed. "You don't have any bargaining to do. Miranda's coming with me. If you want her back you'll tell *Don* Hector that you don't want to take over and that you're happy to have me lead here in Chihuahua."

"Never. You don't know what you're doing."

"But I have Miranda. So I know you'll do what I say."

They stood tense for a moment as both men assessed their situation.

Carlos continued, "When you turn over power to me, you can have your sister back."

While the standoff was going on in Rodrigo's front yard, Dan turned down the street. He saw the two cars parked in front of the house. He stopped the pickup and looked carefully. He could see Rodrigo with his gun drawn. He was staring at someone or something, Dan couldn't see clearly. It didn't look good.

Dan backed up and headed uphill to the next block. He turned left and then left again, going down the side street with the garage. Dan pulled in and ran over to the stash of weapons. He pulled out his Barrett sniper rifle and checked the magazine. He stepped outside of the garage and looked around. Across the street was another partly completed house. The first floor was finished. If it had a roof, Dan would be high enough to be able to look down on the front yard and see what was going on.

He ran across the street and into the house. The first floor was enclosed; there was a roof. He ran up the stairs. When he reached the top, he crawled across the flat roof to the edge which was slightly built up as a parapet. He found a broken section of the parapet and peaked through the gap. Below and across the street he could see Rodrigo and another man. The man had an arm around Miranda's neck and his pistol was pressed up against the side of her head. There was talking back and forth. Dan couldn't hear what was said but it looked like a standoff. Neither man was giving way. Dan slipped his rifle through the gap and centered his sights on the gunman's head.

It was a dangerous shot. Shooting someone in that position could trigger a reactive jerk in their body causing them to pull the trigger even as they were dying. The result could be Miranda's death. Dan knew if he could hit the base of the gunman's skull at the brain stem, that one shot would cut off all activity at once. No secondary reaction, no reflexive response. It was lights out instantly and the body would just collapse without the pistol firing.

He steadied his breathing. The target was about sixty yards, not a long shot, but he had to be perfect, dead center on the spot. There was no margin for error and that made it hard. He adjusted the scope for the close shot; then braced the rifle against the opening and let it settle on the target. The reticle centered on the spot at the base of the skull. Miranda was a full head shorter than the man holding her so he could get a clear look at his head. The shot would enter around jaw level and hit the spot on exit. Slowly Dan's world collapsed into that familiar tunnel. This was what he had trained years for. This was what he was good at. He could see the thread stretching from the muzzle of the Barrett to the target. The shooter and target were locked in that deadly connection.

The standoff could not last. Rodrigo was going to have to give in and allow Miranda to be taken. There was no reason to wait. Dan's target lock was complete, his breathing and heart rate slowed. As he exhaled half of his breath, he paused and in between his heart beats, Dan gently squeezed the trigger. The gun gave a solid *whomp* with the suppressor. In that same instant the gunman's head snapped back, his arms dropped and his body collapsed to the ground. The pistol went off as it hit the ground. The shot slammed into the concrete wall.

Rodrigo spun around, looking up the side street. Dan slowly rose from his position and waved at him. Then he disappeared as he dropped down the stairs. Miranda stood stunned for a moment, then ran to Rodrigo and hugged him.

"What happened? Was there a shot?" she asked.

"It was Steve," Rodrigo replied. "From up there." He pointed to the house across the side street.

"You came just in time. He was going to kidnap me. Why would he risk doing that?" Miranda asked.

"You heard him. He wanted to use you as leverage against me. He figured that *Don* Hector would support me in the end."

Miranda looked back at Carlos's body. The .338 Lapua round had destroyed his face. It smashed into the jaw and there was a large, bloody, open hole at the back of his skull.

Just then Dan came through the gate. Rodrigo turned to him with his arm still around Miranda.

"You took a big chance. Miranda could have been killed by Carlos's reflex."

"Not as big as risk as you think. If you know where to shoot there's no reflex reaction."

"Thank you," Miranda said.

"You're welcome. It didn't look like Rodrigo was going to negotiate any good result from where I was watching. Rodrigo wouldn't dare shoot for your sake. You would have wound up being taken by this man." Dan turned to the corpse for the first time. "Who is this anyway?"

"A rival for control over the Chihuahua gang. *Don* Hector will probably put me in charge which makes helping you even more troublesome."

"And what's your future there? How many more years will you have before you get killed? And what becomes of Miranda and Solana?"

Rodrigo shrugged.

"I predict a short career." Dan gestured towards Carlos. "What do we do with him?"

Rodrigo shook his head. As if coming back to the reality of the moment, "We take him to the dump and burn him and his car."

"We better do it quickly."

Rodrigo dug the keys out of Carlos's pocket and the two men carried the body and dropped it in the trunk.

"I'll follow you in the pickup, Dan said.

"Take the Nissan. It's right here."

Rodrigo grabbed a gas can out of the garage. They drove to an isolated spot at the dump. After pulling the body out of the trunk, they stuffed it in the back seat and splashed the interior with gasoline. Rodrigo lit a rag and threw it through the window.

"A fitting end for a bad man." He turned to Dan, "Let's go."

When they got back, they sat down in the kitchen with Miranda. Solana was in her room occupied by the internet while supposedly doing homework.

"I guess I owe you my life," Miranda said softly.

Dan was silent for a moment. "Maybe you do. I know Rodrigo does. And that was under Tlayolotl's orders."

"So what are you going to do now?" Miranda asked her brother.

"I will tell the men what happened. Only I'll leave out Steve's part. It will make me more powerful and make anyone from Carlos's side think twice before challenging me."

Chapter 35

Hector had finished meeting with the aides to the president. He had met them in Jorge's mansion in Mexico City. The government was concerned about the unrest; a lot of civilians could get killed if the gangs started warring against each other.

"We thought Mendoza had this all under control. We supported him so that things would remain calm," one of the aides said.

"That is what we were doing. Then someone assassinated *Don* Jorge. They also killed two other cartel leaders and now the others don't know who to trust."

"Look, we supported you in order to keep things peaceful. We'll continue to support you, but you must not let this break out into a civil war among the cartels."

"You keep pressure on Los Zetas and Tijuana. They lost their bosses and are looking for revenge," Hector replied.

"Can you handle this?" another aide asked.

"Be careful how you talk," answered Hector. "Remember where all your money comes from. I can handle this. We're sitting here, in *Don* Jorge's mansion, are we not? I am assuming power and control. Everyone will see."

"I hope you do."

Hector pointed his finger at the aide. "Can you find who shot *Don* Jorge and the others? No one seems to be able to solve this killing."

"The highest level of investigation is going on. We have both the Federal police and the military working on it."

Hector stood up. It was useless to waste more of his time on these men. They would not find the shooter, not if he couldn't. They might be more successful in keeping pressure on the other two cartels so they couldn't strike back at him.

"Go do what you can with Los Zetas and Tijuana." With that Hector strode out of the room leaving his men to escort the government officials out of the mansion.

He had to get back to Chihuahua soon and get those terrorists out of his hair and over the border. He would continue importing drugs from Tariq, but he was not interested in more terrorists; not unless it became much more lucrative.

He had not been able to convince Jorge that the terrorist side of the business was not worth pursuing. Jorge was always looking to diversify. Hector did have to admit, though, that his decision to move into meth was insightful. It was easier to smuggle and aggressively more addictive. It promised even greater profits. The Sinaloa cartel was taking in three billion dollars a year and Hector didn't see how smuggling terrorists could create a huge increase in that income. Still Jorge had been right before, so Hector didn't dismiss the idea completely. Yes, it was time to get back to Chihuahua finish this project. As much as he disliked him, he would still keep a channel open to Tariq. After he got the control over the situation here in Mexico, he could consider what other moves he should make.

He had lost Ramón and the rest of the pursuit crew and he wanted answers about what happened. Control over Chihuahua also needed to be solidified. Rodrigo was lost along with Ramón and Carlos had taken charge. Hector knew him only a little and was not impressed by what he saw.

Before Rodrigo left to meet with the other gang members, he and Dan went over the plan. They had walked up to the garage to ensure privacy. "Are you going to do this tonight?"

"I must. You said Hector might be coming back tomorrow or the next day. It's best if all this is completed before he gets here."

"What about Tariq? He's the one in charge of the terrorists."

"If he's caught in the explosions, so be it. I'm not worried about him, only the men who are going to try to enter the U.S."

They were sitting on some boxes in a corner. Dan had the phones out.

"The cell phones are ready. Five of them get attached to the trucks and wired into the igniters. I've got zip ties to attach everything. The five sending phones are programmed. Each with one of the trigger phone's number. When I press the five green 'connect' buttons...boom, boom, boom. Five times."

"It sounds too easy," Rodrigo said.

"It's never as easy as it sounds. But the hardest thing will be attaching the C-4 and phones. The rest should go easier."

"What do Miranda and I do after that? Hector will be coming. He will not be happy."

"I thought he didn't care about the terrorists."

"He doesn't but he cares about things going properly. And the terrorists getting blown up, that's a fuck up. He'll be after my ass."

"Maybe you and Miranda and the kid should disappear after tonight."

"I thought you were going to help us."

"I will. But you have to decide if you want to go to the U.S. You and Miranda need to make that decision now because things are going to happen fast after tonight."

Rodrigo turned to leave the garage, "I'll talk with Miranda."

After Rodrigo left, Dan took two extra burner phones he had purchased and went across the street to sit on the roof of the unfinished house.

He punched in Jane's cell number.

"Who is this?" Jane asked when she answered the phone.

"Your favorite employee," Dan replied.

There was a pause for a moment. "Where are you? Why aren't you using the satellite phone?"

"I've got cell reception where I am and I don't want to be tracked."

"No one's tracking you."

"Maybe, but something's not right. There's a leak somewhere. The pickup team was neutralized, probably dead and some gang members substituted. They almost got me."

"There can't be a leak."

"Don't give me that," Dan said. "How did the gang know where to meet me and how did they get the phone I was calling?" A tone of accusation filled his voice.

Jane was silent. Finally she replied, "I don't know."

"It's a leak, straight to the cartel. I don't know who to trust."

"You can trust me."

"Can I? I almost got killed and now I'm still stuck here in Mexico."

"Where are you? I can send someone to come and extract you."

"No. We're not playing that game all over again. Besides I have more to do."

"You've done enough. Hell, you've got the State Department and the Mexican government all in a lather over the multiple killings. Things have blown up in our face here and Henry's boss is looking for an explanation. This may go all the way up to the DDO."

"All the more reason for me to remain unfound."

"Why couldn't you just do the job I sent you to do? Why improvise?"

"That's what you wanted when you hired me, someone who could and would improvise. It was a target rich environment and I decided to act on it. When it all settles down, there'll be more confusion and disruption. That was the goal, so don't complain."

"I'm not complaining, but it makes things hard on my end."

"That's your job; you have to deal with it. I'm doing my job."

"I just didn't expect the State Department to get all riled up. It complicated things." She paused. "So why did you call?"

"You have to do something for me."

"Besides keep your ass out of hot water and keep this program alive?"

"Yeah. I need you to get three people into the states. I need them to go into the witness protection program."

There was silence on the other end. Finally Jane asked, "Who is it?"

"The guy is a local or regional lieutenant in the Sinaloa cartel. It's him, his sister and her twelve-year-old daughter. He's going to help me and he has a lot of information. But if he helps me, his future here is tenuous at best. All three will probably be killed—"

"I don't know."

"He helps me, we take out more bad guys and you get some good intel."

"The program is run by the Feds, the FBI. I can't promise anything. I'd need to know who it is. They'll want to know who it is."

"No time for that. I need you to trust me. You can stash them somewhere and then negotiate with the Feds."

"Give me something to work with, something for Henry at least."

Dan thought for a moment. "I'll call you back." He hung up the phone and grabbed the other one from his pocket. Jane may not be tracking him, but others would be.

Jane picked up on the first ring. "Changed phones?"

"Just listen. I'll say this quick and then I need a quick answer...from you, not Henry. I don't have time for you to consult with him."

"I'm listening."

"Your worry about the cartels smuggling terrorists into the U.S.? It's real. There's sixty waiting to head across the border any day. Jorge was a step further along than you expected. I can eliminate them. I've got it planned, but I have to act right away, even tonight. Once my contact helps me do this, he's got no future here. Next, what you don't realize is that Jorge's second-in-command, Hector Ortega, has already taken over. He's moved into Jorge's mansion and is contacting the other cartels. He's going to tamp down what you hoped to start, so all this work won't make any difference. But I can take him out before I exfiltrate and there's no one ready at the next level to take over. That will really sow seeds of confusion."

There was no response from Jane's end.

"So? Can you get my guy and his family out? I can't do this without his help."

"I'm thinking. I can't imagine you can get to Ortega at this point. He's going to be well guarded."

"If I can find him, I can take him out. It's worth a try anyway...as long as I'm down here."

"I don't know. I don't want you to get killed. You've already done so much."

"Damn it Jane," Dan said. He squeezed the phone in frustration. "You told me to improvise, you said you were a fighter and you wanted a warrior to take the fight to the bad guys. Well that's what I'm doing. Don't shy away from it. There's no sense in having me out in the field if you won't support me. Hell, there's no sense in having this program if we don't take risks and try to maximize our effect." Dan paused. "Isn't this is what I'm here for, disruption? Are you in? Or was all that talk in Brooklyn just that, talk?"

Jane sighed. "I'm in. I'll tell Henry after we're done. I just don't want you to die trying to do too much. It all seems like it's out of control."

"Good. I'll have my guy go into hiding and I'll get back in touch with how you'll get him out. Try to keep things more secret than before. Check your staff. If there aren't any leaks from you or them, better check your office and phones for bugs. And don't worry, I'm used to chaos.

Dan hung up before Jane could respond.

Chapter 36

Later, in the early evening, Dan and Rodrigo met in the garage after eating a meal cooked by Miranda. "Miranda agrees to go north. She says it's the best opportunity for Solana, even if it means leaving all we know behind."

"Good. You have a rich culture, but right now the current culture could kill all of you."

Rodrigo nodded, almost sadly. "You have torn up my life. Part of me wants to kill you and part of me is looking forward to a new life."

"You probably wouldn't be alive five years from now if I hadn't come along."

"I probably won't be alive next week since you came along."

"Don't discount Tlayolotl. He's playing a part in this somewhere behind the scenes."

"Maybe, maybe not."

"I don't think I have to tell you, but you can't get involved with drugs or gangs when you go north. If you do, the government will drop you and you'll be exposed."

"Maybe I can work for them. I don't think I'll do well standing behind the counter of a convenience store."

"Milk the government for all its worth. If you show some value, you could be involved for a long time. It will be more exciting than being a store clerk."

"*Qué te den.*" Up yours.

Dan shook his head. He could tell Rodrigo was chafing under his demands and his fear of the cartel. He was probably feeling trapped and could react unpredictably. *Better get this going.* "Show me where the trucks are parked and where the guards are."

Rodrigo took out a sheet of paper and pencil he had brought with him from the house. He drew a map of the compound. "You are fortunate. The trucks are here along one side of the metal wall." He drew some boxes along the side of the compound. "It's dark there and out of the way. The guards stay around the entrance. When you get to the trucks, you don't have the warehouse between you and the guards, but the trucks are pretty far away. If you don't make noise, you shouldn't be noticed."

Dan studied the map. "Can I get over the fence in the back? The building will shield me from the guards at the gate."

"You have two problems. One, a guard walks around the warehouse once an hour. You have to know when he's going to come by and then you can climb the wall. If you put a box down you will be able to reach the top and leverage yourself over."

Dan nodded. "I can watch over the fence to see when he comes by."

"Your other problem is that the terrorist, Tariq, walks around at odd hours. You never know. The guards say he doesn't like to be cooped up in the warehouse. They can't lock him in."

"How late at night?"

"The guards tell me often until one or two in the morning. After that, I guess he sleeps."

"So I have to go in after 2:00 am. It will take an hour to attach the bombs. I should be out by 3:00 or 3:30." Both men stared at the map. "I will need a place, preferably a roof top to make the calls."

"Why a roof top?"

"I want to see that it all goes well."

"And if it doesn't?"

"I'll finish the job with my rifle."

"*Estás puto?*" Are you mad? "You will get killed."

"No, they will get killed."

Rodrigo was quiet as he digested Dan's commitment. He had killed many high level-cartel leaders, including *Don* Jorge. He had killed the men sent to ambush him and outlasted the pursuit in the desert. He had killed Carlos and saved Miranda from being held hostage. And now he was going to kill all the terrorists. He was a very dangerous man.

"What happens after the trucks are blown up?"

"You need to have your alibi. You should be with some of the men or something. You should also have a place to hide with Miranda and Solana. Somewhere for a few days, maybe a week at most until I get things set up."

"You have the commitment?"

"Yes, but they have to make arrangements. That will take more time."

"How will I connect?"

"After tonight, they will have your name and you will have a name and number. A woman will be in touch."

"So you will come back here?"

"Briefly. There will be something else. You can help me now and then not worry about me anymore after tonight."

"You want more help?"

"I want you to draw me a plan of Mendoza's mansion in Mexico City."

Rodrigo looked at Dan in disbelief. "You are not going there, are you?"

Dan just stared back at the man, his eyes cold, the eyes of a killer, an assassin.

"*Hijo de puta!*" Son of a bitch! Rodrigo exclaimed. "You are going to try to kill *Don* Hector as well? You are truly crazy, gringo." He shook his head. "Just make sure you give me the phone numbers before you leave. You are a dead man if you go to Mexico City."

Among the many houses Mendoza owned, the one in Mexico City was a showplace. Just outside of town in a green suburb, it included twelve landscaped acres protected by a ten-foot concrete wall that looked as if it could withstand every assault short of a tank. The front entrance was bracketed by two large brick faced concrete pillars with a heavy iron gate. The gate, although ornate, was not for decorative purposes. It would stop a heavy truck. The house enclosed 20,000 square feet of living space. There was a whole wing for María and the children. A formal dining room with a fourteen-foot-high ceiling and a forty-foot banquet table served for official functions. Further into the building there was a party room with a balcony around three sides, giving the privileged guests a bird's eye view of the festivities. In the basement were the storerooms for food, wine, and weapons.

Off to one side was Mendoza's office and private bedroom. He used it when he was not sleeping with María, when she was out of town, or when he brought his mistresses into the house. The office was where he conducted business.

"*Don* Hector, will surely have taken over this wing. He probably leaves María alone in her private suites. Having her present may be enough for him. If you can get to Mexico City, if you can get inside, that is where you will find him."

"Why María? What does he need her for?"

Rodrigo looked at Dan as if he were stupid. "The king is dead, the new king inherits everything. She is part of the trappings of power. He takes over *Don* Jorge's role completely. She is important...and she is a beautiful woman. Any man would want her."

Dan thought about that for a moment. Oddly it made him a bit sad. He realized he had liked what he had seen of her at the hacienda, how she was so attentive to her children. Staying around would not be good for her. But could she ever leave once so far into the gang? Was she just going to have to accept being recycled to Hector as his mate? He hoped there was something better in store for her.

"The wall, does it go completely around the property?"

"In the back is a drainage area, kept natural. I think the back of the property is protected by a chain link fence topped with razor wire."

Dan digested the information and tucked it away in his mind for later. Now was time to execute the first part of his new mission.

"Here's what you do," Dan said. "When Ortega gets here, the trucks will already have been blown up. You can profess ignorance. You just got back out of the desert and had to deal with Carlos trying to kidnap your sister and niece. Play it up. In the end you had to kill him. Before you could get everything back under control, the explosions happened. There will be no terrorists to smuggle, Hector will deal with this Tariq and then if Hector doesn't think about it, you should tell him to get back to Mexico City and solidify his control. You will handle things in Chihuahua."

Rodrigo thought about it. "It sounds easy, but I can't be sure Hector will do what I say."

"There's nothing for him to do here once Tariq is gone. He'll think he's safer in Mexico City and his main task is to solidify his leadership and keep things from blowing up. If the trappings are important, he'll want to do that from Mendoza's mansion." Dan shrugged. "I don't have any other plan. I have to get to him there when his guard is down, where he feels safe."

"He feels safe there because he is safe."

"Not with me around."

Chapter 37

At 1:00 am, Dan was getting his gear ready when Rodrigo came up to the garage.

"You ready to go?"

"In a moment," Dan said.

He packed the plastic explosives in his backpack along with the detonators and phones, separating the calling phones from the receiving ones.

"You found a place for me to trigger the explosions?"

Rodrigo nodded. "The building across the street is empty. You can get on the roof from the back door. I'll go there and jimmy it open after you get into the compound. When you leave, drive down the alley for two blocks and don't come back down the street in front of the warehouse. Go one block further and come down the road until you're across from the compound. You'll see an alley. Park in it. From there you can walk to the house. I'll wait there for you and then I'm going to leave."

Dan nodded. "Got it. Let's go."

He got into the pickup and Rodrigo went down to get the Nissan. Rodrigo led Dan to the backside of the warehouse. They parked a half block away and walked back to the compound. Dan brought his M4 and 9mm, both with their suppressors fitted and the backpack filled with explosives. In the alley they found some barrels and carried one to the metal wall. Dan climbed up to look over. It was dark. It was 1:30 am. If Tariq didn't wander about by 2:00 am Dan would have to take a chance and assume he wasn't coming out any more.

Dan could get in, but how would he get out? He needed to find something to help him get back over the wall after setting the explosives. There was some scrub vegetation along the wall but he could see nothing to stand on.

"How the hell am I going to get out?" he whispered turning back to Rodrigo.

"Nothing to stand on?"

"No."

Dan thought for a moment, then he got down and walked to the pickup. In the bed he grabbed a coil of rope and brought that back to where Rodrigo was standing.

"If I can find something to tie this rope to on this side, I can use it to climb out. But I'll have to risk leaving it hanging over the wall."

"That's dangerous. The guard walks around every hour."

"I know, but I can't see another way out. And it's dark next to the wall."

There was nothing on the outside of the wall.

"The barrel isn't heavy enough to use as an anchor. He looked around the alley. "I'll have to bring the pickup here and tie off to it."

"No. They will hear it inside."

"You have any other ideas?"

Rodrigo looked around and shook his head.

"After I start it, I'll just let it idle in reverse and it will creep back here. It'll be pretty quiet." He set off back to the pickup.

Slowly the truck backed up at idle speed. As Dan predicted it was quiet. The tires crunching in the dirt made more sound than the engine. Rodrigo watched the pickup and then climbed on the barrel to peek over the wall. He could see no one. It was quiet, like a graveyard.

After Dan parked the truck and got out, Rodrigo stepped down. "If you have to shoot your way out, they will know something is wrong. They'll examine the trucks."

Rodrigo had little doubt by now that Dan could shoot his way out. With the suppressed M4 he would probably kill half the guards before they knew what was going on.

"Even if I have to kill the guard who walks around the warehouse, he'll be missed and that will trigger problems. No, I have to be a ghost."

"And you can do this?"

"It's what I'm trained for."

Dan tied the coil of rope to the hitch on the rear bumper, then stood on the barrel and watched for either Tariq or the guard. He would go over the wall after the guard made his round.

"When I go in, wait for a moment and then throw the rope over. Let me test it. If it's working, you go set up at the house across the street."

Rodrigo nodded. Dan watched, peeking over the top of the wall. *Patience, it always involves waiting.* He smiled.

As Rodrigo had reported, the guard came around the warehouse just minutes after 2 am. From what Dan could see, he looked bored and tired. He wasn't very alert, not looking around the yard. That was a good thing. To the guard, it was a chore and he fulfilled his duty by doing the lap. It looked like he was relying on the guards at the gate. Dan had seen many sentries come to a bad end doing much the same thing.

After he rounded the corner, Dan gave him five more minutes to get back inside and then threw his leg over the wall and dropped to the ground. A moment later the rope came uncoiling over the wall. Dan caught it and put all of his weight on it and jerked. It held.

"*Es bueno*," he whispered to Rodrigo.

There was no reply, but Dan heard the footsteps recede down the alley. He turned and quickly walked along the wall to his left. He stuck close to it where the shadows helped to hide him. When he got near the side wall, he began to crawl towards the trucks. He took his time, keeping quiet and low to the ground, pushing the backpack in front of him. The M4 was strapped to the pack and his 9mm was tucked in a holster at his side.

When he had made it under the last truck in line, he rolled on his back. It was even darker underneath but Dan could see the shadows and outlines of the frame. He started at the rear and stuck a brick of the C-4 plastic explosive to the underside of the truck floor. Next he strapped a receiving phone to a frame rail. He then stuck an igniter into the C-4 and ran the wires to the phone. With the clip ends on the phone he connected the circuit. When the phone received a call and began to vibrate, in that instant, a current would run down the wires to the igniter and trigger the explosive. Moving further forward, he stuck a second brick of the explosive to the underside of the floor and pushed an igniter into the putty-like material. He ran the wires back to the phone and connected them into the circuit. He didn't worry about the cab; the driver would be taken out by the explosions from the back of the truck.

Dan crawled forward and quickly moved from one truck to the next in line, attaching two bricks of explosives to each one, repeating the process as he went. He was working on the final truck, the one at the front of the line, closest to the men at the gate, when he heard footsteps. An hour had gone by. *Must be the guard.*

Dan looked out and saw him start for the trucks. If the guard peeked underneath, he would be seen. The guard was headed for the rearmost truck. Dan grabbed the unattached parts of the bomb and, forcing himself to go slowly and quietly he crawled towards the wall side of the truck. His only hope was to hide behind a wheel. He crouched in a small ball behind the front wheel as the guard walked forward, looking under each truck as he went.

"Hey Juan, what're you looking for?" one of the guards called out when he noticed him.

"I thought I heard something."

"Maybe a big raccoon, or a big rat," the man replied.

"Maybe it's the *chupacabra*," another said. The men at the gate laughed.

"*Vete al demonio idiota*," go to hell dumbass, the guard replied.

There was general laughter and the guard quickly finished giving the remaining trucks a cursory look. He then went up to the gate and cigarettes were lit, their tips glowing in the dark. *Make good targets*, thought Dan as he watched.

When the guard went inside, Dan finished attaching the explosives under the first truck and then worked his way back to the rear truck, going down the gap between the trucks and the wall. He was shielded from the front gate and could move faster than crawling underneath. It was already after 3 am and he didn't know how early the caravan would set out.

At the end of the line, he took off his backpack, now relieved of most of its contents, and pushed it in front of him as he crawled along the fence line. After turning the corner, he continued to crawl along the back wall until the building shielded him from the front gate guards. At that point Dan moved in a crouch to the rope. Slipping on his backpack, he pulled himself to the top and swung his leg over the edge. He pivoted the rest of his torso over and slowly let himself down, dropping the last two feet to the dirt.

Dan gently pulled the rope back over the wall and untied it from the hitch. He laid it in the back of the pickup, walked around to the driver's door and quietly opened it. The light went on and he threw the backpack into the passenger seat and slid in. After gently closing the door enough to shut off the light, he reached up and took out the overhead bulb. Then he reopened the front door, placed the shifter in neutral and stepped out. He pushed hard against the door frame and finally got the truck to rock. It kept increasing with each push until the truck began to roll forward. Trying to keep his puffing quiet, Dan pushed the truck until it was clear of the warehouse compound. Then he got in, started the motor, and idled down the alley.

When he got to the alley across from the warehouse, Dan parked the truck. He checked all his phones and his Barrett sniper rifle, and started down the alley. Soon he could see Rodrigo standing in the shadows behind the building. When Dan came up to him, Rodrigo pointed to the door.

"The stairs go to the roof. I don't know if that door is locked. You're on your own. Now who do I call to arrange pickup?" he whispered.

Dan gave him Jane's number.

"Use a burner phone and don't stay on the phone too long; it may be monitored and she may not know about it.

Just give her a pickup address or coordinate. Don't make it the same place you are hiding out. Tell her to get a burner phone and call you with instructions. When she calls, get her number, and use another phone to call her back. Change the pickup location. Make sure you leave the first phone far away from the meeting place. Then you have a good chance of being secure."

"I hope you are correct. It sounds like you can't trust your own people."

"Just do as I say and you might get out alive."

"You are a crazy gringo." With that Rodrigo faded into the darkness of the alley. Dan turned and went into the building.

He found the stairs and was happy to find that the access door wasn't locked. He crawled across the roof to the parapet and settled into a good spot to observe. He could not see the guards close to the wall but he could see the trucks. Dan laid out the phones in a row in the same order as the trucks. He punched in the numbers for each truck. He had the phones set up to not let the screen go to sleep for two minutes. Of course they would while he waited, but when the drivers came out and the men were loaded, he would have time to wake them up and hit the green connecting icons. Next he checked his Barrett to make sure it was ready to fire. Then he settled down to wait; the familiar waiting.

He didn't think about the next part of his mission. It was almost 1,500 kilometers to Mexico City, about 900 miles. It would take him seventeen hours of non-stop driving to get there even with good roads. If they were bad it would take longer. He would have plenty of time to come up with a plan.

It was 5:30 am. The sky was getting lighter in the east. The night's chill had crept over Dan. He had hunched down with his coat wrapped around him waiting for the dawn to come. There was some commotion in the warehouse. Instantly he was alert. Three guards came out. A two other men followed. They were dressed differently from the guards and didn't look like cartel members. Dan guessed they were the terrorists. Everyone stood outside the door smoking.

Dan watched carefully. Soon things were going to get exciting. A half-hour later, the sky was lighter, the sun just about ready to break over the horizon. Suddenly the men came out of the warehouse. Someone was directing them. *Probably the guy, Tariq.* Dan waited. The back doors of the trucks were opened and the men began to climb into the boxes. Tariq was moving around from truck to truck talking to the men, probably saying goodbye with some words of encouragement. Finally they were all loaded and the doors closed. The drivers headed for the cabs. Dan woke the five phones. The drivers started their engines. Tariq took one last look, turned, and walked towards the front gate. Dan pressed the connect buttons, one after the other.

Before the second call was completed the first truck in line exploded. The blast threw Tariq and the guards to the ground and shattered the cab of the second truck; then the whole line went up in explosions. The shock waves slammed into Dan causing him to fall back from the parapet of the roof. The pressure knocked the wind out of him and he struggled to get his breath as he lay on the roof.

When he got back up he crawled back to the edge of the roof and looked out. Men were running out of the warehouse. The guards at the gate were down. Two of them were moving but the rest lay still. Through the scope Dan could see they were covered in blood as they lay twisted on the ground. The boxes of the trucks were completely shattered; only parts of the cabs and the engine bays remained. Body parts were strewn around the dirt yard. Fire erupted among the ruins of the trucks and smoke billowed into the air. The warehouse wall closest to the trucks was caved in from the blast. Out on the street, people emerged from the surrounding buildings and looked towards the warehouse.

There was no need for the backup plan; no one from the trucks survived. Dan collected the phones, crawled back to the door, and went down the stairs. He peeked out of the door leading to the alley. It was empty, so he walked back down it, away from the carnage he had caused. Dan didn't see the large raven lifting from the adjacent roof and flying off.

Chapter 38

Tariq was up before dawn. This was the day. By 5:30 he began rousing the men to wash and say their prayers. After, he gave them a short speech of encouragement, telling them to not be seduced by the west, to seek support within their own community, and to be ready to act. He worried more about the ones who were to be sleepers. They would have to blend in for years. The others could take action right away, as warriors should, and then try to find their way out of the country. The men headed outside. Tariq counted them off into groups of twelve for each of the trucks. Sixty warriors to strike the U.S. Tariq smiled. Despite the odd events, the insertion was finally taking place. Once he saw the men off, he could conclude his business with Hector Ortega and head back to Karachi.

The men were finally loaded and the doors closed. As the drivers headed for the cabs, Tariq turned and started towards the gate. That turning probably saved his life. He was halfway to the front gate and the trucks were starting their engines when the first explosion went off. The pressure wave threw Tariq to the ground. Chunks of metal flew past him, some of it cutting his back, and some of it killing anyone unlucky enough to still be on their feet.

Then more explosions in rapid succession. In a moment it was over. Tariq turned in a panic to see only shattered remains where the trucks were once parked. The ruins were in flames. He staggered to his feet and lurched towards the inferno screaming out the names of his men. The fierce heat burned his face and singed his hair; his back was wet with blood. He fell back. He tried again and again to approach the burning remains until some of the guards grabbed him and held him back. It was no use. He could not get close. Then he noticed the body parts strewn around the yard; there was no one alive to pull from the burning wreckage.

The flames rose high in the air with black smoke billowing above them. Tariq stood back from the fires staring in disbelief. How could this happen? All the plans laid waste in a single moment of explosions. Who did this? No one knew about the men except for himself and the cartel. He sank to the ground. His mission had failed. Not only failed but he lost sixty of his finest men. All the money and planning were now gone to waste. He thought of Rashid al-Din Said. What would he say? He had offered up 500,000 dollars to help with this mission. He would hold someone accountable. And that someone would be Tariq.

The gang members gathered. One of them yelled to call Carlos, another said to call Rodrigo.

"What will *Don* Hector do when he hears of this?" one asked.

"We'll let either Carlos or Rodrigo deal with that," another replied.

Soon the sirens of the fire trucks could be heard. The men ordered Tariq into the warehouse to remain out of sight.

Rodrigo got the call as he was driving up to his house.

"The trucks were blown up. With everyone in them. They're all dead." The man on the phone shouted.

"When?" Rodrigo asked.

"Just now. I called Carlos but he doesn't answer. Should we call *Don* Hector?"

"No. Get the fire out, get rid of the fire department, and tell the cops that it was a gang attack and to not interfere. I'll be there shortly."

Rodrigo hung up the phone. He could possibly play this out for a while although it might get awkward to explain how he got out of the desert but no one else did. Would *Don* Hector suspect the gringo? Rodrigo could throw suspicion on Los Zetas. They were brutal. But he didn't know how far *Don* Hector had gone in making peace. *Better to play dumb. After all I just got back.*

He went into the house and woke Miranda and Solana.

"We have to pack and get ready to leave," Rodrigo announced.

"What's happened?" Miranda asked.

"Some trucks at the warehouse were blown up."

"The gringo, Steve?" Miranda asked.

Rodrigo didn't say but his look betrayed the truth.

"But why do we have to go away?" Solana asked.

"Because some people may suspect I had something to do with it. I still have to explain myself to *Don* Hector." He pointed his finger at Solana. "And remember. You have never seen the gringo. He was never here."

She nodded; her eyes wide with fear.

"Are we in danger?" she asked.

"Yes. That is why we have to pack and be ready to leave. I'll play this out as far as I can but we may have to hide."

"Where will we go?" Miranda asked.

"*Tía* Milagros. She lives near Torreón. We can get there in two hours."

"And what then? Wait for them to come for us?"

"Wait for people in the U.S. to get us out. I have the number to call."

"I'm scared," Solana said.

"So am I," Miranda responded. "But we have to do what Uncle Rodrigo says. The gringo gave him a number for people who can get us away and hide us. Rodrigo thinks we can trust him since he saved our lives once already."

"Go pack, both of you. I have to go down to the warehouse," Rodrigo said and turned to leave.

Dawn had come and when he opened the front door, he saw the raven perched on the wall. Rodrigo stopped and stared. Why was it here?

He turned back to the house and called to Miranda and Solana. When they came to the door, Rodrigo just pointed to the raven.

"What does it mean?" Miranda asked.

"I don't know, except that the raven is the sign of the shaman. He sees us. I told you this was all true and now you see for yourself.

"It's just a bird," Solana said.

At that the raven let out a harsh squawk and jumped into the air. The three on the porch shrank back at the size of the bird's wingspan. It flew at them and then swooped into the air before setting back down on the wall.

"It is not just a bird," Rodrigo said. Slowly he began to walk to the car under the watchful gaze of the black bird. He noticed the red and black eyes. It was the same bird as in the desert. It was Tlayolotl.

Dan headed south out of Chihuahua on highway 16, then 24 towards Mexico City. When he had put fifty miles behind him, he pulled off and tried to sleep. Sleep wouldn't come. Dan's thoughts were a swirl of confusion.

Things blowing up, getting lost in a dark mansion and seeing a beautiful woman only fleetingly drifting around dark hallways, always out of reach.

The day was beginning to heat up. He would get no sleep now. He got out of the pickup and splashed some water on his face. *Get something to eat, get some gas and press on. You can sleep later.*

He drove down the empty road, being careful to keep to the speed limit. With his rumpled ball cap on and the Mexican plates on the very beat up looking pickup, Dan hoped he presented an unlikely candidate for extracting a bribe. Still he was happy he had his 9mm under the seat, close at hand.

His mind drifted to María as he droned along the road. He had only seen her through his telescopic sights and here he was creating a whole persona around her. She seemed to Dan to be sad. A beautiful woman stuck in a trap with two beautiful kids whom she seemed to love. Maybe she had nothing else in her life but the kids. How long had it been that way? *This is dumb.* What did he know about her? Nothing except that she was beautiful and had two kids. Yet his mind kept returning, teasing her back into his thoughts. Maybe it was the idea of Ortega taking her over, as a prized possession and her life remaining like a caged bird without escape. *What do you care?* He kept telling himself. But his mind didn't seem to listen.

The red and blue lights flashing in his mirrors jarred Dan out of his thoughts. *Damn. This is not going to be good.* He slowed and pulled over to the side of the road. It was a lonely stretch of highway with desert on both sides. It had been miles since he passed a building and probably miles before he would pass another.

While he was pulling over, Dan grabbed the 9mm from under the seat and put it under his jacket on the seat next to him. Now he kept his hands on the steering wheel. The cop got out of the patrol car, adjusted his equipment belt, and began to walk towards the pickup. Dan could see he was with the *policía federal*. That was not a good thing. Dan felt the rush of adrenalin run his body. This was dangerous. Earlier he had looked at the registration in the glove box and noted the name of the owner. He'd try to play the scene out and bluff his way through. If not, there was the 9mm.

"License and registration," the patrolman said when he reached the driver's window.

Dan slowly pulled his wallet from his back pocket and removed his U.S. license in the name of Steve Mason along with his International Driver's Permit.

"The registration is in the glove box," he said.

The cop looked up from the documents and nodded to him. Dan opened the glove box and retrieved the paper. The truck was registered to a Diego Ramírez. The cop looked at the documents and then looked at Dan.

"This is not your truck," he said.

"That is correct. I'm delivering it to my friend Diego in Mexico City. He had to fly there earlier and wanted me to drive his truck down to him."

"What is your business with Diego Ramírez?"

"He is a friend of mine. We sometimes work together."

The cop raised his eyebrows. "And what work is that?"

Dan silently cursed himself for giving more information than was necessary. "I help him with his crafts business."

"What kind of crafts?"

"He makes carved figures. I help him."

"That is odd. He gets a gringo to help him make figures? Why does he not use someone local?"

"We met some years ago and became friends. I got interested in what he was doing and wanted to help out. I don't have a regular job so this worked for me."

"And you sell these things in the U.S.?"

"Sometimes when I go back I sell some to friends back home."

"And you smuggle them out of our country."

"No. I take them in my luggage and declare them. They are gifts that I purchased. I don't smuggle them."

"But you don't purchase them and they are not gifts." The cop looked suspiciously at Dan.

"It is not what you think. Most of Diego's business is here in Mexico. Look, if I was speeding, I'm happy to pay the fine. I'm just trying to get to Mexico City to meet my friend."

The cop smiled for the first time. "That could be expensive. You might be a smuggler who should go to jail. Or you might need to pay a lot of money to stay out." This last was said with a smirk.

"How much do you want?" Dan asked.

"How much do you have?" the cop answered.

"Enough. It is in my backpack."

Dan moved to reach into the back seat.

"Stop!" The cop commanded.

Dan looked back at him. The policeman drew his side arm.

"Get out of the truck. Keep your hands where I can see them. I'm putting you under arrest until I can determine if you are a smuggler. I'll check your backpack."

With the C-4 and wires, the backpack would get him put in jail. That and the weapons in the other bag would keep him there for a long time. He got out as the cop backed up.

"Put your hands against the roof of the truck." He frisked Dan with his left hand while holding the pistol in his right.

"Now bring your left arm down and behind your back."

He was going to handcuff him. It was now or never. As he brought his left hand down, Dan spun and pushed the pistol to the side. The cop fired but the bullet went into the back door of the truck. Dan continued with his right hand and smashed it into the neck of the cop. He reeled back and shot again. This time the bullet hit Dan in the left leg. Dan surged forward against the policeman grabbing for the gun again, trying to control it. They were both grunting as they struggled against each other. The cop beat at Dan's head and face. Dan ignored the blows. He knew he had to win the wrestling match quickly. His leg would not hold up. With a huge surge of energy, he forced the gun against the officer. With both men's hands fighting for control of the weapon, the gun went off. The cop staggered back a look of surprise on his face. The gun fell from his hand. A red stain spread out from his chest. He put his hand to it and looked down at the wound as he fell to the ground. Dan fell back against the pickup.

The bullet had entered below the man's chest and traveled up, behind his rib cage to nick his heart. He lay on the pavement bleeding out internally. In a minute he was unconscious. In two minutes he was dead.

Dan sagged to the ground. The bullet had hit him in his outer left thigh. Thankfully it had traveled through his leg so less energy had been deposited in his body. There was steady bleeding, not pulsing; the bullet had not hit an artery. Dan took off his belt and tied it around his leg above the wound. He limped to the rear door and opened it. Climbing in, he opened his backpack and took out some QuikClot dressing and antiseptic powder. Opening the belt, he slid his pants down and applied the powder and then the QuikClot pad to the entrance and exit wounds. He then tied everything off with some gauze bandage wrapped around his leg.

After watching to see that the bleeding was under control, he pulled his pants back up and sat back. He drank some water. *What a mess. Got to get the cop off the highway.* He looked around. *What do I do with the patrol car?* He could drag the body out into the desert and hide it behind some rocks but the police car was a bigger problem. There were no obvious places to hide it from view. *Best thing is to get far away from here. It's useless to hide the body if the car is still visible.*

Dan decided to put the cop's body back in his car with the pistol in his hand. It might look like a suicide at first glance and create some confusion. A hidden body would indicate that someone had killed the cop. He took a deep breath, got out, and limped over to the cop. The bullet had not gone through his body so he wasn't bleeding out of his back and onto the pavement. That gave Dan some hope he could set a realistic scene. Dan dragged to body back to the patrol car and, with some effort, got him back inside. He arranged his pistol in the man's hand, lying on his lap, where it would fall after shooting himself. The deception wouldn't survive a close scrutiny, but it would delay the conclusion that the cop was killed by another person.

He rubbed scuff marks out of the pavement as best he could and got back into the pickup. He had been fortunate that no other vehicles had come past while the encounter was being played out. Now it was time to go. He drove off. His leg was throbbing and had started to bleed again. He would need to attend to it soon.

Jane sat in her office staring at the phone for a full five minutes. *A leak. Where?* Finally she got up and started pulling the drawers out of her desk. She examined the tops of the drawer cavities and the underside of the frame. Next she grabbed a chair and placed it under the smoke detector. With a letter opener, she pried the cover off and checked the insides; no bugs. She looked around. There were so many places; it would take an expert a full day to scour the room. It could really only be done properly with electronic gear.

She sat back down. After a few minutes she got up and left her office for Henry's down the hall. She knocked on the door and received an invitation to enter.

"Henry, let's have a drink after work. I'm a bit fried and need someone to lean on while I decompress."

Henry gave her an odd look. Jane put a finger to her lips and picked up a sheet of paper from Henry's desk. She quickly wrote on it: *My office may be bugged, yours also. We need to talk off site.* Jane crumpled the note and put it in her pocket after Henry read it. He nodded.

"I'm free at 3 pm. Want to leave early?"

"That works," Jane replied. "See you in a couple of hours."

She turned and left the room.

Three hours later Jane and Henry were sitting in the Bethesda diner where they'd had coffee with Dan months ago.

"Why do you think our offices are bugged?" Henry asked after they had sat down.

"They're either bugged or one of my people is leaking information." Henry just looked at her quizzically. "Think about it. Someone had to give the cartel the exfiltration contact info. They most likely killed the men the embassy sent. They had the sat phone and they knew what the routine was going to be. Who knew that outside of you, my staff and whoever you told at the embassy?"

"The embassy is probably where the leak is," Henry replied.

"But who would have told them that this request was something important enough to kill for? The plan had to be divulged and the embassy didn't know what the plan was. They had no idea what was going on."

"What about your staff?"

"Fred and Warren. I picked them because they were outsiders here, misfits. This assignment let them join a small team and be a part of something where they could be comfortable. We're the outsiders, let's face it. They sensed that from the start and knew this assignment would be where they'd fit in. I can't imagine them being moles."

"Still, we should check them out."

"And if they clear, Warren can help us sweep the offices."

"I'll arrange a lie detector session as quietly as I can for each of them," Henry said.

"I'll work on the questions," Jane replied.

Chapter 39

Rodrigo looked at the burned out wreckage of the five trucks. The fire department had gone and the police were just finishing up. Rodrigo let them know clearly that he and his boss, Hector Ortega, now the head of the Sinaloa cartel, would take care of the incident. He had nothing to say to the police except they were to leave this to *Don* Hector.

When they were gone, Rodrigo put in a call to Hector.

"*Don* Hector, it's me, Rodrigo. I made it out of the desert. I'm the only one who did." He went on to explain to Hector how some of the men rebelled and walked off leaving him and Ramón alone with two other men and how the truck rolled down a hill and caught fire, killing everyone else. He explained that he walked back to the pickup the gringo had abandoned and managed to get the flat tire changed and drove out of the desert.

"Where is the pickup now?"

Rodrigo didn't answer. A panic began to rise in him.

"So where is the pickup? Does it have any weapons? Any evidence of who this gringo is?"

Hector was too interested in the truck which was on its way to Mexico City.

"It finally broke down, another flat tire. But I was close to the road by then and could walk until I got a ride."

He knew that if Hector went looking for the truck or the cop who stopped them was ever heard from, his story wouldn't hold up, but it would keep *Don* Hector satisfied for now.

"I found nothing in the truck to tell me who this man was. And he took his weapons with him. There was nothing left but gas cans and some rope." Rodrigo paused and then went on. "I called you to tell you that someone blew up the five trucks that were to take the terrorists to the border. The terrorists were in the trucks. They are all dead."

There was silence on the line, then an explosion of swearing and cursing.

"*Hijo de puta!*" Son of a bitch! Is it the gringo?"

"I don't think so. He couldn't have gotten out of the desert. I had a truck to drive. He would have had to walk all the way and there was no water."

"Maybe he had more water than you knew of."

"Maybe it was one of the other cartels." Rodrigo kept the suggestion vague as he didn't know how much progress *Don* Hector had made.

Ortega kept swearing but didn't directly answer. "What about Tariq?"

"He's here. He insists on meeting with you. He holds you responsible."

"What about Carlos?"

Rodrigo thought for a moment. Should he tell Don Hector or just let Carlos be missing for a while? The body would be found eventually and it would look bad for him then to not have told. But would he be here when that happened?

"Carlos is dead."

"What? How?"

"I caught him molesting my sister Miranda. He thought I was lost in the desert and decided to take her against her will. I caught him and killed him. I hope you understand, but I can't let him kidnap and rape my sister."

Hector didn't answer the implied question of honor but only said, "I'll be there later today. I want to see you at the warehouse."

He hung up the phone.

Rodrigo pondered his next move. Was it time to run and hide or should he play things out for a few days more? What advantage would it give him to wait any longer? Just then Tariq approached.

"Where is Hector? I want to talk to someone about this outrage." He pressed up close to Rodrigo. "My finest sixty men are dead. We stayed in this compound for weeks and what did it get us? All killed." His face was a mask of rage and hate. "You are valueless dogs. The next men I send here will be to kill you."

"Maybe I should kill you now. Then I won't have to worry about you."

"You kill me and you will have the vengeance of al Qaida on you, dog. But I don't want to talk to you. Where is Hector or Jorge? They are the ones who need to explain what happened."

"Jorge is dead, killed by a sniper. *Don* Hector is now in charge of the cartel."

Tariq stepped back. "Dead? That explains much."

"*Don* Hector had to get matters under control so civil war didn't break out among the cartels."

"He should have moved my men to the border right away. He wasn't able to protect them." Tariq turned away declaring, "He will have to pay for this."

Rodrigo didn't respond. He'd let Hector deal with the man. His phone rang.

"Hola," Rodrigo said.

"I'll be arriving at the airport by helicopter this afternoon at 2 pm. Meet me there with an armored car. Bring two." It was Hector. The phone went dead before Rodrigo could answer.

There were three armored SUVs in the warehouse compound. Rodrigo grabbed four guards and told them to be ready at 1 pm to drive to the airport.

"Take AKs and handguns. Bring extra magazines. We don't know how dangerous it is for *Don* Hector right now and nothing else bad can happen."

Henry made quiet arrangements to test Fred Burke, Jane's research assistant and Warren Thomas, her tech guy. They both passed the lie detector test. Afterward Fred, Warren, Jane and Henry met in the Bethesda diner.

Warren had a sour expression on his face. "I don't appreciate the fact that you didn't trust me. I could have faked out the machine for all you know, it can be done and I can do it, but I played it straight because I don't have anything to hide."

"Don't be offended," Henry said. "Everyone has to go through the test, you know that. And we seem to have a breach in confidentiality within our ranks."

"Now that we know you two aren't involved, I want you to sweep our offices for bugs," Jane said.

"Yours and mine and Fred's?" Warren asked.

"And Henry's," she said.

"If you find anything, identify it but don't disturb it. We don't want whoever is doing this to know we're on to them," Henry said. "If we remove the bugs, they'll just come back at us another way. Better to leave them in place and work around them."

"They get scraps for intel and we keep our dark secrets to ourselves," Fred said.

"You got it," Henry replied. "Whoever it is will catch on eventually, but we'll have time to try to identify them."

"What will you do when you find out?" Warren asked.

"That depends on who it is," Henry said. "Can you get some sweeping equipment without attracting too much attention?"

"I can purchase some good equipment on the market and won't have to go through office requisition. I do have some favors to call in over at tech, but you may not want me to use that route."

"You're right," Jane said. "Let's keep this as quiet as possible."

That afternoon Warren went into Arlington to an electronics store, essentially a covert device shop. He purchased a wide range radio frequency, or rf, scanner. He brought it with him to work the next day. Being a tech guy and a known geek, no one was surprised at any electronic equipment in his backpack.

"This will find most anything after you turn off all electronics in the room," he told Jane. "If we need more, we have to spend big bucks for a nonlinear junction detector."

"How much is big bucks?" Jane asked.

"Ten to twenty thousand," Warren replied.

"Let's see what we find with this," Jane said. "If we have to take the next step, we may have to take a chance and use the tech department here."

The sweeps took only a couple of hours. Warren found a bug in Jane's office and one in Henry's. The room where he and Fred worked was clean.

"I guess they don't think we're worth bugging," Fred said. "We don't rate."

"That's a good thing," Jane replied. "We can use your space to discuss critical issues.

Later Jane and Henry sat in Fred and Warren's office while the two men were at lunch.

"So who do you think it might be?" she asked.

"Don't know. I have a good sense of who it isn't. I don't think it's my boss Roger. He's on board with the program. Was so from the beginning and is now supportive, even with the blowup in Mexico."

"The DDO?"

"No. If Garrett wanted to shut us down, he'd just do it. No, it's someone who doesn't have enough rank, but doesn't like these black ops, especially the ones that go out and eliminate the bad guys. Someone who wants the CIA to be a tame organization, more politically correct and not in danger of having some congressional investigation uncover anything uncomfortable."

"That doesn't rule out a lot of people, unfortunately," Jane said.

"I'll talk to Roger. I don't think he'll like the fact that someone is intruding on his turf. He'll want to handle it quietly, but maybe the two of us can go through some possibilities."

"So how do we shut it down?"

"Depends on how much horsepower the person involved has. We don't want things to blow up in our face and we get 'outted'. That's as good as killing the program. It has to be clandestine."

Chapter 40

Rodrigo was nervous. He rode in the lead SUV. They drove out onto the airfield and up to the helicopter landing area. The two armored vehicles were there when Hector's chopper arrived. It was the same one Jorge and María had used, the Airbus H155. Rodrigo got out and held the rear door open for Don Hector as he emerged from the helicopter. Four other men got out. Rodrigo recognized only two of them. They were aides and bodyguards. They had worked for Jorge and now took orders from Hector. They were high up on the pecking order and one had to be careful not to mess with them or get on their bad side. Rodrigo's worry increased. Three of them got in the trailing SUV and one got in the front of the lead vehicle. Hector and Rodrigo sat in the back.

"You have let things go very wrong here," Hector said.

"*Don* Hector, *por favor*. I just got back from almost dying in the desert. Then I find Carlos is attacking my sister. I couldn't let that stand. She's my family. I had to protect her. If I didn't, I wouldn't be a man and no one would respect me."

Hector ignored his remark. They drove through the town and pulled into the warehouse compound. "When shit happens, you have to move quickly to stay ahead of it.

It is how you survive. You let the guards get lazy, since no one was in charge. You kill Carlos who had been filling in for you and then you don't immediately take over. Someone then gets into the warehouse compound and does this." Hector pointed to the burned wreckage of the trucks.

"I am sorry, *Don* Hector. I am now focused and will make sure nothing else goes wrong."

Hector looked over at Rodrigo with cold eyes. Rodrigo could sense Hector felt challenged on all fronts and he knew that Hector would be ruthless in making sure he eliminated any weaknesses.

"I know you will," Hector replied in a hard, cold voice. "I'm leaving Raúl here to help you. If I don't think you are up to the job, he will replace you."

Hector got out and the men followed him into the warehouse. Tariq tried to approach, but was shoved away.

"Hector Ortega, you have to talk to me. You are responsible for this," Tariq shouted as the men went into an inner room in the warehouse.

The door closed and Rodrigo spoke. "*Don* Hector, you don't have to do that. I will make things go smoothly. I did so in the past."

"You had me helping in the past. Now I have to work on bigger things and can't cover for any of your mistakes. You will do things right or Raúl will take over. You see what I have to deal with now? That is my final word on this."

"*Sí, Don* Hector."

"Now, who did this?"

Rodrigo didn't speak. He knew, but it wouldn't make sense to Hector and would only increase his suspicions of him. But what cartel could it be and how could they know about the terrorists?

"Can you speak?"

"I, I don't know. I guess it's a rival gang."

"But how would they know about the men at the warehouse?" Hector looked at Rodrigo. "We have a mystery here."

"But I know nothing of it since I just got back, almost from the dead."

"Yes, we will have to talk more about that. But for now we have to find out who did this? Who knew about the men waiting to go to the U.S.?" Hector got up. "I have to take care of this man, Tariq. I'll be back." He turned to leave the room.

Rodrigo was left with a sinking feeling in his gut and the unsympathetic stares from the four men who came with *Don* Hector.

Hector came out of the room and Tariq was on him immediately.

"You have ruined my plans. You will pay for this."

Hector looked at him. He wished he could have his men kill him right now, but that would end the drug connection.

"I am not at fault. *Don* Jorge was assassinated and I had to find out who did it to save us from a gang war."

"And someone got into your warehouse and blew up the trucks with my men in them. You had incompetent men protecting us. It is very much your fault."

"I am trying to find out who did this. Believe me, when I do, they will pay."

Tariq shook his head in disgust. "And will that bring my men back? Men I trained for months to do this job? You have set us back a year with your carelessness. I'm not sure we can do business with you again." He looked at Hector with his dark eyes filled with anger and hate.

"So you will go somewhere else with your plans?"

Tariq felt a stab of caution. He felt a trap. "No. We may have to do something completely different."

"I am the best one to receive your drugs. And you have been well paid for this first shipment."

"But you can't protect my men and get them smuggled into the U.S. That is something I want to accomplish as well. How can I trust you with more of my men when you have failed me now?"

Hector paused. Tariq could see he was holding back from what he wanted to say. Tariq had said the right thing and not provoked him. Hector's response was diplomatic.

"I can't do anything to replace these men, but I can make it up to you. I will pay you for your loss with the next drug shipment and I will make the changes to see to it that your men are moved quickly to the border after they arrive."

Tariq chose to not argue any more. He would decide later.

"I need to gather up the remains and give them a proper Islamic burial."

"If my men can help, let me know." Hector turned to go back inside.

"You will help me take them out into the desert to bury them properly, then take me back to Veracruz. I will fly home from there."

Hector waved his hand but didn't turn around. Inside the warehouse, he directed a man to help Tariq gather the remains.

"Rodrigo, you will dine with me tonight at Café Montenegro, downtown. We will talk in detail about your adventures in the desert and what you did to Carlos. I'm eager to hear all about these things. Then we'll go and find the pickup. I want to see it for myself, the truck the gringo used to outsmart us and get away from us."

"He is dead *Don* Hector. The desert has claimed him."

"I would be happier if I could see his dried up body for myself. Right now he is a ghost and I've lost fifteen men going after him, including Ramón."

Rodrigo knew the noose was tightening. "May I go home to change *Don* Hector? I have been sweating in these clothes all day."

"Be at the restaurant at 8."

Rodrigo nodded deeply and turned to go. He got into his Nissan and drove back to his house, watching to see if *Don* Hector had anyone follow him. When he pulled up to the house, he ran inside and collected his bag.

"Miranda, Solana. Come, we have to go now," he shouted.

The two came running downstairs with their suitcases.

"Wait here," Rodrigo said and ran upstairs to grab fifty grand in cash that was stuffed into a hole in the back wall of his closet. After retrieving the cash, he took his AK 47 and two extra magazines, his .45 automatic and ran back down the stairs. They went out to the car and put their bags in the trunk. Rodrigo slid the rifle under the bags and put his pistol on the floor under the driver's seat. With Miranda in the passenger seat and Solana in the rear, he set out for his aunt's house in Torreón.

Chapter 41

D an drove into the night but by midnight the pain in his leg forced him to stop. He pulled off at a truck stop. Really just a café with fuel pumps, primitive showers, and a large dirt lot where trucks could park. He found an inconspicuous spot away from the trucks. After checking to see that no one was about, he stretched out in the back seat and opened his pants. The leg was swollen and red but he saw no sign of infection traveling from the wound. He removed the bandage and poured another dose of antiseptic powder on the wounds. Then he applied a fresh clotting pad and wrapped his leg with the gauze bandage. He drank a whole bottle of water and sighed. Everything was now in danger. Would he be able to walk in tomorrow? How was he going to get into the mansion, kill Hector and get out with a bum leg? Dan cursed his luck. He didn't worry so much about being tracked by the police. There had been no camera in the car. After the police figured out it was not a suicide, they would not have any clues to follow. He locked his door and rolled up his jacket into a pillow. He needed rest. He lay back and his body slowly relaxed.

There were dreams of dark corridors. Dan was in a large building. He was chasing a woman who kept disappearing.

There were phantoms closing in around him. He couldn't catch the woman and he didn't know the way out. He limped slowly. The phantoms were surrounding him. He tried to force himself to go faster but his movements were in slow motion. He tried harder to move, to escape to no avail. Dan sat upright, jerked awake from his dream, panting. *Hope that isn't prophetic!*

Sunlight was shining through the windshield. The day was well along. He swore. It was going to take more time now to reach Mexico City. But he had to admit to himself that his body needed the rest after the previous day's activities. His leg hurt like hell but the throbbing was less intense. He pulled his pants down and checked his bandages. They looked good; there had not been much bleeding during his sleep. *Leave it alone for now.* He drank some water and dug through his backpack for a power bar.

There were showers advertised, but Dan didn't want to try that. *Better to not be seen here, on the road, with a wound. Don't want anyone to connect dots leading to me.* He drove around to the gas pumps. Oddly there was no attendant. It was a prepay station. He would have to go into the store to pay the gas. He walked slowly across the lot, trying hard to disguise his limp. There was a dark stain on his pants. Thankfully the clerk was watching the TV and Dan got up to the counter before he looked up. Dan gave him enough to more than fill the tank and paid for a cup of coffee. He took his time, messing with his coffee, while waiting for the clerk to turn back to the television. Once back at the truck he quickly filled the tank. Should he risk another walk into and out of the station to get his change? He had thirty-five pesos due, just over two bucks in dollars. *Leave it as a tip.* He got in the truck and drove off.

He was on pace to arrive in Mexico City by the afternoon. He would have to find a hotel and clean his wounds. The hotel would have to be one that didn't ask too many questions. Then he needed more rest, more time to recover. After, he would push ahead, getting ready and hoping his leg held out.

As he drove along he thought about Rodrigo. *Hope he knows when to bolt for cover.* If Hector Ortega put pressure on Rodrigo, his story would not hold up. The pickup would not be found and that would make Rodrigo more suspect. Hector would want some answers.

When Rodrigo didn't show up for dinner, Hector sent one of the local gang members to his house. The man soon returned to the restaurant.

"He is not there. No one is. The house is empty."

"You went in?"

"*Sí, Don* Hector. The door was unlocked. It looked like they packed clothes and left."

"Where did he go?"

The man shrugged his shoulders. "I don't know. Probably a relative, but I don't know who they are or where they live."

"Why would he run?"

"I don't know that either. I know he was in a battle with Carlos over control in Chihuahua—"

"He killed Carlos," Hector said.

"He ran for that reason?"

Hector ignored the question. "You will bring the men to the warehouse tomorrow. I want to talk to them." He dismissed the man with a wave.

"Something is wrong here. There is no violence from the other gangs, yet the trucks get blown up. Then Rodrigo runs off."

"Do you think he blew up the trucks?" Raúl asked.

"Maybe. Maybe one of the cartels got to him. Offered him a lot of money. Maybe one of them is behind the assassinations and Rodrigo was to sabotage the chase. Maybe that is why he survived."

"But it was a gringo who did the shooting," Raúl said.

"Maybe they hired a gringo so we would think it was the U.S. government."

Hector's mind swirled with the possibilities. He risked getting confused with the lack of hard information.

"Here is what we do," he said leaning forward. "Raúl, you remain here. You are now in charge. I will make that announcement tomorrow. Find someone who knows where Rodrigo might have gone. I'm going to send for a *sicario* from Mexico City. He will track Rodrigo down and kill him and anyone in his family."

"Who will you send?" Ramón asked.

"El Serpiente."

"Emilio?" Raúl shuddered at the thought. Emilio, also known as 'The Snake' because he was thin and deadly, was someone the gang members avoided. Darkness seemed to surround him. He would walk into a room and conversation would quickly die out. His dark countenance and black, beady eyes that seemed to target you more than look at you, made everyone around him uncomfortable. It didn't bother Emilio. He didn't get along with people and enjoyed working alone.

Hector continued, "When Emilio gets here make sure you have some information for him so he can go after Rodrigo. I don't want him to wait around. But first help Tariq do what he needs to do and get him out of here. Have someone take him to Veracruz. Don't respond to anything he says. He is still angry and wants to provoke a fight. I want him out of our hair. Things are quieting down here.

The police are leaving and the other gangs have not struck. Keep it that way and get the drugs moving through here again to the border. Purchase new trucks and modify them for the smuggling.

"I'm going back to Mexico City. I have to keep the other cartels from going to war with us. Hector Beltran-Leyva is on our side. I must make sure Escobedo and Chacón are as well. Then I have to convince the Tijuana and Los Zetas cartels not to go to war with us. If they know all the others are with me that will make them think twice."

The next day Hector made his announcement about Raúl being in charge. He included the fact that Rodrigo had run off and was responsible for the sabotage of the trucks. If anyone knew where he might have gone they were to tell Raúl so they could go find him and bring him and his family back for some bloody revenge. Then he headed for the airport with the three other men he had brought and flew back to Mexico City.

The four of them, Henry, Jane, Warren, and Fred were sitting in Fred and Warren's office.

"The bugs weren't too sophisticated and not all that well hidden," Warren declared. "Whoever it was, it wasn't a tech guy and he didn't use the company's resources." They were meeting in the room Warren shared with Fred.

"I'll go through the org structure to find possible candidates," Fred said. "That's not hard research to do."

"We're looking for someone without a lot of horsepower to authorize this," Henry said. "Someone who has to do it on his own. Can you get a read on their views from the files? We want someone who wants the company to follow a safe, non-controversial path."

"I can get a feel from the records. It's not exact, but it will give you a starting point," Fred replied.

"Good."

Jane spoke up. "Do you think you should let Roger know? His office may be bugged as well."

Henry thought for a moment. "I may let Roger know, just to keep him in the loop. He won't like it. But I doubt whoever did this bugged his office. Being the SAD, Roger's further up the ladder."

"Still he ought to check," Jane said.

"Agreed. In the meantime our 'recorded' communications will consist of the fact that we don't know where Dan is and we don't know what he's up to. We have to look like we don't have any connection to him at this time. That should lower their interest in us. If they think this operation has gone off the rails since the exfiltration was sabotaged, it might make whoever did this think they won the day."

"I still wonder how the exfiltration plan got to the cartel." Jane said.

"Maybe our eavesdropper has a drug gang connection in the embassy. They hire locals for some work. Maybe the DEA got involved and didn't want things upset."

"So why didn't they stop it ahead of time?"

"They didn't know about it then? Maybe stopping Dan's exit was all they could do. The plan might have been to capture him. After that they would torture him to reveal our operation which would have led to us getting cancelled."

"So they could shut things down even after Dan completed his operation."

"And with that information, the gangs wouldn't go to war with one another."

"With Ortega taking over, their plan is working even without Dan's capture. His blowing up the terrorists won't have that much of an effect. But if he can take out Ortega, that would cause major chaos to erupt."

"That's a big 'if'. I think he's on a suicide mission." Henry said.

Jane frowned. "I hope not, but it sounds foolhardy," she replied. "But if anyone can pull this off it will be him."

Rodrigo called before he arrived at their aunt's house. She had some food prepared and beds set up. Solana ate and quickly went upstairs to go to sleep.

"Why are you here?" Milagros asked. She lived alone. Her husband had died two years ago in an industrial accident. She had two grown children, both married. One had moved to Veracruz and the other still lived in Saltillo.

"There are some bad men that will be coming after me soon. They will kill me, Miranda, and Solana if they find us," Rodrigo said.

"They won't find you here?"

"Not for a while. We'll be gone in a few days. I have to make arrangements."

Milagros stood up and began to pace the room. "If they come...these bad men, they will kill me along with the three of you. Even if you are gone, they will kill me if they find I hid you here."

"No they won't," Rodrigo replied.

"So you say, but they are gang members, no?"

"*Sí*, gang members." Rodrigo hung his head. "They will think I have betrayed them."

"So they will seek revenge, if not on you, then anyone near you. That means family."

"I am sorry *Tía* Milagros. We had nowhere else to go in a hurry."

"But you now need to find somewhere else. Somewhere that doesn't put me in danger."

"*Tía* Milagros may we stay the night at least?" Miranda asked.

The older woman looked at her niece with sad eyes. "*Sí.* It may be dangerous, but stay and rest. Think about where to hide and then you must go in the morning."

In the morning they discussed where to go.

"Try Saltillo. It's a larger town and you can easily hide there," Milagros said.

"Maybe we should go to Monterrey. It's even larger," Miranda said.

Rodrigo nodded his head. "It also has an airport. We'll go there."

After a quick breakfast, they put their bags in the Nissan and hugged Milagros goodbye.

"Hide well. Make sure nothing happens to Solana."

Chapter 42

When Hector arrived at the mansion he went to Jorge's quarters to clean up and change clothes. He had moved his clothes in when he took up residence. Then he went to María's wing. He knocked on the door to her suite of rooms.

"*Adelante,*" Come in, a woman's voice said.

Hector opened the door and stepped into the room. María was at her desk going through papers. When he entered she closed the folder and looked up at him.

"Eduardo, my attorney, left some papers for me to look at."

"Do they have anything to do with cartel business? If they do, I should review them."

There was a small hesitation before she replied, "No. I think they are all personal things."

"Still it might be a good idea for me to review them as well."

María smiled at Hector. "What brings you to my room?"

"We have things we must do together. Things that are important to keep the cartel together and protect you and the children."

"What sort of things, *Don* Hector?"

He smiled at the honorific she gave him. "The assistant to the Sinaloa president is coming to see me. He should see you by my side so he knows that I have your blessing to take over leadership. He flies in tomorrow and will be here at noon. We must have a nice lunch for him."

"And my being with you will make him feel everything is fine?"

"As much as it can. Everyone is nervous, including the politicians. The more quickly we can establish we are in control, the sooner we can calm things down."

"I don't know that my presence will have any effect on him. I suspect it is more what you say and do."

"We must maintain an image of control and succession. Our leader has passed and you are showing support for the new leader."

"Can you lead the cartel? I know you did much to help Jorge, but can you lead it by yourself?"

"Don't worry about that. For one, there is no one else. For another I know how everything works. If I have your support, it will keep others from challenging me. A revolt will not be good for you or your children."

"How long do you want me in this role?"

María posed the question with some dread in her heart. She sensed Hector wanted so much more and she was beginning to feel trapped. She had felt that way with Jorge, but he doted on the children. He loved them and wanted only the best. He wanted María, also, as a glamorous prop and for some sex now and then. But he spent so much time with his mistresses and the prostitutes that she felt abandoned. He must have enjoyed their wilder tastes, certainly when he was drinking and taking the drugs. With his sudden, shocking death, María had begun to think about getting away from the mansion, the cartel, the life, but now Hector had put his claim on her. Had she lost the opportunity? Eduardo, the family attorney had been encouraging at the start, but now he was more reluctant and not very optimistic.

"That depends on how well we work together. My desire is to protect you and to keep the cartel intact and dominant. That means much money for you and your children going forward. You may not have much for your own right now, but if you stay with me, I will make sure you have millions for yourself and the kids. You will live in luxury the rest of your life."

María smiled yet her heart sank. *He wants me for his woman.*

"I will be there tomorrow for your meeting with the president's assistant. I will smile and be supportive."

"Good. This will all work out well. You will find greater security and wealth for yourself with me. Your fortune will not be mixed with your husband's. That is your current problem. Your husband's wealth is going to be reabsorbed into the cartel."

María frowned.

"But don't worry. Stay with me, help me, and I will make you personally wealthy."

María nodded to say she understood. Hector stood. He looked like he wanted to say more. She hoped he wouldn't. Finally he turned to go.

"Thank you," he said on leaving.

The next day Alejandro Pérez, the Sinaloa president's assistant, arrived at the mansion. He came in two armored SUVs with two aides and four heavily armed bodyguards. Hector met them at the front door with María at his side. Everyone was ushered into a reception room. The bodyguards were posted outside and the president's assistant, his aides, Hector, and María sat in comfortable leather chairs. Drinks were served and Hector offered a toast.

"Here's to our continued cooperation to keep things peaceful and keep the prosperity going."

"To peace and prosperity. A good campaign slogan if I ever heard one," Alejandro said.

"The president has an election coming soon, doesn't he?" María asked.

"In the fall," Pérez said.

"Let me know what you need for resources," Hector said. "I know *Don* Jorge was generous and I want to continue the same way."

"That is good to know, *Don* Hector."

The small talk continued until a servant informed them lunch was ready. It was a sumptuous affair with champagne, fresh iced shrimp, carved duck, and small filets of beef. Brandied peaches, vodka infused pineapple and fresh fruits along with imported chocolates finished the meal.

"So you are taking over the mansion?" Alejandro Pérez asked.

"It is important for everyone to see continuity in our leadership. María was gracious enough to invite me to set up my residence and office here."

Alejandro looked over at María who smiled back at him. "I am sorry about what happened to *Don* Jorge. He was a great friend to us and was trying to make the business work without so much violence. Now he was the victim of it." He was not sure about Ortega and wondered if this whole lunch was a false show of strength.

"Thank you for your concern, *Señor* Pérez. I know my husband was in a dangerous business that sometimes got violent, but he always sought a better, smoother way."

"And that is what I am going to work for as well. It is the least I can do...carry on *Don* Jorge's work." Hector declared.

"And so you support *Don* Hector in this?" Alejandro asked. He looked closely at her, measuring her response.

"Yes I do," María smiled again.

Alejandro smiled back. The woman put up a brave front but something in her voice betrayed her. Still if she was a willing supporter of Hector, it would help him maintain control. That was the important thing for him and his boss: maintain control, which would keep the violence down and the money flowing.

After the lunch, Hector and Alejandro moved into a small smoking room while María excused herself, and the aides went off to relax in the living room.

"Can you control the other cartels *Don* Hector?" Alejandro asked when they were alone.

"I can but I also need you to do your part."

"What is that?"

"What you did for Jorge. I need you to help us and keep pressure on the other cartels that try to operate in your state."

"And the arrangements? They will continue?"

"Yes. I have the details in Jorge's books. You and your men will be paid as always. Just keep them in line. Don't let them try to double cross me or try to find a better deal. I will be ruthless when it comes to challenges. I can't afford any right now so there will be little warning if someone crosses me."

"No one will cross you. Just keep everyone happy."

"We have an understanding. But remember, you have to keep any investigations by the *Centro de Investigación y Seguridad Nacional* or *Policía Federal* under control."

The meeting ended by three in the afternoon. Hector and María saw the convoy off at the front door.

Hector turned to María. "You did a good job. He is satisfied that things will go smoothly and I warned him of dire consequences if his people don't obey orders." He reached up and stroked her cheek. "It was nice to have you with me and to hear you voice your support. I hope you mean it."

"You will keep things together. I am grateful for that."

"Remember, I'll do more than that. As we go along, if things go well, you will become a very wealthy woman. I'll see to it."

She smiled at him. "I must go see to the children now. They are done with the tutors."

María turned to go. She could feel Hector's eyes on her as walked down the corridor. How soon would he be coming around to her bed? A chill ran through her body.

Dan arrived in Mexico City at 4:30 in the afternoon. His leg had started to bleed again. There was no way to elevate it to relieve the throbbing pain. He wanted to go to the Lomas de Chapultepec neighborhood where Rodrigo had said Jorge's mansion was located. But when he got to the neighborhood he realized his dirty and battered pickup stood out in an uncomfortable way with all the new, expensive cars on the street. He made a quick decision and turned away from the area. He couldn't risk attracting unwanted attention from the police which he surely would have done by cruising the streets. Dan had the address and knew where the neighborhood was. He would scout it later. What he needed to do now was find a place to stay and take care of his wound. He turned and headed back towards the central part of the city, slogging his way through the traffic.

Chapter 43

Dan found a cheap hotel at the edge of the *Doctores* neighborhood, near *Roma Sur*. It was an area that tourists avoided and prices were cheap. Not a lot of questions would be asked and he wouldn't attract any undue attention. In short, it was perfect for his needs. He was happy to finally be out of the traffic and out of the truck.

The lobby was old and tired. The desk clerk looked bored. Dan limped up to the counter hoping the clerk would not notice the blood stain on his pants. He paid for a week's stay in cash. After registering, he got directions to a garage where he could rent a space for the pickup on a weekly or monthly basis. Dan climbed the stairs and limped to his room.

He dropped his bags on the floor and lay down on the bed. It was a relief to get his leg elevated. He lay still, letting the throbbing slowly subside. *Just like to lay here for ten hours.* He allowed twenty minutes and then made himself get up. After checking the bandage, he limped back down the stairs and drove to the garage. There he paid for a week of parking and left the truck in the garage.

It was a three block walk back to the hotel. Dan was exhausted when he got back to his room. He stripped off his clothes and took off the bandage. The wounds looked angry. There was red around the entrance and exit holes. He wasn't sure it was infected; there were no threads of red running from the damaged tissue. Could he risk cleaning the leg in the shower? Or were there bacteria in the water that would infect the injury? Dan knew the water system in Mexico City was not the cleanest. He lay back on the bed. *I have to go out and find some more supplies.*

Dan needed more bandages, more gauze wrapping, antiseptic, clotting pads and something to wrap his leg that would strengthen it for the work to come. *But first I need to rest.* He relaxed. He would go out in a half an hour.

An hour later Dan jerked awake. *Damn. Got to get moving.* He got up and put the last of his bandage supplies on his wounds, got dressed and went down to the check in counter. The clerk gave him directions to a pharmacy that carried medical supplies and Dan gave him a five dollar bill. *Want to keep him happy.*

Dan limped out to the street and looked for a taxi. The street was crowded with locals; not many tourists went to this part of the city. Most people ignored him. A few touts were shouting out the attractions in front of the shops that employed them, trying to get anyone passing by to stop and enter. He finally was able to flag down a cab and gave the driver the address.

At the pharmacy Dan found all the supplies he needed. They didn't have any clotting pads but the antiseptic powder would help the wound to clot. Dan hoped time would be on his side and he would have less of a problem with the bleeding by tomorrow.

Back at the hotel, he stripped again and this time got into the shower. The water pressure was not very good, but the water was warm. He let the water run over him, flushing away the dirt and grime from the last few days.

He felt weariness in his body, deep in his bones, something he had never felt before. *Am I getting old?* The thought rose in his mind and he laughed out loud. *Of course you are. Everyone is from the day we are conceived. We get older and older.*

He stepped out, toweled off, and, with the towel under his leg, poured a liberal dose of hydrogen peroxide on the wounds. It burned and foamed but Dan knew it was doing its work. When he was satisfied, he lay back on the bed, naked. *The question is, are you too old? Not finished with your first mission and you're already feeling old and worn out?* He stretched. *Fuck it. I'm just tired...and wounded.* He put his hands behind his head and began to think about this final part of his mission as he started to relax.

When he awoke it was dark. He was thirsty and hungry. There were only two bottles of water left in his pack. Dan drank them both. Now he needed food. He put new bandages on his wounds. They still were red, but the throbbing was gone. *Probably start again when I start walking.* He went downstairs and into the street. Within a block were four vendors selling food. Dan stopped at the one that smelled the best and ordered two meat and cheese burritos. The vendor had bottled water and Dan purchased six bottles from him.

His hunger satiated, he looked around. He would have liked to walk the streets but his leg had already started to throb again. He needed to blend in with the city; he needed some new clothes. The dusty, dirty clothes he was wearing would stand out. He needed a car as well, something nice to blend into Mendoza's neighborhood. *Tomorrow.* Tonight he needed to just sleep. He walked back to the hotel favoring his wounded leg.

His rental of an upscale BMW sedan raised some eyebrows due to his disreputable clothes but his money convinced the agent. The car was clean, modern, and didn't look overtly like a rental. Just the sort of nice vehicle one would find in Jorge's neighborhood. He paid cash and had to put a thousand dollar deposit against damages. *Wonder if I'll see that back?* He drove the BMW back to the hotel and arranged to park it in their short driveway. The car leant some upscale ambience to the place so the clerk allowed it was okay to park in the drive. The extra fifty-dollar bill didn't hurt to convince him either.

Next Dan took a cab to *Centro Histórico,* a neighborhood full of tourists and shopping. He found a men's clothing store and purchased two new pairs of slacks, a pair of sturdy shoes to replace his boots, and four casual collared shirts. He looked properly business casual. He could be a salesman or a security analyst and would fit in around the *Lomas de Chapultepec* neighborhood. He had shed the look of the desert and now blended into Mexico City. After getting dressed in his new clothes, Dan hailed a cab to take him to the *Tepito* district. Here he wanted to purchase some tactical clothing for his mission and replace his soiled desert gear.

Tepito was almost a city unto itself. Many of the streets were covered over with canopies reaching out from either side to meet in the middle. Vendors shouted out their wares, touts proclaimed the delights of various bars and sex parlors. The stalls were filled with an abundance of clothes and shoes, all from China and other places in the Far East and probably all smuggled into the country. You could purchase anything including weapons. Dan knew the gangs did some of their purchasing here. The police patrolled the neighborhood but didn't intrude on the illegal trade. They only kept public disturbances under control.

He moved along the narrow, canopy covered streets with people jostling him. The odors from the many vendors competed with each other to fill the air with an exotic mix of cooking aromas. His senses were overwhelmed by the assault of the sounds and sights. He made multiple inquiries as he walked the labyrinth of streets. His questions were met with suspicion and no information. He was wandering, still asking where he could find some special clothing, when a large man came up to him and asked him what he was doing there.

"I need some tactical clothing for an expedition," Dan answered in Spanish.

"What kind of expedition?" the man asked.

"That is not important for you to know. I am not with any government or *policía*."

The man looked at him. Dan stared back, confident in his abilities, not afraid, even with his wounded leg. Maybe the man recognized something familiar in Dan, someone who knew how to operate outside of the law. He nodded.

"Follow me," he said.

He led Dan through a back alley to a shop that was filled with tactical and camping gear including knives and other weapons, everything short of firearms. No one walking the streets would have found the shop, only those directed to it or with advance knowledge of its location. He purchased some black tactical pants, black shirt, sweater, and knit facemask and two twenty-liter plastic jugs. After leaving the store, he found an electronics shop and purchased two more burner phones and a coil of 12-volt wire.

Dan exited the warren of awning covered streets into the sunlight. It was still crowded, he was still in the Tepito district, but he felt he could breathe easier now that he was out in the open. He walked along, weaving through the people. No one made eye contact. They were all in their own private spaces as people do when they are in dense urban environments. The occasional tout would try to catch his eye with a shouted phrase or shaking some piece of merchandise in his direction. Dan just did as the others, avoid eye contact with them, and not change his pace. The buskers, playing their instruments, added music to the sound track of the scene. Dan stopped to drop a ten-dollar bill into the violin case of one particularly talented young man.

His limp increased as he walked towards the wider streets where he hoped to catch a cab. He continually scanned the crowd out of cautious habit. No one looked back but he registered most of the faces as he limped along. Then his eyes passed over an old woman. She was standing across the street from him. Her stare halted his scanning. She was looking straight at him. Not just looking but seeming to see *into* him. Her eyes were intense. They were dark, almost black, but they shone like they were lit on fire. He had the uneasy feeling she knew who he was and why he was in Mexico City.

When she had Dan's attention, she dipped her head slightly and started walking. She was only about five feet tall, wrapped in a shawl over a dark skirt. The shawl covered her black hair. She had the prominent, sloped Mayan nose barely mixed with Indian traits and without any trace of the conquistador's blood in her. Dan could not take his eyes off of her. He watched the woman shuffle down the street. Dan walked forward, in the same direction but on the opposite side of the street. She stopped occasionally to look back, directly at him, as if to make sure he was following. After a block and a half, she stopped at a narrow alley and turned to look at him. When their eyes locked, she nodded to him and stepped into the alleyway. The gesture seemed to be an invitation.

He walked forward until he was across from the alley. It was narrow and dark. Not inviting after the sunshine of the larger streets. He could see the woman walking slowly with her stooped shoulders. Did she know who he was? She acted as though she did. He paused. She had deliberately made eye contact with him in a way that was clearly purposeful and now seemed to be inviting him to follow her. To what end?

His mind jumped between caution and intrigue. So many strange things had happened to him in Mexico, but he couldn't deny the events. They had saved his life; they were too real to dismiss. Was this another encounter he should experience, or a trap? Then Dan remembered. Tlayolotl had spoken of an old woman in Mexico City who would help—a Watcher like himself. Dan crossed the street and followed after her.

Entering the alley, he was immediately in deep shadows from the buildings. It took his eyes a second or two to adjust before he could see the woman. He was on high alert. The alley was confining and there were so many places for an ambush. The woman stopped at a door and turned again to him. Her eyes were just as fierce in the dark shade as they were in the sunlight. They focused directly on him. Then she turned and entered the door and disappeared.

Dan paused at the entrance. Should he go in? He'd already gone down a rabbit hole out in the desert and found Tlayolotl. Was this more of the same? There was no one who could give away his mission except Rodrigo and he was probably on the run by now. Besides, Rodrigo wouldn't know where Dan would be in the city. Dan hadn't given away any of his plans; in fact he didn't have any formed when he left for Mexico City. How did anyone know where he was? Was this the woman Tlayolotl had spoken of? There was only one way to find out; Dan opened the door and pushed into the dark room.

He stood still as his eyes adjusted to the even dimmer light in the room. It was square, about twelve feet by twelve feet. There was a wooden floor that creaked as he shifted his weight. At the back was a hallway leading further into the building, to what, Dan had no idea. There were no windows facing out onto the street. The woman sat in a chair at a table in the far right corner of the room. The small overhead light on the ceiling cast a dim glow in the room and left dark shadows in the corners, but Dan could see the woman. Up close her gaze was even more penetrating than it had been on the street. It was as though she was looking through him. She motioned for him to come over and sit down.

"Sit here. I want to talk to you."

Her Spanish sounded odd, difficult to understand. Her dark eyes continued to burn into him. They were black as midnight and seemed to glow. He went across the room and sat down opposite her on a wooden chair. There was an uncomfortable silence between them.

Finally he asked, "Do you know me?"

"I know who you are."

"How did you find me?"

"I knew when you came into the city. After, I searched and found you."

"But here? How did you know I'd be here, on this street?"

"You ask many questions. Questions not needed."

"Did Tlayolotl tell you?"

She ignored his last question.

"I know why you are here. You are to strike deep into the darkness and shatter it. This is what is important. Pay attention."

Dan nodded and didn't speak.

"I am a Watcher, like Tlayolotl. I saw the darkness grow here in Mexico City. It is centered at the mansion. The man who took over the mansion wants to increase the dark and overcome what you did in the desert of Chihuahua. Your strike here will defeat him."

"So I'll be successful?"

She didn't answer him.

"How many of you are there?"

The woman continued to look at him without answering.

"I mean 'Watchers'. How many of them are there?"

"Still the questions that do not matter."

"It matters to me. Tlayolotl helped me. But are there Watchers who will try to stop me? Will I have to look out for them?"

"We are many. We are all over the world. Wherever you go some will find you...to help you. This is what you must understand so you can trust and use the help to fight the darkness. Your battles are important to many."

"But what about those who may try to stop me? Do I have to worry about them?"

"They exist, but they are afraid of you. You have been given a gift. From Tlayolotl. It will protect you."

Dan shook his head. "I don't know of any gift from Tlayolotl except that he saved my life and I must do this for him."

"You have it. You must learn how to find it so it can protect you."

"How?"

"Turn off the noise in your mind." She reached out to him. "Give me your hand," she commanded.

Dan held out his right hand. She grabbed it. Her hard, calloused fingers closed pressing her palm to his and her other hand covered the back. Her grip was vise-like. She closed her eyes.

After a minute she spoke. "You have much strength within you. You will have to draw on all of it. You will have to be smart. The darkness will not yield easily, but you are stronger."

She paused, and then opened her eyes. "You are injured. Your leg is damaged." She released his hand. "Show me your wounds."

Dan hesitated but finally unbuckled his belt and lowered his pants. He turned sideways as the old woman came around the table. She looked at the bullet wound. She made him twist around in the chair so she could see the larger exit hole.

"It is angry. Infection is ready to break out and flow through your body. We must stop it now."

She got up and disappeared down the hallway at the back of the room. Dan sat there with his pants part way down, feeling both foolish and apprehensive. Two minutes later the woman returned with clean bandage cloth and a bowl of some green paste.

"This will kill the infection so it cannot attack you. I will unwrap your bandage and put this paste on the wounds. Then I will sew them closed. The leg will be sore, but it will not get bad with infection."

She began to work without waiting for Dan to reply. He started to resist and then relaxed. If the salve was anything like what Tlayolotl had applied, it would be effective. When she was done applying the paste she took out a needle and thread that had been wrapped in the cloth.

"You are ready?" She asked.

Dan nodded.

He gritted his teeth and grunted as the woman began to sew the flesh together. She offered no sympathy or any relief. She just attended to her sewing. He was sweating profusely by the time she was finished. She wrapped the clean cloth around the leg and bound it tightly. Picking up the bowl, she disappeared down the back hallway. In less than a minute she returned with a cup of liquid.

"Drink this. It gives you strength and relief from the pain."

"No drugs," Dan said.

"Not drugs. Strength herbs."

Dan swallowed the bitter liquid and sat back. Within a minute he felt energy flowing through his body. The pain was still intense in his leg, but it didn't feel debilitating. Still needing some specific help for his task, he looked at the old woman.

"How will I know when Hector Ortega is at the mansion?"

She had sat back down on the other side of the table. "He is there now. From his actions he will be there for many days. When I am strong enough I can see into the dark. And when I look I can see he will do his work from this place. He wants to make the woman his own but you can change that."

"Is there a way into the mansion?"

"Go through the trees."

"Is the mansion guarded?"

"Always, but use your skills. Observe and choose wisely."

"So I will be successful?" Dan asked again.

The woman shrugged and looked at him, now with softer eyes, eyes that showed her concern, as if he were someone embarking on a dangerous, perhaps fatal mission.

"It is not for me to say." She turned from him, indicating he should go.

Back on the streets Dan marveled at the odd world he had entered. He could never in a million years have dreamed of these encounters now happening to him yet they had saved his life. Life truly was more complex than he had ever thought it to be. There were Watchers, all over the world. They would help him. He had a gift from Tlayolotl, but he didn't know what it was and had to discover it...somehow. It was all so strange. Could he ever explain this to Jane? She was a part of this drama. And when he asked about his chances, the old woman had looked at him with sad eyes, like he was a doomed participant in what was going to be played out. Tlayolotl said she could see the future. What did she see? She had given him some good information but left him with a sense of foreboding. He found a cab and sank back in the seat as they headed back to his hotel.

Chapter 44

The next day Dan drove back to the *Lomas de Chapultepec* neighborhood. He had the street address for Mendoza's mansion and quickly located it. The front entrance was impregnable with a ten-foot high wall and a stout, sculpted steel gate complete with a guard just as Rodrigo had described. He kept going past it and turned left at the next corner. At the next intersection, he made another left turn and was now on a street paralleling the back of the mansion's lot. The lot seemed to be about four acres in size and backed up to a natural drainage area that was preserved in its semi-wooded state. It was a good hundred yards wide and ran beside the road he was on. The drainage preserve ran for a mile with the cross roads going over it on bridges.

I can park blocks away and hike to the back of the lot. That will make it easier to leave the area unseen...if I can get out. He tried to keep his thoughts professional and focused on planning the mission but dark thoughts kept intruding. The old woman had spooked him.

When he thought he was across from the back of the property, Dan parked along the road and, after a careful look around, climbed over the fence and disappeared into the wooded area. It was easy terrain to navigate with enough cover to protect him from being seen from the road. Hopefully the cover would hold right up to the property line. He limped, favoring his wounded leg. It was painful but worked. The drainage preserve was a natural swale. Dan went down and across it. On the other side the ground gently rose. The cover held right up to the fence at the back of the mansion. It was tall and made of chain link topped with razor wire. The ground inside was mowed and continued to slope upward before it flattened out into an expansive lawn with strategically planted trees and shrubbery. The effect was not quite a garden. It was more English than French. It looked natural but was enhanced somehow. It mimicked nature but accentuated some of the views.

More importantly, Dan took note of concealment opportunities on the approach to the house. In the middle of the grounds was a fully cleared circle with close cropped grass and ground lights surrounding it; a helipad. Dan took out his binoculars and studied the grounds and mansion. He examined the fence and found no electrical wire triggers present. He would use a bolt cutter on the links. Getting through it would not be a problem. At the back of the mansion was a courtyard, created by two wings sticking out to the rear from the main house. There were double doors leading out to the stone patio.

The doors will be alarmed. I may need to cut out a windowpane. He couldn't see any perches for rooftop lookouts, at least in the back. If there were any facing the front they would not be a problem. It seemed as he examined the property that Mendoza worried more about an assault from the front than from a stealthy intrusion from the rear. That made getting in easier. However, getting out would be an added challenge.

Rodrigo, Miranda and Solana had left their aunt's house right after breakfast. As soon as they were gone, Milagros called her son and informed him she was going away for two weeks and couldn't tell him where. Next she called her daughter who still lived in Saltillo. Milagros told her that she must also leave town for a week. When asked why, Milagros said gang members might be coming to town and they were after her uncle, Rodrigo. Milagros added that they would be brutal and would take their revenge on her as well as Rodrigo.

Milagros was packing her bag when there was a knock on her door. Her heart leapt in her chest. *Who would that be? Could the cartel have found me so soon?* She looked around in a panic but there was no place to go. Another knock came, this time harder, more insistent. Milagros ran to the kitchen and grabbed a large knife. Just then the door burst open.

A thin, dark man stepped in with his gun drawn. His dark eyes scanned the room and focused on Milagros, off in the kitchen, back against the wall with the knife held in front of her. He smiled. It was an evil smile with no warmth in it.

"You were expecting me?" he asked.

Milagros just stood there, unable to speak, her breath coming in gasps.

The man noticed her bag on the floor. "You were going somewhere?" He stepped into the kitchen. "Where were you going?

"Who are you?"

"They call me 'El Serpentino' but the name is not important. I think you know what I am. Do you have something to tell me?"

Milagros just shook her head.

"Ah, I think you do. And I think you will. The question for you is how quickly you will tell me."

"I don't know what you want. Please don't hurt me," she whimpered.

"You do know what I want. And I *will* hurt you if you don't tell me. I can hurt you so much you will beg to tell me everything."

"No, no, please—"

The man stepped closer.

"I'll stab you. Don't come any closer," Milagros said, now in a more forceful voice.

Again the man smiled. He fired a shot that hit the counter just next to Milagros. She flinched and in that instant he was on her, grabbing her wrist and wrenching the knife from her grasp.

"Sit down," he commanded, pointing to the kitchen table.

She sat down.

"You are Rodrigo's aunt. Don't deny it. I know he was here. Now you tell me where he went and it will go well for you."

"How do you know he was here?"

"The men in Chihuahua City spoke of you. He's run away after selling out his brothers. He would come here for help."

"He wasn't here," she protested.

The man leaned forward, putting his face close to hers. "I will cut you to pieces, slowly, if you don't tell me. Do you want to die like that?"

Milagros couldn't answer. She just shook her head.

"Then tell me," he shouted.

She shook her head again.

"You have a daughter."

Milagros looked up at him with her eyes wide with fear.

"Yes, I know about her, and her brother. If you don't tell me you will not only die painfully, but so will your son and daughter. I will leave no one alive in your family." Again he leaned close to her. "Do you understand me?"

"Are you going to kill us all?"

"If you tell me, your children will live...and it will be better for you."

Milagros slumped in her chair. "You won't touch my children if I tell you?"

"You have my word."

"Can I trust you," she asked looking up at him. "Will you keep your word?"

"You can trust me. If you don't tell me it will only be worse."

Milagros sighed, "He has gone to Monterrey."

"Where?"

"I don't know." She looked at the assassin with pleading eyes. "I truly don't know. I don't think he knew. But he felt it safer to hide in a bigger city."

The man smiled and stepped back.

"So you will not kill my family? Not kill me?"

"I will spare your son and daughter. And it will be better for you now that you have told me." He brought his gun up and pointed it at her face. "You will not feel pain like I have made others feel." With that he shot her in the head. She was dead before any pain could register.

The man turned and went out through the broken front door. He felt he had made it better for her.

In two hours Rodrigo, his sister and niece were in Monterrey and had found a small hotel on a side street. It was anonymous. If the gang managed to follow him this far, it would still be a challenge to find them. After checking in, Rodrigo bought a burner cell phone and called the number Dan had given him.

"Who's this," a woman said on answering the phone.

"Rodrigo. I'm a friend of Steve's. He told me to call you."

Jane paused for a moment before she realized Rodrigo was using Dan's alias.

"He said you would arrange a trip for me and my family."

"Yes. I can and will. Where are you located?"

"Near San Luis Potosi." Rodrigo used a city that was not too far from Monterrey.

"Okay, I'll make arrangements and call you back. Give me the full names of you and your family."

"Not on your phone. Dan said it might have been compromised. You should buy a burner and then call me back on this number. Call me tomorrow morning."

With that he hung up.

Jane sat there thinking. Dan had counseled Rodrigo. He didn't trust Jane's phone. She was now unsure herself since they had found bugs in her office. She got up and put on her jacket. She would purchase a burner phone that afternoon.

After watching for two hours, Dan satisfied himself that, at least during the day, there were no patrols around the mansion. He hiked back across the preserve and, after checking the street, climbed the fence and got into the BMW.

As he drove back to the *Doctores* neighborhood, he got caught up in the city's infamous traffic jams. Cars milled about switching lanes, blocking intersections while the police tried to keep order. Horns honked incessantly and the exhaust fumes filled the air. Dan was glad the air conditioning worked in the BMW but still he could smell the pollution.

When he reached the neighborhood, he had to drive around for some time, still in heavy traffic, but he finally found a store that sold glass cutters and suction cup handles. With this final purchase, Dan headed back to his hotel, happy to be done with the intense traffic.

Back in his room, he lay on his bed and reviewed what he knew. If he could believe the old woman, Ortega was at the mansion. He could get on the grounds through the drainage area at the rear and, if he got lucky, there would be no night foot patrols. That was something he'd have to check on. He would take out any guards he found on the inside with his suppressed weapons. Once he had found Ortega and killed him, he would plant the explosives spread the gasoline.

He had the two extra bricks of C-4 and igniters that Rodrigo had procured in Chihuahua. He had anticipated needing the extra explosives for this part of the mission. The bricks would be planted in different parts of the mansion to weaken it. They would ignite the gasoline and a conflagration would erupt gutting the house before any fire equipment could arrive. He would escape out the back and travel through the drainage preserve to his car. After stashing his weapons and tactical clothes in the trunk he would drive back to his hotel in his good clothes. That night he would leave and put some miles between him and Mexico City. No one would be looking for a gringo; they would assume it was the work of a rival gang.

Sounds so easy thinking about it. Forget it, everything you do sounds easy but is hard and dangerous in reality. He got up and went to the bathroom to splash water on his face. *It's what you signed up for.* After putting his gear away, he got up and went out to get something to eat.

Reconnoiter tonight and then do the mission tomorrow night.

At midnight Dan set out for Mendoza's neighborhood. He drove down the road bordering the preserve and went past the position of the mansion for another half mile where he found a corner grocery mart that was closed and had a small parking lot. He could park the car here for the scouting tonight and perhaps for the operation tomorrow.

There was a gap in the fence where it butted up against a bridge going over the swale. Dan was able to slip off his pack and squeeze through without cutting any fencing. After retrieving his pack, he faded into the middle of the wooded area. Once concealed from the street, he put on his night vision goggles and walked down the middle of the swale. He favored his wounded leg as he navigated through the brush and trees in the green light of the goggles. He stopped three times to check on whether or not he had gone far enough to be at the rear of the mansion. The third check was successful and, with his knife, he slashed the bark off of a tree, leaving an easy-to-see blaze to mark where he needed to turn towards the fence. At the fence he settled down to wait, watching through the goggles.

He was not lucky. There was a foot patrol at night. *Be too easy otherwise.* He smiled. The circuit took twenty minutes give or take three minutes. From the day's observations, Dan knew there were cameras. He had to assume they were not equipped for night vision as they were mounted with floodlights. If there were an alert, the lights would go on allowing anyone monitoring the cameras to see activity in the yard. He just needed to get in without triggering an alarm. *They should not be able to see me if I move carefully.* With the timing of the foot patrol, he gave himself only fifteen minutes of movement before he would have to settle down to wait for the guard to pass. He'd have to plan his approach and be in a hide position when the guard reappeared on his rounds. Cutting the glass and getting inside would be the final step that also had to be done in between the guard's circuits.

After two hours of watching, Dan was satisfied he had as much information as he could gain and retraced his steps to the car. He waited to make sure no one was about and slipped through the fence and got into the BMW.

Chapter 45

The next day Dan woke late. He lay in bed going over the plan. It was the best he could do, but with so many possibilities where it could go wrong or nasty surprises could appear. *You plan and then you improvise because plans never work the way you expect.* That was the wisdom of his trade and he had seen it born out many times. Still he felt uncomfortable. This plan had so many loose ends. The old woman kept coming back to mind. *What did she see for him? Success in killing Ortega but getting killed himself?* She had not answered his question. He shook his head. *No use thinking that way. Just execute the plan and be ready to adjust it. They don't know who they're up against. The old woman said, 'Use your skills and choose wisely.'* She also said something about a woman. *Was that María?*

After going out to a local stand-up food counter and getting a burrito for breakfast, Dan went back to his room and laid out his gear. He rigged the two bricks of C-4 with igniters and wired them to the burner phones. Then he entered the phone numbers on a third phone's speed dial. When finished he carefully placed the devices in his pack. He checked his M4 and 9mm, made sure he had extra loaded magazines and put them into the zippered bag along with the Barrett MRAD. He put the night vision goggles, glasscutter, suction handles, his tactical flashlight, tactical knife, bolt cutters, and his operational clothes in the backpack. In a side pouch, he put some water and energy bars. He was ready. He only needed to fill the two plastic jugs with gasoline on his way to the jumping off point.

With everything packed and ready, Dan sat on the bed and examined his wound. His leg throbbed, but when he unwrapped the old lady's bandage the wound looked calmer, less red than the day before. The salve was doing its work. He put clean pads on the wound and wrapped the leg in fresh gauze. Then he lay back on the bed to rest. He propped his leg up on some pillows to ease the throbbing and focused on relaxing his muscles. In this quiet state he went over his plans once more. They were as good as he could make them. The operation was dangerous, but not beyond hope of success. *I can do this. Even if the old woman is worried.* The plans floated into a dream as he fell asleep.

When he awoke it was later in the afternoon. He got up, stretched, and put on his street clothes. He left his room and went out for a walk and food. The neighborhood was a mix of apartments, modest houses, street front vendors and small shops. In one block there was a car repair shop; in another was a local taxi garage where the cabs were dispatched, parked and repaired. It had the unkempt, busy look of a place thriving but only through constant hard work and pressure from its owners.

A few hustlers tried to approach him, guessing his good clothes indicated money in his pockets, but Dan gave off a vibe that said, "Don't mess with me." After a futile try, they quickly backed off. He scanned the crowd keeping an eye out for anyone with intense eyes focusing on him. After a

while, he chided himself for worrying about what Tlayolotl
called Watchers.

He grabbed two chicken tacos with refried beans at a
street vendor's stall and went back to his hotel room. He
ate and then lay back on the bed to rest again. He was
going to start the operation at midnight. At ten pm Dan
took his gear and went down to the front desk to check out.

"But you have paid for a week and only stayed four
days," the clerk said.

"My business finished early and I want to get back
rather than stay. You can refund me two days and keep the
third day for this late notice."

That seemed to satisfy the clerk. Whether or not he'd
report the extra day's cash or pocket it himself was of no
concern to Dan. After completing the checkout, he loaded
his bags in the trunk of the BMW and drove to the rental
agency. It was closed so he parked on the street and put
the keys in the drop box. He grabbed his bags and hailed a
cab to take him to the garage he had rented.

He picked up the truck and set out for *Lomas de
Chapultepec* only stopping to fill the pickup and the two
plastic jugs on the way. He drove slowly and in a roundabout
fashion, out of habit, making sure he wasn't being
followed. Even at this late hour, traffic was still thick. It
was 11:40 pm when he got to the corner store. It was
closed. Dan went to the front door and read the sign that
said they opened at 6 am. He had to be gone by then. He
parked in a dark corner, out of the way.

From the back seat, he took the M4 and 9mm out of the
gun bag. He put the pistol in his backpack and strapped
the M4 to the back of it. Shouldering the pack and
grabbing the two jugs of gasoline, Dan hurried across the
street and walked to the end of the fence. He realized he
couldn't run well. *Hope I don't have to do much of that.*

He unhooked the carbine and slipped it through the gap. Next he stuffed his pack through. Just then he saw some headlights coming over the bridge. There was no time to get inside the fence. As the lights approached, Dan dropped to the ground and lay up against the fence. He hoped no one in the car would be looking to the side and they would just go past. The car stopped at the intersection and then rolled through going straight down the road. Dan let out a sigh, slid the two gas jugs through the fence and then squeezed himself through the gap. Grabbing all his gear, he moved into the undergrowth.

Once shielded from the street, he changed into his black pants and shirt. He left his facemask in the pack for later use. With his pack on his back, his M4 over his shoulder, his 9mm strapped to his waist, and both gas jugs in his hands he began limping down the preserve. Like the night before, the goggles made navigating through the trees and undergrowth an easy task.

In twenty minutes Dan was at the turning point, marked by the large blaze he had made on the tree. He now moved quietly and carefully towards the back yard. When he reached the fence, he settled down to wait for the guard. Once he had passed, Dan would cut the chain link and slip into the yard. He scouted his route forward, from tree to bush to tree. He picked out spots to stop before the guard came by, estimating he would be crawling slowly so as to not be noticed on any camera. From the camera angles, Dan figured he could approach the patio doors by moving along one of the house's side walls; the cameras seemed to point over them into the patio and yard. While there was illumination on the patio, the walls were shrouded in shadows.

Five minutes later the guard appeared. Like last night, he was not very alert. After many nights of walking around the mansion, Dan guessed the act had become so routine as to lose any sense of urgency and need. *Just like the warehouse.* He smiled. The gangs were brutal but not well trained; probably not very good shots either, which boded well for him. After the guard turned the corner Dan took the bolt cutters and applied them to the fence. There was a small snap as each link was cut. He rolled the cut links back, slipped his gear through, and crawled into the yard.

After closing the links with some twist ties, he started crawling to the nearest tree. He took his time noting on his watch how soon the guard would appear again. He was behind the tree when the man came back. Again, when the guard disappeared around the corner, Dan crawled towards some bushes that edged a bed of flowers. No one could see him. He repeated the maneuver three times, finding hiding spots before the guard came around. He skirted the helipad which was flat and open. The last move to gain the wall would be the most dangerous. He had to cross the edge of the patio. There were no plantings there, although some benches offered minimal cover. *If I'm discovered this will turn into an all-out assault and I won't have time to do what I came to do before police or reinforcements arrive.* Everything depended on gaining access to the house undetected.

The guard's path took him just outside the patio, skirting a planting bed that lined the outer border of the stone pavers. Dan lay inside the bushes of the bed as the guard walked by only ten feet away. He held his breath and pressed himself against the dirt, trying to be a part of the landscape. Again, the guard's casual approach played into Dan's hands and he was not spotted.

After the guard turned the corner Dan started crawling along the back edge of the patio towards the left wall. The guard would have the least direct view of that wall as he was walking from left to right along the back of the patio. He forced himself to move slowly since there was no cover and the patio illumination spilled over. When stationary Dan would show up as a dark lump in a dim picture on the monitor screen. Only when moving would he attract attention. *Hope the guy monitoring the videos is just as bored as the one outside.*

He finally reached the wall and had only a moment to huddle flat on the ground, against the wall, before the guard reappeared. The guard was looking forward as he walked past, never glancing over his shoulder, a pattern Dan had observed on the previous rounds. He turned the corner and Dan began to move along the wall. He had to move down the wing to the main house wall and then to the glass area to the double doors. He moved in a crouch rather than a crawl, wanting to get as much done as possible before the guard came around again. Lying on the stones next to the windows he would be most exposed and he only wanted to risk that once. The only help was some patio furniture that broke up a clear view of the base of the wall.

When he reached the windows he took out the glass cutter and began to work, checking his watch. A few minutes before the guard's expected return, Dan took out his 9mm with its suppressor and lay on the patio against the glass walls facing outward. If seen he would take out the guard immediately. The shot would probably not be heard; it was the best he would be able to do. If the guard didn't come around, eventually someone would come looking, but Dan would be inside and could take down the others as they entered to look for the intruder.

He was in luck. The guard didn't notice him and walked past again. When he turned the corner, Dan finished cutting a pane at the floor level and pulled it out with the suction cup handle. He set the cut piece down, shoved his gear inside, and crawled through the window. Then he brought the cutout pane into the building. Only a lack of light glinting on glass would give away the missing pane.

After getting inside, Dan pulled his face mask over his head. With his backpack on, his M4 slung over his shoulder and hanging down in front of him, and his 9mm in his hand, Dan began to move forward.

He had memorized the map Rodrigo had drawn him. The first step would be to locate his position. Then he had to find and take out any interior guards; if no one came in from the outside, all the better. By the time he finished all hell would be breaking loose and he would have a chance to run for his exit in the confusion. *That's the plan, anyway.*

Chapter 46

J ust inside the patio was a room that seemed to be an arboretum. It had a polished stone floor and was filled with huge plants, water fountains, and basins. Throughout the room there were benches where one could sit. The air was moist, tropical-like; an oasis from the dry high desert air of the city. *Must be quite an expense to maintain this tropical space.* Dan slipped through the room without a sound and entered a hallway. Part of the way down the hall was a large, commercial type kitchen with an eating area. It was empty. He crept further down the hall towards the front of the building. At the end of hallway the space opened up. There were rooms to the right. One looked like a dining room, the other a reception or sitting room. To Dan's left, the space remained open like a hotel foyer. Further to the left were a pair of double doors that he knew opened to a grand banquet or ballroom hall. Past that, Dan remembered from the map, was a formal library and office.

He remained crouched at the edge of the larger foyer space going over the map in his head. Through the dim light he could see a guard sitting at a desk near the front door. He was facing the front door and had earphones on, probably listening to music. Dan crept quietly along the foyer to his left, behind the guard, heading towards the ballroom. Ortega might be in the office that was beyond the large room.

The double doors leading to the grand room were closed. Dan tried them. They were not locked but when he pushed down on the door handle it gave out a loud screech. Dan quickly slipped through the opening and flattened himself against the other door. He heard a chair scrape. The front door guard had heard something and was coming to look. Dan unclipped his carbine and laid it on the floor. He took out his knife.

The man came through the door, sticking his head in first. Dan grabbed him and pulled him through. Before he could do more than grunt in surprise, Dan stuck his knife in the guard's back, puncturing the man's lung. He heard the hiss of air escaping. The man stiffened. Dan immediately pulled his knife out and thrust it into the base of his skull, where the neck and head meet. The guard went limp in his hands.

Dan let the man down gently to the floor and looked around. He needed to park the body where it couldn't be found. If anyone saw the guard missing, they would assume he'd gone to relieve himself or slip off somewhere to sleep. If they found a body though, alarms would be raised. He moved along the inside wall. The room had a forty-foot table in the center. The ceiling was fourteen feet high. It looked like a European castle banquet hall, a place where the lord could preside over sumptuous feasts. The outside wall faced out to the formal front grounds with ten-foot-high windows. The inside wall was paneled wood. There had to be a door hidden somewhere in the paneling; an entrance to a passageway to get food from the kitchen to the dining hall without going through the front foyer. The door would open to a corridor that would connect back to the hallway he had used and from there one could access the kitchen. He moved along the wall feeling for an opening. Halfway back into the room he found the door. It was not locked. He dragged the body down to the entrance and put it inside the hallway.

He next moved down to the door leading into the large office and library. He listened outside the door. There were no sounds coming from the room. With his 9mm at ready he slowly turned the latch and opened the door. He quickly scanned the room, ready to shoot. It was empty. *He must be upstairs in his private wing.* Rodrigo had explained that Mendoza had a private wing of his own in the mansion as did his wife, María, all on the second floor. Mendoza's wing had a master bedroom and bath suite, a sitting room and a private office. It was there that he had spent most of his time. *Ortega will likely be either in that office or asleep in his bed. Time to go upstairs.*

Dan retraced his steps back to the foyer. Just to one side of the hallway leading back to the arboretum was a grand curved staircase that ended in a balcony landing. It was designed so the lord of the manor could look down on the people arriving. Everything in the house was designed to accentuate the prestige and power of the owner.

From the drawing he knew that at the top, from the landing there were three doors. The one to the right, on the same side as the banquet hall, was Mendoza's wing. At the rear of the balcony was another door that led to an upstairs lounge and sunroom. To the left was María's wing that incorporated her personal bedroom suite, sitting room, children's bedrooms, and playroom.

As Dan reached the top of the stairs the door to María's wing opened. Dan brought up his 9mm but hesitated; it was a woman. She looked at him wide eyed and then backed out of view, closing the door. It only took a second, but Dan thought he recognized María. He hurried to the door and slowly opened it. Down the hall he saw the woman turning a corner in the hall. Dan followed and reached the corner in time to see her enter a door.

He went to the door and gently knocked on it. There was a moment of silence. He knocked again, only a bit louder this time.

"*Adelante.*" He could barely hear the woman's voice from inside the room.

Dan opened the door and stepped into the room. The lights were low, but he could see her standing to one side of the room. She was staring at him wide-eyed, direct, but not fearful.

"You have come to kill me?" Her voice was clear and lilting.

He shook his head 'no'.

"Who are you? Why are you here? You are masked like a bandit or assassin."

Dan realized he had his facemask on. He must look terrifying to the woman, yet she stood there asking him about his business in the house. He reached up and removed the mask. He didn't know why, but once done, it was too late to undo the act. There he stood, face to face with the wife of the man he had assassinated. She was tall. She had brown hair that fell over her shoulders. Her face was that of a classic beauty, high cheekbones, full lips and dark brown, slightly almond shaped eyes.

"Are you the one who killed my husband?"

Dan nodded, not sure of his voice.

"Why?"

He forced himself to speak. "He was a bad man and was going to hurt many people."

"You did this alone?"

"Many people wanted it done. He was going to smuggle terrorists into the U.S."

"So the U.S. government had him killed."

"No."

"*Vigilantes?*"

"Something like that." Dan continued, "He has killed many people. He has enslaved many through his drugs, here and in the U.S. And now he was going to send terrorists into my country. He was not a good man, your husband."

"Why not arrest him? Put him on trial? Isn't killing him just doing what you accuse him of doing?"

"Your government is too corrupt. He would not be prosecuted. You must know of all the officials and politicians he has bought off."

She didn't reply and her look betrayed her knowledge of Mendoza's corrupting influence.

"He said it was necessary to do his business in peace, without violence."

"María, that's your name isn't it?"

She nodded.

"María, he ordered many killed to gain power and control. Hector Ortega did most of it. You seem to be a smart woman, you must know of some of that."

She seemed to sag slightly as if the weight of that knowledge bore down on her. She shook her head and tossed back her hair to look back at him again. "So you killed my husband. You were judge and executioner and now you are here. Why?"

"I'm going to kill Hector. He can't be allowed to take over. I didn't expect to find you here." Dan paused and stepped forward, "Why are you here?"

María didn't answer.

"And your children? Are they here as well? I understand Hector taking over your house," he waved his hand around, "this mansion, but how are you a part of that?"

María lowered her eyes as if embarrassed. "He wants me by his side...to make me his woman."

Dan was silent. This was something he never expected to hear. "He takes over the mansion and Jorge's wife. That gives him all the trappings of power and leadership, helps solidify his position. And the kids? They're going to be part of this arrangement?"

She didn't answer, still not looking up at him.

Dan fought to find the right words but he didn't know what to say. He didn't know what he wanted from the conversation. He just stood there, fighting his emotions. The news disturbed him in a way he couldn't fathom. It seemed a violation of the image he had developed about her. *Fool*, he thought to himself.

"I watched you at the hacienda, before anyone arrived," he said. The woman looked at him intently. "I watched you through the binoculars. You looked like you were a good mother, even from that distance, that you cared for your children. I don't understand how you could bring them into this. If there was violence with Jorge, there will be even more violence with Hector; he is the enforcer."

"I had no alternative. This was the only safe place to go after you killed Jorge and the others. You, yourself are a violent man."

"Not to you. And now you have made an agreement that locks you into violence. What will happen to your children? Will the boy grow up to be a drug dealer? Will Hector force you to have his own children so he can groom them to follow in his footsteps? You have bargained away any stable future for your children and yourself...for what?"

"What do you care? You killed my husband. You caused this situation."

"Your situation was bad before I acted. I saw how he used you and the children to create a picture. To create the effect he wanted to give to the other drug leaders at that meeting. That is the only reason you were there. You were his pawn. I know he had his mistresses. There must have been so many insults you had to endure without complaint."

"So now, *Señor* Assassin, you judge me?" She looked up. Her eyes flashed in anger.

"No. I just describe what I see. And from your reaction I see it is the truth." He stepped up close to her and spoke in a quiet voice. "You were a kept woman. A bird in a cage. It was a fancy cage but still you were captive. And now you have let yourself become a captive again...you and your children."

She looked at him, her gaze not wavering, but tears started to form in her eyes.

Dan continued, now in a softer voice. "You must leave, now, with the kids. Hector is a dead man. I am going to bring death and destruction to this house. This is your chance to break free." There was urgency in his voice now. He couldn't fully understand, but it was important to him to save this woman and her family. Was it to bring some salvation out of the carnage he was going to reap?

"I have no place to go. My attorney says I have no money that is not part of the cartel...that is my own."

"It does not matter, this is your chance. You will have no protection without Hector."

María thought for a moment. "Come with me. I want to show you something before you act."

She strode past him to the door. "There is a set of back stairs we can use so we don't have to go down the main staircase. I want to take you to the basement. There is no one down there. It is underground and considered secure."

They went into the hall and continued past her door. At the end of the hallway was a small door leading to a narrow staircase. They went down two flights and exited in the basement. They walked down the hallway past multiple rooms with pull down grates holding an enormous collection of wines and liquors.

María stopped at a door, took out a key, and unlocked it. Inside she turned on the light. There, in a stack ten feet across by twenty feet deep and four feet high were neat bundles of U.S. currency of various denominations. In front was a smaller stack of only one hundred dollar bills. There must have been more than twenty million dollars in the two piles.

"This is money waiting to go off-shore. The Mexican banks get overloaded and Jorge and Hector cannot deposit there for a while. This is waiting to get flown to the Caribbean banks. It builds up daily."

"How much comes in each day?"

"Millions? I don't really know. Hector says this pile may get larger with how things have been disrupted since Jorge has been killed."

Dan turned to her and took her arm. "Is this what holds you here? Is this why you accept your cage?"

She pulled away from him, her face now angry. "It takes money to live, money to protect oneself and one's family. I am lost if I am destitute."

"María, here is your exit. Pack up some of this. You could take out a million and leave tonight. You are a smart, beautiful woman. You were once a top model. You could become an independent woman again. Everyone knows your husband is dead. They do not know of the bargain you made with Ortega. And he will be dead tonight. No one will know about all of this and it will seem natural to everyone for you to be on your own. There may be risk, but you are taking the risk for your children's futures. A million dollars will help you get started in a new life."

María looked into his eyes. Her face softened. "I wish I could believe what you say."

"You must believe me, because I am going to destroy this place and everyone inside. I'm offering you a way out before I bring hell down on Hector and the gang."

"You are an angel of death."

Dan just nodded. He walked over to the stack of the hundred dollar bills, took out his knife and cut open the covering. He picked up handfuls of the wrapped hundreds and put them in two side pockets of his backpack. It took less than a minute to load what he guessed was a half million in hundreds into his pack.

"Have your children pack up backpacks, only essentials. You do the same. You can purchase new clothes after you get out. Then come down here and load a pack or suitcase with twice what I just put in my pack. Then go to the arboretum. Next to the back door there is a panel missing from the window. Use it to get out without triggering the alarm. Wait for the guard to go by before you leave the room and head straight to the back fence. You need to look along the fence. You will find the links are cut at the bottom; you can pull them back. The guard comes around every fifteen minutes so just lay on the ground against the fence if he comes back before you find the opening. He will not see you. Take the kids, walk across the swale and all of you climb the fence to the street. Call a cab and disappear. This," he raised his pack, "is my exit money, just like you. If you hear gunshots, don't wait for the guard to come by, just run for the fence."

"I should hate you. You are a murderer and are going to kill again."

"I don't have any more time to argue. Think of me how you will. I had a wife and a gang killed her along with our unborn child. I am now the 'angel of death', as you say, to gang members who kill and destroy. Take what I am offering. You have a half-hour to get out of here."

He pushed past her and headed down the hall. When he reached the stairs, he noticed she was right behind him.

Chapter 47

María exited the staircase and went to the children's room. Dan headed down the hall towards Jorge's wing. He slipped out of the door onto the landing and stopped. There was a guard down in the foyer calling out for the missing guard. Another guard came in the front door.

"He's probably gone to take a piss," the man said.

"Or go to sleep, lazy bastard. *Don* Hector will kick his ass if he finds out."

"Well I'm not going to try to find him. We better get back outside."

The two men went back out the front door and Dan crossed the upper landing. He took out his 9mm and tried the door. It opened. Just inside was a guard sitting in a chair leaned back against the wall. The man lurched forward.

"*Qué demonios?*" What the hell? He shouted as he got to his feet, reaching for his gun.

Dan's pistol gave a muffled spat and the man crashed back on the chair and to the floor. Dan ran to the office door and burst through it. Hector was on his feet and reaching for his gun.

"*Basta!*" Dan shouted. His pistol was aimed Hector's chest.

Hector froze.

"What do you want?" he asked.

Dan only stared at him. The gang leader sat down heavily and put his hands in his lap.

"Put your hands on the desk where I can see them," Dan ordered.

Hector did as he was told. "Who are you and how did you get in here?"

"I am your executioner."

"*Santa Muerte*," Hector said almost under his breath.

"*Ángel de la Muerte*," Dan said, Angel of Death; "I'm the deliverer of death."

"You will not get out alive."

"Maybe, maybe not, but you certainly won't. I hope you enjoyed your short reign as boss. Now it is time to go."

He heard footsteps running up the stairs. Hector must have pushed an alarm button underneath the desk. Dan squeezed off a shot and Hector's head snapped back with a hole in his forehead. Two more quick shots into his heart and he turned, crouching, towards the door. Two men crashed through firing over his head and Dan shot them both in the chest. He jumped to the side, out of the doorway and holstered his 9mm. He brought up his M4 and put a short burst down the hallway. Two more men fell and two others ran back onto the upper landing. Dan took the moment to run forward, the M4 at ready. One of the men put his head around the corner and paid with his life. The other ran down the stairs. Dan dove through the doorway and flattened himself on the landing. The man below loosed a long burst of automatic fire. The bullets whistled harmlessly over Dan's head. The guards were armed with what sounded like AK47s. They made a loud bark which could be heard throughout the building. Dan's suppressed M4 emitted a muffled "pop" when he fired. Dan crawled to the edge and when the man paused to see if he had hit anything, Dan fired. One clean shot, center mass, which dropped him.

Dan heard a car drive up; probably from the front gate. He ran back into María's quarters and caught up with her and the children just as she was leading them down the hall.

She turned with a panicked look in her eyes as he ran up to her.

"Change of plans," he said. "We'll go together. Meet me in the arboretum after you collect the money. I'll escort you out."

They flew down the steps of the back stairwell and Dan exited on the main floor while María and the kids went to the basement. From the hallway, Dan went forward and waited, lying on the floor and against the wall. It was only a moment before four gang members came bursting through the door with their weapons ready. Dan opened up with an automatic burst from his carbine and three of them fell. The fourth man let loose on full automatic in his direction but the rounds flew too high. Dan's second burst dropped him.

He took out the spent magazine, inserted a fresh one from his pocket, and ran back down the hall to the arboretum. There he grabbed the gas cans and headed back to the front. Just before entering the foyer, he took off his backpack and removed one of the C-4 bricks and igniters with its cell phone. He placed the explosive on the floor next to the staircase

Then he grabbed his pack and a gas can and ran back upstairs. He placed the second brick just inside the door of the hall leading to the office where he had shot Hector.

Then he poured gas along the corridor and into the office. Retracing his steps, he went back down the stairs splashing gas along the way. He took the second can and sloshed gas into the banquet room and the smaller dining room to the right of the foyer. He could hear two more cars drive up. Dan retreated to the hallway just in time to see María and her two children enter the arboretum. He grabbed his pack and went into the kitchen where he turned on all the burners of the gas stove without activating the igniters. Then he ran to the arboretum. The front door was opening as Dan led María and the kids out onto the patio. They ran to the fence where Dan took out his phone.

The men entered and, seeing the dead bodies, they crouched down not wanting to join the body count. They began to search the foyer for the intruder or intruders. Not knowing how many shooters were inside, they were very cautious. After seeing no one in the foyer, one of the men headed towards the hall past the staircase. He glanced to his right and saw the brick of C-4 attached to the staircase.

"*Mierda!*" He shouted just as the phone rang.

The explosion took out the men who had entered the foyer. Fire erupted in both the dining and banquet rooms. In the next moment the upper floor exploded and tongues of flame ran down the hall to the office. Back on the main floor the fire followed Dan's trail of gasoline down the hall and into the kitchen where it ignited the gas coming out of the stove burners, producing a third explosion and a large fireball.

From the fence line the children and their mother looked on in horror as the explosions boomed out across the grounds. They gasped at the force of the shock wave as it hit them even back at the fence. Then they saw the light of flames through the windows. The mansion would be burning beyond salvage before any fire department could arrive.

Dan pulled back the chain link and hurried everyone through. He led them down to the center of the swale.

"Now go straight ahead. The road is only fifty meters away. You will have to climb the fence on the other side, but it is only five feet high. You have a cell phone?"

María nodded.

"You get the money?"

She nodded.

"Good. Then this is the start of a new life for you and your children. I wish I could help more, but I think you are smart and talented enough to make it. At least that is what I'm going to believe."

"What will happen to you?"

Dan looked at her. A feeling of sadness swept over him. What could he say? "That is not part of your story." A part of him wished he could stay and help this woman, their stories becoming entwined. "You have your own story to write. You will struggle and you will have set backs but you will succeed."

"How do you know?"

"I don't know how I know." Dan paused for a moment. He didn't have time to fully explain. "But I do know there are people who are watching over you. They are good people. I think they wanted me to save you tonight from a darkness that was enveloping you. And so, that is what I tried to do. The rest of the story is up to you."

He turned to go. María grabbed his arm.

"Thank you for not killing us, for getting us out," She said.

He turned to her and almost smiled. "I only kill bad people."

She touched his face. There was a wistful look in her eyes.

"I don't even know your name," she said.

"It doesn't matter. I'm happy that I could bring something good out of all this destruction."

With that he turned and limped off through the brush.

Chapter 48

It was 4:30 am when Dan reached the pickup. The street in front of him was empty, as empty as Dan felt inside. He should have felt a satisfaction with a job well done but...nothing. There was a feeling of sadness about never seeing María again. Had he fallen in love? That was a stupid thought. But would the woman take the opportunity for a new life that he had given her? Dan shook his head. He had done what he could. The Watchers, Tlayolotl and the old woman had hinted at a woman, probably María, and Dan had done what he thought he should do, maybe what they wanted him to do. In any case, it was over. Now was not the time for melancholy reflection, now was the time to leave; to get out of Mexico. He could hear sirens from across the drainage swale. Forcing his mind back to his present situation, he started the truck and drove off. A half-hour later he was hammering north out of Mexico City, his pack and weapon bag on the passenger seat, his 9mm under his jacket next to him.

At six in the morning, Jane's cell phone rang.
"Do you have a burner phone with you?"
"Dan is that you?"

"Yes. Do you have another phone?"

"No."

"Go out now and get one and call me back. Don't wait. Do it now."

The phone went dead. She sat there on the bed wondering what was going on. Of course, Dan would suspect her cell phone was bugged. Even she worried about it, although Warren's equipment had not detected any bugs. She sighed and got up to put on some clothes. *Better to humor him. He must be under a lot of stress.*

A half hour later she called his number.

"You got a new phone? Good. Give me the number and I'll call you right back."

In a minute Jane's prepaid phone rang.

"We should be able to talk now."

"You changed phones?"

"Yeah, I finished my work. Ortega's dead and the mansion is burning as we speak. There's no one below Ortega who can immediately take the reins of power so whatever damage control Ortega was able to institute, will disappear and the disruption you hoped for will break out in full."

"I'm so glad to hear your voice. Henry thought you might be on a suicide mission. He didn't give you much chance of success. But I wanted to believe you could pull it off and survive. It's amazing you succeeded. How did you do it?" Her words came tripping out in rapid succession.

"Never mind that. Just know it will be bloody and people are going to be screaming. Just be prepared. You'll probably hear the blowback before the end of the day."

"Where can we meet to exfiltrate you?"

"You can't. That didn't work before. I'll get myself out. You need to contact the DEA or others in our agency. Get them and some honest Mexican authorities over to the mansion right away. There's twenty million or more in U.S. cash in the basement and it will probably survive the fire. Someone needs to collect that money and keep it out of the cartel's hands."

"I'll get right on it."

"I've got to go."

"Dan, congratulations. I'm glad you're alive. And, please, come back to us...to me."

"I will," Dan replied and hung up the phone.

After Dan hung up, Jane called Henry. "Henry, let's meet at our usual spot this morning before going in to work. I have something to discuss with you."

In an hour they were sitting at a booth in the rear of the diner.

"Dan took out Ortega and destroyed the mansion. He's devastated the cartel. There's no one below Ortega that can step up. Any control Ortega set up will now be gone."

Henry gave out an appreciative whistle. "How the hell did he pull that off? It will be chaos...open warfare between gangs," Henry replied. "The Sinaloa cartel will assume it was a hit by another gang. They will suspect the Los Zetas, or Tijuana cartels."

"They'll be at each other's throats, looking for revenge, new territory, new smuggling routes."

"You know we've unleashed a bloodbath."

Jane stared down at her coffee. "I know. It's what we aimed to do." She paused. "And it will catch civilians." She looked up. "But it will interrupt the drug flow. And, remember, Dan also took out sixty terrorists heading to the U.S."

Henry looked at her, his face displayed no emotion. It was undecipherable. "I know. It's just a shame there are always civilian casualties."

Jane changed the subject. "Dan says we should get some of our people down there to the mansion along with DEA agents and any honest Mexican officials."

Henry looked at her now with a quizzical expression on his face.

"He says there's about twenty million in cash in the basement that will survive the fire. It needs to stay out of the hands of the cartel."

"I can make that happen." Henry shifted into action mode. "Are we exfiltrating him?"

"No, he doesn't trust the process."

"Did you make any headway on who planted the bugs?"

"Fred is whittling a long list down. We'll have maybe twenty or more suspects when he's done."

Henry got up and put some money on the table. "Good. Let's get going." He took out his phone and started making calls before they were out of the diner.

When Jane got to work, she received a call from Rodrigo. "When are you going to get us out? The cartel is closing in."

Jane outlined how a car would pick them up tomorrow and drive them to the Texas border. They would have U.S. passports and the car and driver would have diplomatic credentials so they would breeze through customs.

"Where will we cross?"

"Nuevo Laredo"

"Have them pick us up in Monterrey. We'll be in Fundidora Park, in front of the shiny metal ball. The road runs right past it. Ten o'clock. We'll be waiting on a park bench by the road."

"You're not in San Luis Potosi?"

"No. We had to move." With that he hung up.

Emilio "The Snake" arrived in Monterrey the same morning as Rodrigo placed his call to Jane. He had already contacted the cartel members and told them to scour the hotels for a man, woman, and young girl who might have checked in during the last two days. That evening he met with the local leader and got a list of a dozen hotels that had received such guests. He told the man to mobilize his men and check all the hotels.

"We must find them tonight. Tomorrow may be too late."

If they found Rodrigo they were to capture him. Hector wanted information and then he wanted Emilio to kill all of them in a very gruesome way. He wanted their heads on poles and on display in Chihuahua City.

Rodrigo turned to Miranda after speaking with Jane. "Tomorrow we will be entering the U.S."

She ran to him and hugged him. "Thank you Rodrigo." Her tears said the rest.

"Yes but now we have to make a new life in a new country. You will have to learn English, along with Solana. And I, I don't know what I'll do. I don't want to be a brick layer or gardener for some rich gringo."

Miranda grabbed his face in her hands. "You can help the U.S. government fight against the drugs. That is what you know. That's how you can help."

Rodrigo looked serious. "That's dangerous work."

Miranda kept smiling and holding Rodrigo's face. "But I'll bet it pays well. And you are not afraid of dangerous work."

"That is what Steve said, 'milk the government as a consultant'."

"I wonder if we'll see him again. I didn't like him at first. I thought he meant nothing but trouble for us. But he helped us in the end."

"He *was* nothing but trouble for us. But he saved my life. I would have died in the desert except for him." Rodrigo went silent as he thought about the other events in that story. "And that shaman, Tlayolotl and his raven. They frightened me."

"Tell me what happened to the others. What happened before the gringo found you."

Rodrigo recounted the chase, the insurrection of the men and the final rush through the desert ending in the crash. He told how he alone escaped and walked, finally going in circles until he was near death. Then Dan showed up with a coyote and a raven.

Miranda listened wide-eyed. "What happened to the men who went west?"

"They probably died. There was no hope in going in that direction."

"And now we're on the run because you helped the gringo."

"I had to. The shaman would have killed me and cursed my spirit if I didn't help. There was no choice." He shook his head as if to clear it. "It is good we are going. There is no place for me here now."

Late that night Rodrigo was awakened by some shouting in the lobby. He went to the door and listened. Men were shouting questions at the desk clerk. It sounded to Rodrigo like they wanted to know the room number of a man, woman, and girl that had checked in recently. On hearing that, Rodrigo ran to the night table next to the bed and took out his .45. He shook Miranda to wake her.

"Get up. Some men are here. They're after us."

"Who?" she asked sleepily.

"Cartel men. Wake Solana, we have to leave now."

Miranda went to the other bed and woke her daughter. "Hurry, get dressed and pack your things, we have to go now."

"Just put your clothes on, there is no time to pack," Rodrigo said.

He went to the window and opened it. It opened on to an alley. They were eight feet off the ground. As soon as the women were dressed he had Solana climb out of the window and he held her arms and let her down until she was only two feet off the ground. Then he did the same with Miranda. Finally Rodrigo climbed out and dropped to the pavement.

"This way," he whispered and they ran down the alley away from the front of the building.

They were around the corner before the men burst into the room. Seeing the window they looked out but there was nothing to see. The men ran back to the lobby and out the front door. By the time they got down the alley, Rodrigo and the two women were two blocks away and still running.

It was late but people were still out on the streets. Rodrigo led his family running through the streets until they got to a busy street where he could hail a taxi. After they climbed in he sat back, his chest heaving.

When the others had also caught their breath, Miranda asked if he was sure the men were after them.

"Did we just leave our belongings behind for nothing?"

Rodrigo gave her a sharp look of reproach. "Don't doubt that the men were after us. Escape is only for those who act quickly. If we had stayed to talk about the situation or pack our bags we would have been captured. And you don't want to know what would have happened to us then." He shuddered.

"How did they find us?" Miranda asked.

"Some of the men knew we had family in Torreón."

"You mean they came to Tía Milagros' house?" There was an hysterical tone in Miranda's voice.

Rodrigo nodded. "Maybe."

"Oh my God," Miranda exclaimed. "Poor Tía Milagros. Will they kill her?"

"I hope not. She must have told them. That is why they are looking for us here. I hope they let her live."

"God help us," Miranda wailed. "How will we get out?"

"They don't know where we are meeting our ride. And they don't know when. We just have to hide for the night and then be at the park tomorrow."

"Where will we go tonight?" Miranda asked.

"We can't go to a hotel, they will call the cartel. We can't go to the police either. Let me think."

He had his .45 in his pants and his pockets were still stuffed with the fifty grand he had taken from the house. It was for this reason he hadn't left the money in his backpack. In his pants, it would always be with him. He leaned forward to speak to the driver.

"How much do you want to park your cab for the night and go home to your wife?"

"Why do you ask?" the driver responded.

"We need to stay the night in your cab. You take the keys. We are not going to steal it. I will pay you for the night."

"That would be very expensive, *mí amigo*."

"How expensive?"

The driver thought about how much he could get out of this situation. He might make only the equivalent of fifty dollars in a night, but this request offered the possibility of more.

"I will do it for five hundred dollars."

"Okay. Drive to a parking garage and I'll pay you."

The driver did as Rodrigo asked while wondering if he shouldn't have asked for more. They were on the run, from a gang it sounded like to him; a gang that had connections all through the city. It was one of the cartels. Maybe he could make some more money out of this by selling them some information.

When the taxi was parked, Rodrigo pulled out five one hundred dollar bills and gave them to the cab driver. The man nodded and walked off.

"Are we safe now?" Solana asked.

"Not quite yet," Rodrigo replied. He got out and got into the front seat. He took out his knife and jammed it into the ignition switch. The knife wrecked the lock and he was able to turn the ignition and start the car. He backed out of the space and exited the garage.

"When we change locations we'll be safe," he said to Solana. "If the driver thinks to sell us out for more money, we won't be here when they come."

"That may be bad for the driver," Miranda said.

"It will serve him right," Rodrigo replied. "In the morning we will take a bus to the park and be gone by 10 am."

Chapter 49

After burying the remains of his men in the desert, Tariq had been driven to Veracruz and from there he had flown out of the country. On the drive to the port town, he called Rashid al-Din Said to report the killing of the terrorists.

"This is very unfortunate," were the only words Rashid spoke about the incident. "I will have someone meet you when you arrive in Karachi."

"I can refund some of the money you gave. It is not all spent."

"The money is not important. The failure of the mission is. We will talk further when you arrive."

Tariq was left with a cold knot in his stomach. This failure could mean his death. Rashid was not a man who allowed for much failure in those who worked for him.

After layovers in Houston, Frankfurt, and Dubai, he arrived some thirty-five hours later in Karachi. Tired and unkempt, Tariq was met by two serious looking Arabs in dark business suits. They loaded him in their car and proceeded to drive to the Gulshan E-Sekandarabad section of the city. As before, the labyrinth of streets confused Tariq. He was uncomfortable. Would Rashid eliminate him in order to send a message to others? Tariq had proven useful, even if this venture had ended in failure. Bitterly he thought that was not his fault but that of the cartel leaders. Jorge had not wanted to deal with him and Hector liked him even less. Then Jorge got killed and things had come undone.

But who had blown up the trucks? Could it have been the people who killed Jorge? Was it the work of rival gangs? Tariq shook his head as if to clear his jet-lagged mind. It didn't matter in the end. His handpicked and trained infiltrators were dead. He had buried their remains in the desert and left Mexico. The mission failed and now he would face the consequences.

They arrived at the same nondescript entrance. Tariq was frisked for weapons and two other men silently led him up the staircase. The lead escort knocked gently on the door.

"*Udkhul,*" came the response.

Tariq was escorted inside. This time no dinner was set out. Rashid sat across the room in an overstuffed chair. He motioned Tariq to a smaller chair across from him.

"Tell me what happened." Rashid looked at Tariq with a calm expression. His black eyes gave away nothing.

Tariq explained how the trip went well and how the men spent a week recovering in Chihuahua at a warehouse compound owned by Jorge Mendoza. But that week had stretched into three weeks with no explanation. He was relegated to dealing with Hector Ortega, Jorge's second in command. Only later, Tariq explained, did he find out that Jorge, along with some other gang leaders, had been assassinated. When Hector had settled things down, he ordered the men to be delivered to the border but the morning they were to leave, the trucks were blown up, killing everyone.

"And you weren't killed."

"No *Sayyid*. I was not going with them to the border. I planned to complete my dealings with Hector and then depart."

"Who killed Jorge?"

"Some say it was the Americans, some say another gang."

"Did the same people blow up the trucks?"

"No one knows for sure, but I suspect it is so."

"Who would know about the trucks and our fighters besides Jorge and this Hector?" Rashid's dark eyes bore into Tariq.

He shrugged. "I have no idea." The answer felt dangerously inadequate. "Other gang members knew. Maybe there was a traitor among them who spoke to another gang."

"Or, if it was the Americans, someone spoke to them."

Tariq nodded. His body slumped.

"So the Americans may know about this attempt."

Tariq nodded again.

"And they may know about you?"

Tariq looked up at Rashid. Fear showing in his eyes. He didn't answer.

"Do you agree that is a possibility?"

Finally Tariq nodded. "Yes," he said; his voice barely audible.

"This is not good. First you fail, then you may be exposed and our work thus exposed."

"This was always a risk, *Sayyid*. We know the Americans are listening everywhere and have many sources of information. It was worth the attempt. Next time we will not fail." Tariq leaned forward. "We can do this on our own. We don't need the cartel to smuggle our men. We can rent the trucks, a warehouse and deliver the men to the border ourselves. And we can make money from the drugs. The cartels are hungry for our product. They cannot get enough."

"The Americans cannot get enough."

Tariq nodded in agreement, his hopes rising.

"But that will take time. You have been there, but you may not have the skills for this. Perhaps you are best suited for the mountains and caves."

"I am a warrior for Allah. I will serve wherever I can be useful."

Now Rashid leaned forward and riveted Tariq with his eyes. "Can you be useful? Can I make good use of you, for our cause? If the Americans have identified you, then you may lead them to our work...to me."

"Never! I was not identified. How would anyone know me except for Jorge and Hector?"

"I don't know. But it worries me."

"I would never betray our cause, *Sayyid*."

"No. Not knowingly." Rashid waved his hand in dismissal. "Go, rest for now. We will speak later about your future."

Tariq stood. He wanted to say more, but he couldn't find the words. There was nothing more to say. With his head bowed he went out the door in between the two large men.

They drove to a large landfill. It was night. There they had Tariq kneel down and say his prayers. When he finished, one of them shot him through the head. They wrapped his body in a cloth and bundled it in the trunk. They drove the body to a mosque in the Manghaphir district and laid him near the door. They pinned an envelope with a note in it giving Tariq's name and instructions to bury him as a devout Muslim. In the envelope was a thousand dollars.

Back in his apartment, Rashid closed his computer, packed his bags, and dismissed his staff. He was closing the apartment and everyone would leave, to disappear into Karachi, or travel back to Saudi Arabia with Rashid. He would find another path into the U.S. He would continue with the drugs and make another attempt to smuggle terrorists into the U.S. If the cartels were unreliable, he would do it with his own operatives. The fight would go on. Tariq was just a setback along the way.

Chapter 50

Dan took one of his burner phones and called Jane. He was driving north towards Monterrey.

"Do you still have a burner phone so we can talk?" he said when she answered.

"I'll call your number right back. I have one."

"Good." Dan hung up and his phone rang a minute later.

"Where are you now?" Jane asked when Dan answered.

"Heading north out of Mexico City."

"Can I arrange someone to get you out?"

"You asked that before and the answer is still no. I'll find my own way across. Once on the U.S. side I'll be fine."

"If you carry your weapons back with you they could be a problem if you are stopped."

"I know, but I hate to abandon them, especially the Barrett MRAD."

"It's not worth it."

"Well I'm going to have to bring in at least one weapon. I'm not going unarmed, so, in for a dime, in for a dollar."

"Ditch the rifles at least but keep the 9mm if you have to have a weapon." It's much less conspicuous."

"Yes ma'am."

"I just don't want you to get caught this late in the game."

"Are you always so nervous about your agents?"

Jane changed the subject. "We have a car picking up Rodrigo and his sister and niece. They'll be covered by diplomatic passports so they'll breeze through the checkpoint. We're bringing him in at Laredo."

"Thank you...I mean that."

"You're welcome. Things are certainly stirred up, but that is what we aimed for. Congratulations on a job well done."

"Thanks."

"You mentioned an incredible story earlier. Can you tell me about it?"

"Later, when I'm back in the U.S. We'll talk in person. It's complicated but just know that there are others out there who are aware of you and what we're doing together. Don't worry, they're on our side...sort of."

"You're being very mysterious."

"That's because it's all a bit of a mystery. I'm going to hang up now. I'll contact you when I'm in the States."

Dan shut the phone off. He felt a mix of emotions. There was sadness at leaving María. He hoped she would find the will to make her own way. There was anticipation at seeing Jane again. That feeling was more real to Dan than the mix of feelings swirling around in his mind about María. She was more of a dream, a fantasy, and the children created an element of unfulfilled hope surrounding the fantasy. Since Rita's death along with their unborn child he had become a sucker for children. *Frustrated desires for fatherhood.* Jane was more real. She was in his life; she was full of opinion and action; she was not fearful. He found himself projecting some of Rita's qualities onto Jane and was pleased to find they seemed to fit. He drove until noon when his eyes started closing and his head started to nod. He stopped in Matehuala at a rundown hotel and rented a room. He was asleep almost as soon as his head hit the pillow.

Jane met with Henry outside their offices.

"Did you alert Roger about the bugs?"

"I told him. He's not happy. He wants to see the list as soon as Fred is done whittling it down."

"What can he do?"

"He has connections. If we determine who it is, he'll work through his superior to shut the action down."

"What if his superior is in on it?"

"Doubtful from what you said about the technology. Someone high up would use the company's resources."

"I just hope we can nail this down before Dan gets back. He doesn't need this. It will only make him paranoid and not trust us." Henry nodded. Jane continued, "That trust is vital to his well-being in the field. I've seen how things can go sour when the asset stops trusting his connections."

"So have I. Where is Dan now?"

"Driving north. He's going to cross illegally. Once in the U.S. he should be okay."

"Will he come in? Come to DC?"

Jane shrugged. "Not sure. It may depend on what we have to tell him."

"Tell Fred to get me that list."

It was dark when Dan awoke. He washed his face and body as best he could from the bathroom sink; there was no shower. Next he checked his wounded leg. It was swollen from the activity and the driving but it didn't look infected. Pulling out a shirt from his pack, one that was less dirty than the one he was wearing; he got dressed and went out on the street. The night was warm and full of smells. The mix of aromas from the street vendors competed with the fragrance of the night blooming flowers that filled the air with their perfume. He stretched and walked along the streets of the town, taking deep draughts of air into his lungs. *Clearing out the crap.* Finally his appetite kicked in; he hadn't eaten for a day. He stopped at a particularly good smelling stall and ordered what looked good. The chicken burrito came with a corn side dish. Dan ate ravenously and then stopped in at a cantina and bought a beer. He sat in the corner and drank the beer, letting his body relax. He remained alert to the street, watching everyone walk by and noticing who came into the bar.

But evening was mellow. The people seemed to be happy to be out relaxing after the day's work was done. He didn't get any sense of danger or threat. Everyone was just enjoying the pleasant evening when the fierce heat of the day had departed and the air was filled with exotic smells and a sense of anticipation, of wonder. It was a simple town with a priceless ambience. *We try to recreate this in our fake downtowns up north only to end up with a pale copy. People might think they're having an experience, but they are missing the real thing. You don't find it in a developer's imagination but in a small Mexican town, dusty and hot in the day and magically transformed at night.*

I hope I haven't unleashed too much blood on them. Deep inside he was afraid that there would be much blood spilled and many civilians would be caught in the deadly violence. *Still, how do they put up with so much corruption? Can the people ever rise up and demand more from their officials?* Dan shook his head. The reformers were so few and so easily eliminated. It took great courage to be a crusading reporter in Mexico—to print the truth. *Have I helped your cause?* He didn't know the answer. He did know that he had disrupted the cartels, which meant disrupting, at least for a while, the drugs flowing into the U.S.

Would all his jobs seem so fleeting in their effect? He needed to strike at the key players among the terrorists. And they needed to be aware there was someone out there gunning for them. They needed to feel fear. *They will go to ground. That is how I'll slow them down, have them go silent, afraid to stick their heads up for fear of me—some unknown assassin—Ángel de la Muerte.*

Dan finished his beer and stepped back into the street. He heard a sharp screech and looked up. There on the edge of the low roof perched a large black bird, a raven. Dan stopped and looked carefully at the bird. From the streetlights he could see one red eye and one black eye. He smiled and started for the hotel.

I wonder if that's Jane's vision, to strike fear as well as to assassinate? I wonder if that is what Tlayolotl wants of me. His mind went over the all he had experienced here in Mexico. Yes, the world was much more complex than he had imagined. It was not so neat and tidy and there was a larger drama going on; one in which he had a part to play.

Early the next morning Dan departed Matehuala. Along the way to the border he stopped at a remote spot in the desert and pulled off the highway. He was reluctant, but he knew he had to leave his long guns behind. He took his weapon bag and walked out into the desert. He dropped the bag behind a large boulder. Inside were the Barrett MRAD and the M4 with their suppressors, magazines, and unspent ammunition. He stared at the bag. *Such a waste. Forget it. It's a tool and you probably won't use them again. The right tool for the job, and all jobs are different. But what if someone finds the bag?* He shook his head and turned around; he couldn't worry about that. He walked back to the pickup.

By noon he was in Nuevo Laredo. He cruised along the riverfront, looking for a good place to cross. He wanted to be able to quickly blend in to the pedestrian traffic on the Laredo side. It was an unsatisfactory search. He didn't have enough intel to make a good choice and this was not the time to screw up.

As he drove around his mind kept going back to the mission: the assassination, blowing up the trucks, and the killings at the mansion. He had killed close to eighty people in the course of three weeks. He didn't feel remorse. He guessed most people would; but most people would not do what he did. These were all bad men, bent on destroying lives for their enrichment. It was true some of them became gang members due to their poverty and lack of opportunity, but Dan figured that was their choice. The terrorists, he had no further thoughts about; they needed to die before they could get into the U.S. and kill innocent people.

Maybe it was the carnage that would be unleashed on the civilians here in Mexico that bothered him. The cartels going to war with one another was the goal of this mission and that would lead to collateral damage. Dan felt twinges of remorse for that, but it wasn't a reason to not act. He had done what was necessary to protect his country and would continue to do so. His encounter with Tlayolotl showed him he had a mission, an appointed task, and Jane, without knowing about the larger struggle, had correctly recruited him to the work. For now, this was going to be his future.

After an hour and a half, Dan stopped a scruffy looking teenage kid walking along one of the streets.

"Do you know where the best place is to cross the river?"

The boy looked at him warily. The man's Spanish was good but not native. "You're not Mexican. Just drive over the bridge."

Dan shook his head and smiled at the kid. "I can't."

"The river is deep. You need a raft or you have to swim."

"I can swim, but I need some plastic bags to keep my gear dry."

"This is strange. You're a gringo and you want to sneak into your own country? Are you trying to get me into trouble?"

"No, no. I need some advice." Dan leaned out the window of the truck. You help me and there is a reward for you."

"What help? You can swim anywhere."

"I want to go across where I can get into Laredo the quickest."

"I can show you a park down by the river. I hear many try to go from there, but it is watched. I would not try there."

"Get in. Take me to a store where I can get some plastic bags and then show me where I can get across."

The boy hesitated.

"It will be worth your time."

The boy lifted his shirt to reveal a knife in his belt. "You try anything funny, I'll stab you."

Dan almost laughed. "Don't worry. No funny business," he said with a smile.

They weren't dry bags, but by using multiple layers along with duct tape Dan figured he had a pretty good chance to protect his gear.

"I would cross outside of town," the boy said.

They drove north, out of the city. The houses gave out to the desert. A few miles out of town they came to a 'T' junction with a few houses, a cantina, and a gas station. To the right of the road were footpaths leading down to the river's edge. Dan pulled over and parked where the boy directed him.

"You go down to the edge, in the thickets. You wait until dark and then you can swim. If you swim well you won't drown. Who knows if you run into patrols on the other side? All I know is that they patrol the river banks but not as much here as in town."

"You've been a big help. I want to give you something. Reach into the glove box."

The boy opened the box. "Only papers in here."

"Hand them to me."

In the stack was the registration to the truck. There was a place on the back where the owner could assign it to a purchaser.

"You know how to drive?"

The boy nodded. He had driven his uncle's car a couple of times. Dan signed the owner's name on the transfer section.

"I'm signing this pickup over to you. You can do with it what you want. Register it if you're old enough, or sell it if you want. It's yours." He handed the boy the papers.

The boy's mouth opened in surprise. He had hoped for maybe fifty U.S. dollars for what would be an afternoon's work by the time he got back to town, but a pickup? It must be worth a thousand dollars. He looked at the papers.

"This is not you," he said pointing to the owner's name.

"Yes, but I signed for him. And he is not coming back to claim the truck."

Dan grinned and grabbed his gear, now limited to his backpack and the plastic bags, and got out.

"It is yours now. Drive carefully," he said as he turned to head to the water. He would wait in the thickets until late that night. With his Night Vision Goggles he could even his odds, seeing the patrols as easily as they could see him. The swim would be no problem. He had done harder ones in sniper training. He'd just wait for a break in the patrols, they couldn't be non-stop, and then he'd swim across. After that he'd stand an even chance of avoiding the border agents, moving as slowly and quietly as needed in order to reach the city. It might take all night and he might have to hole up for the day, but Dan felt confident in his skill at avoiding detection.

"Gracias," the boy finally managed to say as he slid over into the driver's seat.

The old man sat in the front of the cantina, under the porch. He came here every day. He would nurse a beer for hours and often fall asleep. He watched the traffic going by and wondered where they were headed. He knew many of the people who came to the bar at lunch time. Sometimes one of them would buy him a beer. They would always say hello. After school he watched the kids playing in the empty lot next door. They played football in the dirt yard with more energy than the old man could remember. The *coyotes*, the people smugglers, would come in the evening and drop off people. They led them down to the river. Often they would leave them alone by the water with flimsy rubber rafts and depart. They had collected their money and didn't want to risk crossing over and getting arrested. The people had to fend for themselves, sometimes with disastrous results. The old man didn't witness these things, he usually left before dark. But he'd heard of them.

He guessed he had seen most everything there was to see in his life. Nothing surprised him anymore. He had lived through the waxing and waning of drug violence many times. He had navigated corruption all his life, playing his hand carefully to avoid getting caught in it. Now he was old, the world ignored him, and the world showed him few surprises.

But today was different. He saw three things he had never seen before and he began to wonder again at how the world could surprise even someone as old as him.

The pickup pulled off just beyond the cantina, on the other side of the street closest to the river. A man and boy were in the truck. The old man watched. The man wrote something on some paper and handed it to the boy. Then he got out with a bag. He looked like a gringo. The boy slid over into the driver's seat and started the truck. The old man realized the driver had given the boy the truck and he was headed to the river. But why would a gringo give away something so valuable to a boy? And why would a gringo need to sneak into his own country?

The next thing the old man noticed was a large raven that perched on the rail of the fence next to the cantina. The bird looked at the old man. He saw that it had one red eye and one black eye. He had never seen that before.

When the gringo walked off, headed to the thickets by the river, the raven let out a screech that startled the old man. It flew into the air and circled higher and higher. Then it flew over the man as he approached the thickets. The gringo stopped and looked up at the bird for a long time, the bird circling above him, the man staring up. The gringo then waved and disappeared into the thickets. The raven let out another screech and turned, flapping its wings to fly into the desert.

The old man marveled: a gringo giving a pickup to a poor Mexican boy, a raven with one red eye and one black eye that seemed to know the gringo and then flew into the barren desert, away from easy food found near the city. This had been a special day. He had seen three wonders. He got up. He would walk home early and tell his old woman what he had seen.

The End

Afterword

The Shaman is the second book of a new thriller series featuring Dan Stone. Book 3, *The Captive Girl*, continues Dan's adventures in Europe. Look for subsequent novels with Dan Stone and Jane Tanner going on other missions.

If you enjoyed this story, please consider writing a review on Amazon. Reviews do not have to be lengthy and are extremely helpful; they provide "social proof" of a book's value and help the reader take a chance on it. I very much appreciate your support.

Other novels published by David Nees:
The After the Fall series in order;
    After the Fall: Jason's Tale
    Uprising
    Rescue
    Undercover

The Dan Stone Assassin series in order:
    Payback
    The Shaman
    The Captive Girl
    The Assassin and the Pianist
    Death in the Congo

For information about upcoming novels, please visit my website at *http://www.davidnees.com* or go to my Facebook page, *fb.me/neesauthor*.

You can also sign up for my reader list to get new information. Scroll down on the landing page on my website and hit the "Follow" button. No spam; I never sell my list and you can opt out at any time.

Thank you for reading my book. Your reading pleasure is why I write my stories.